Under the Sea

Tyrant Books
9 Clinton St
Upper North Store
NY, NY 10002

Via Piagge Marine 23
Sezze (LT) 04018
Italy

www.NYTyrant.com

ISBN 978-0-9913608-8-8

Book design by Adam Robinson
Cover design by Brent Bates

"K-4" was originally published in *Jerry*. Thank you to Dan Bevacqua. "21 Extremely Bad Breakups" was originally published by Newfound Press as a chapbook. Thank you to Levis Keltner and Chelsea Martin. "21 Extremely Bad Breakups" was also adapted for the stage in 2018. Thank you to Amy Rummenie and Walking Shadow Theatre Company. The clumsy "translation" of the Sappho fragment in this story owes a debt to Julia Dubnoff's more faithful and illuminating translation. Thank you to Giancarlo DiTrapano and Sam Axelrod for their edits and to the many people who have given feedback on these stories over the years.

UNDER THE SEA

MARK LEIDNER

tyrant
books

CONTENTS

BAD-ASSES

I WAS ON THE COUCH WATCHING A CARTOON ABOUT ANTS when there was a loud-ass knock. Rawls walked out of the kitchen with the butter knife he'd been packing dimes with. He looked at me like I knew who it was. Whoever it was knocked again and he frowned and went to the door. For a second I went back to watching the ants on TV, but I could tell by Rawls' silence that something was wrong. I got up and walked to the window. Casey Bentley was out in the yard in his jersey like he'd just come from practice.

"The fuck do you want?" Rawls shouted at him.

"You," Casey said, "to come the fuck outside. I ain't tryna beat your ass in your own house."

A couple of Casey's friends were in our driveway. I knew they wouldn't jump Rawls because he was friends with them too. Everybody in Oak Park was friends with Rawls… except Casey. They'd hated each other since day one.

"Get the fuck outta my yard before I do come on down there," Rawls said.

Casey Bentley's glare broke into a smirk. "Heard you was up at school the other day." He glanced at his boys. "Thought you'd dropped out."

That was their cue to laugh, and they did, even the ones who had also dropped out.

I pressed my cheek to the window screen to see Rawls' reply. He was giving Casey the same go to hell look he gave Daddy when Daddy was wasted, which he always was, which is why Rawls always had that look on his face.

Rawls'd quit school because Daddy couldn't work and Momma was gone and somebody had to buy groceries. He worked nights at the fertilizer plant and sold weed on the side. Casey was still in school, supposedly to play football, but everybody knew it was more about them amphetamines. As long as we made the playoffs, which we did every year, nobody cared that Casey had a monopoly in the form of tenth, eleventh, and twelfth grade. I figured he must've heard Rawls had been swinging by the school to sell dime-bags to band kids while Casey was hitting the tackling dummies at practice.

"You think you're a bad-ass, Casey," Rawls said, pointing the butter knife at him, "but you ain't shit." He looked at the others. "I got bills to pay. That's why *I* dropped out." Then he looked back at Casey and said, "And I gotta pay em however I can."

"You ain't the only one struggling, mother-fucker," Casey spat. He pointed at the gathering crowd, which now included nosy-ass Keisha and Amy smoking by the road. "We all got ends to make. But I done told you too many times, school's mine."

Rawls held up a tiny blue ziplock full of weed. "It ain't nothing but green, man," he said. "It's fucking gas money."

"Don't care. I cut you a break, I gotta make exceptions everywhere."

"Go the fuck home," Rawls told him. "Before I pull that jersey over your head and whoop your fat ass."

There were some oohs from the driveway. Casey lowered his eyes. Now some old people with barefoot kids had walked up, one in just a diaper. I got scared. It felt like folks wanted to see something go down. I guess everybody had been waiting for Casey and Rawls to hash it out for good. My brother was a bad-ass, but Casey was big, and their history was long, and I was afraid of what they would do to each other if it went to war.

Casey had taken a step forward, and I thought it was on, but then our phone rang. Rawls and I turned to look back in the kitchen. He'd have to answer it, and that would defuse it. But then he just let it ring.

"Better get it," Casey said, wiping sweat off his face. "Might be your crackhead-ass momma looking for money."

Casey smiled at the driveway boys and they all laughed again.

Rawls looked like a statue now.

"Rawls, don't," I whispered. "Daddy'll be home soon."

Casey looked at me through the screen. "Daddy'll be home soon!" he mocked, his voice even squeakier than mine. Then everyone in the whole yard laughed. Casey pointed at me: "After I beat your brother's ass, I'm gonna come inside and make you make me a sandwich. Then when your daddy gets home I'm gonna beat his ass too, and then me and you gonna play pattycake."

More whoops of laughter. I was so humiliated that I didn't realize Rawls had jumped off the porch.

Casey was caught off-guard, and Rawls got in a ton of quick licks, bloodying Casey's face right up. Hell, I felt bad for Casey for a second, but then he flipped Rawls over and slung him like a rag doll. Rawls was small but it was a shock to see him bounce across the dirt like a toy like that. Rawls got back up and they circled each other, Casey towering over him.

A feeling of dread spread out from my stomach. I left the window for the door to see better. By the time I got there, Casey had Rawls in a headlock. Rawls was gut-punching Casey, but Casey was too fat, plus he was cutting off Rawls' circulation and working his face. They spun and kicked up dust and I caught a glimpse of Rawls' open mouth and eyes covered in black blood, helpless.

I ran to the kitchen and took the butcher knife out of the drawer. I put it behind my back and ran back to the porch. The crowd had grown, and everybody was chanting, "Fight! Fight! Fight!" Casey let Rawls out of the headlock as a trick, because when Rawls tried to run, Casey tripped him. Rawls fell. Then Casey dropped a knee into his back. Rawls screamed. The knife handle was slippery in my sweaty hand. Rawls clawed backward at Casey, but Casey rolled him over, then reared back and slugged him. Rawls' neck flopped like rubber. I screamed for them to stop, but no one heard me. Casey slugged my brother again, and this time I jumped off the porch and, after a hop-skip to get where they were, I swung the knife down into the big white number on the back of Casey Bentley's practice jersey. I must have closed my eyes though, because I don't remember seeing anything. I just remember shouting, and then being knocked silly across the yard, and then my mouth full of dirt and blood. When I opened my eyes, I was facing the sky with Casey's fat face filling it up. He yanked me off the ground, ripping the neck of my shirt, and I heard Keisha screeching above everybody, "What the fuck did you do, April!?"

Rawls was still on his belly, cheek covered by a blanket of blood. The knife was sticking out of his back. I'd accidentally stabbed my own brother. My first thought was that Rawls was dead, and in my mind, my whole world ripped apart. I felt like the horrible dark destiny of my life had finally come to pass. Because he wasn't moving or saying anything. I'd killed my own brother. I couldn't breathe. I couldn't think of anything but the weight of everything, and it nearly broke me in half. Then I saw him move, and groan, and it felt like light from the heavens. Everything wasn't fucked, I thought. Maybe it would be okay.

Casey was looking at the knife in Rawls' side. Then he looked at me and shouted, "You coulda killed somebody, you dumb bitch!"

He squatted and pulled the knife out of Rawls, almost like a doctor. Rawls writhed and coughed. I ran to him, but before I got there Casey grabbed me by the shirt again and shook the knife in my face. "That's fucking murder, bitch! If he dies."

Staring into Casey's big, dumb eyes, I was paralyzed, mostly because he was right. He waved the knife at our trailer. "What you waiting for? Call a fuckin ambulance!"

I ignored him and ran to Rawls' side apologizing a million times. I put my hand over the wound, then stopped, not knowing if I shouldn't touch it or what. The blood was trickling out, mingling with the dirt and making mud. "Rawls!" I screamed.

He blinked at me between busted eyelids and lips and said, "Call 911. I got this."

He grabbed his side and rolled onto it and curled up like a baby.

I ran inside faster than I'd ever run in my goddamn life and grabbed the phone with his blood on my hand. The last thing I remember seeing and hearing before the operator picked up was Casey grinning like a maniac and pointing at our trailer with the butcher knife and saying, "That bitch is crazy!"

SUMMER PASSED AND OAK PARK went back to normal, but I changed dramatically. I was hanging out with different people, and had formed a fast friendship with a girl named Sasha Shaw. Sasha had big eyes and big boobs and round white teeth and any boy she even looked at got hypnotized. She lived a county over, but she worked at our Applebee's so she crashed with us a lot. Her and Rawls almost had a thing but Rawls was so quiet and distant after the fight with Casey that he never went for anything like he used to, and he had quit partying. Daddy finally lost his job for real, and so except for his government checks, what Rawls got from watching the fertilizer plant at night was our only money. After Sasha came onto him and he didn't do shit, I asked him why because she'd asked me to ask him, and he told me that he didn't want anything to do with any young-ass girls, though that had never stopped him before. I had also started partying and smoking weed and doing coke and X and me and Sasha had shot up a couple times, but we never did meth. Casey got kicked off the football team and then dropped out with only a semester and a half left to graduate. He was around Oak Park a lot more, but he and Rawls kept a wide berth. Rawls had had to put his emergency room visit on a credit card, which by the way I didn't even know he'd had, so I had tried to find a job to help him pay it off, considering I had stabbed him, but the Baskin-Robbins was the only place in town that would hire me, and I quit after three days because my boss was a fake-ass Christian who liked to stand behind me and rub himself on me pretending it was just the tight space between the wall and the freezer. Plus it was only five bucks an hour and I spent almost everything I made on the cigarettes it took to get me through a shift. I also hated all the rich-ass church bitches who were the only people who ever came in there. One of them tried to get me to come to some revival. He was kinda cute, too, but I couldn't even picture myself holding hands and singing songs and shit like that without busting out laughing. By day two of Baskin-Robbins, I had probably the first actual idea of my life. I realized I could make more money in half an hour selling weed than I got in a week scooping ice cream, so that's what me and Sasha started doing. There was this cool dude named Reggie who had a Cadillac and sold weed on the other side of town who worked with Sasha at Applebee's. Sasha would hook up with him occasionally in exchange for a discount quarter-pound, so we sold it in Oak Park and all around town. I was selling it at school, and making bank. Don't get me wrong, life still sucked a million asses, but I could go to McDonald's or buy cigarettes whenever I wanted for the first time in my life. Sometimes I wondered if stabbing my brother had changed me, or if I'd always been this way and it just took something that fucked up to wake me up to the fact of who I was.

ONE HOT DAY IN NOVEMBER I got home from school to find Rawls had gone to work early, so I rolled a joint and smoked it on the front steps because Daddy's one rule was we couldn't smoke in the house. I was halfway through, looking down at the mosquito bites on my legs and wishing it would hurry up and get cold enough to wear something besides shorts when Sasha pulled up in her baby blue Corolla and got out red-faced and crying.

"What's wrong?" I said.

She hid her face as she walked over. Then we hugged and she sat beside me on the steps. I gave her the joint. She hit it a couple times and passed it back, then put her head on my shoulder.

"We got robbed," she said.

"Robbed? By who?"

"You know that fool, Tyler?"

I stared at her. Tyler was a new face who'd come into town earlier that summer from somewhere down in Florida. He had wavy black hair that always looked like he'd just stepped out of a shower. And dimples. And cold eyes that made him look cooler than he probably was. Honestly, the first thing I felt when Sasha said his name was a little jealousy that she'd hung out with him without me. He wasn't in school, and nobody knew how old he was. The only thing I knew about him was that he lived in his own house off the highway like a half hour walk from Oak Park. I knew he sold weed and what-not, but I would've thought me and Sasha were too young and unimportant to be fucked with by somebody like that.

"He paged me," Sasha started, "and said he wanted a quarter pound, and that's about all we had, so I brought it over and he just took it. I was like 'Where's my money,' and you know what he said?"

I was mad at her for not telling me she brought our whole stash to some random shady dude's house without telling me but I let it go.

"What."

"He said I could have it if I sucked his dick. So I didn't and he kept it. I fucking left in tears. He was laughing. I've never been so embarrassed in my life."

"He just took it?"

Sasha took the joint back and hit it. "He thinks he's some kinda bad-ass."

"All of it?"

She nodded. "I'm sorry."

"He's still got it?"

"Yeah. I guess. If it ain't sold yet."

"That's our fucking property, Sasha."

"Well, I know. What do you want me to do, go fuck him? Get it back?"

I snatched the joint out of her fingers. "No," I said. "Hell no." I hit it, thinking. Then I started nodding. "We're gonna fuck him up."

She looked at me like I was nuts. "How?"

"I don't know yet."

THAT NIGHT, AFTER DADDY PASSED out, I knocked on Rawls' door. He was rocking out to some classic rock bullshit. When I heard him turn it down, I went in and put a plastic bag with a six-pack of High Life in it on his dresser.

"Merry Christmas."

He looked at me, then at the beer. Then he took one out and offered me one, which I took.

"Where'd you get it?"

"Dixie Stop."

"How?"

"Fake."

"When'd you get a fake?"

"Sasha got us both one. Her momma's a hairdresser."

"What's hairdressing got to do with it?"

"She knows people, Rawls." I took a sip. I hated beer, but I liked how it made me feel, not just the buzz, but knowing I could drink something I hated and look like I liked it.

He took a sip of his, then looked at it, then looked at me. "You need to watch it around her. And you don't need to be buying alcohol neither."

"Why not?"

"Because look around, dummy. You wanna end up like Daddy? You wanna end up here for the rest of your life?"

"What's wrong with here?"

His jaw dropped. "What's wrong? Everything's wrong. This is a goddamn nightmare we're livin in."

"Well, you're right about that," I said. I was leading him.

"What?"

"You know that dude Tyler who lives down the way?"

"What about him?"

"He stole Sasha's weed."

Rawls looked back at the six-pack again, then at me. "Good. Y'all too young to be smoking, too."

"You smoked weed in fifth grade."

"Things were different back then."

"Nothing's ever different," I said, feeling smart.

He looked at his beer again. "What'd you bring me this for? You want me to get your weed back? You trying to bribe me?"

"No!" I said. Then I said, "Maybe."

Rawls pointed his beer bottle at me again. "You're dumb as shit, April. You know that?"

"Fuck you! Don't talk to me like that."

"I'll talk to you however I want. I'm your brother. I ain't got nothing but love for you, girl. But you're fucking up."

"Don't tell me what I'm doing," I said. "And I'm not. And you ain't a fucking schoolteacher, so you need quit acting like one."

I took two bottles from the six-pack and was about to leave his room, but then I stopped in the doorway and said, "That fool Tyler thinks he's a bad-ass. And we both know what happens when somebody thinks he can push people around and take their shit. And there was a time when I didn't have to ask you twice to get my back."

I waited until I saw that I'd hurt his feelings, then I shut the door on him.

SASHA WAS IN HER APPLEBEE'S uniform when she picked me up from school the next day. "Well?" she asked. "Is he gonna help?"

"I don't know," I said, lighting two cigarettes as we left the parking lot. I passed one to her. "I think he's depressed."

"Well, we gotta get our weed back."

"I'm thinking," I said.

"It was six hundred dollars' worth, April. My car payment's due in a week. My momma's gonna kill me. That was the whole point of this. To get ahead, not behind."

"I know!" I said. I was frustrated with her because I should've been the one to deliver the weed. Sasha was too easy to scare. Dudes saw her and only saw a piece of ass. People saw me and saw the crazy bitch who stabbed her brother. I think that was even the reason Casey Bentley had never tried to fuck with us since we'd been selling. Or maybe it was just the fact that we didn't move weight.

"Did you ask Reggie?" I asked her.

"Yeah but he just laughed."

"I figured."

"He said he couldn't front us nothing either. Too risky."

"Well, he ain't a dumbass."

"What're we gonna do?"

"Well," I said reluctantly, "I know one thing that would solve the problem."

"Damn it, April, I'm not fucking nobody for weed."

"That's the only reason Reggie gave us that first bag."

"I like him! There's a difference!"

"I don't really see it," I said, looking out the window. We were passing the Methodist Church where I'd once gone to hell in the form of a summer camp.

"There's a big difference," Sasha said.

"I guess."

"Would you fuck Tyler for it?" she asked.

"I ain't the one with those," I said, pointing at her boobs with my cigarette. The seatbelt helped me make my case.

Sasha rolled her eyes, then thought about it and asked, "Well, if you had these, would you?"

I thought about it.

"I guess not," I said.

"So let's think of something else," she said.

"ARE YOU SURE THIS IS a good idea?" Sasha said.

We had parked in front of Casey Bentley's trailer. There was two trucks besides his in the drive, and a dog was barking its ass off somewhere nearby. I didn't answer her question. I was getting my nerve up.

"Why do we have to do this now?" she said.

I turned to her sharply. "Getting our shit back today is gonna be easier than tomorrow. The day after that, it's gonna be even harder."

Sasha looked at me sideways.

"It's like cancer," I said. "You either cut it out or it kills you."

I opened the door and got out of the car. I walked through Casey Bentley's yard. When Sasha caught up, I told her to let me do the talking. She nodded, and I knocked on the door.

A dipshit I hated named Chuck answered it. "Oh shit," he said when he saw me.

"Fuck you, Chuck."

He took a good long look at Sasha then hollered for Casey. I could see another jersey-wearing loser inside too. They were all football rejects. The guys who played because they were big or fast and it gave them something to do that got them laid for a little while, but everybody knew they weren't going nowhere with it and, even more pathetic, after they quit the team they still wore the jersey. Maybe on some level I didn't

even blame them. Maybe I would've wore a jersey if I could. I
don't know. Maybe everything would be different if anything
was, but everything is what it is and probably always has been.

Casey smiled at me when he came to the door. "What's
up, Apeshit." That's what some people had started calling me,
and I did hate it, but I'd yet to let a single person know it.

"Sup, Casey."

His glassy eyes looked past me as if at a prize. "Sasha
Shaw. You wanna come in?"

"Hell no," she said.

"Yes we do," I said.

We walked in and it was dark and smelled like ass and
a million cigarettes. It was times like this that I was grateful
Daddy never let our house get to smelling like a goddamn ash-
tray. On the TV was some kind of machine gun killing video
game, and I saw Chuck slide a flat-looking tackle box under
the couch with his heel as we sat down. I had to wait until they
all got done eyeing Sasha again before we could get anything
done. Finally, Casey looked over at me.

"So what's the deal, April?"

"You know Tyler, that son of a bitch from Florida?"

Casey and Chuck exchanged a look. Then Chuck looked
at me.

"You talking about Mad Dog?"

I shrugged. "I don't know his fucking nickname."

"That's what they call him," Chuck said to Casey.

"Mad Dog?" Casey asked, flicking a Zippo with a fat thumb and toasting half his cigarette trying to light it. "He some kinda bad-ass or something?"

"Naw," Chuck said. "I mean, I think his name's just Maddux."

The guy whose name I didn't know was wearing a backwards Denver Broncos hat, and he nodded. "Like Greg Maddux," he said, still playing the video game. "Future Hall of Famer."

Casey nodded as if this was somehow significant, then pointed his blackened cigarette at me. "So, what about him?"

"He stole our weed," I said plainly.

Casey raised his eyebrows. "So?"

"Casey," I said, leaning forward. "Ain't no Florida pretty boy just gonna come up outta nowhere and start stealing shit from people like me and Sasha. We're from around here."

"Sasha ain't," Chuck said. "She's from Luther County."

"Shut the fuck up, you fat piece of shit," I said.

Casey and the guy in the Broncos hat laughed.

"Fuck you, slut," Chuck growled.

"You wish I was a slut," I snapped back. Then I said to Casey, "Listen. Everybody knows all the shit you got going on. With me and Sasha though, it's just green. It's just spending-money. But this fucker Tyler, he's just gonna keep getting bigger until one of y'all steps up."

Casey took a long drag, looked at Sasha, then back at me. "Your limp-dick brother know where you are right now?"

"Oh shit," Chuck boomed, snapping his fingertips like he was packing a can of dip.

I stayed staring at Casey. "No," I said. "He don't, and that ain't got nothing to do with anything."

"What're you saying I should do then, Apeshit?"

"I'm proposing that me, you, Chuck, Sasha, and your booty buddy over there if he wants to, all go over to Tyler's and get our weed back. We'll let you take half." I glanced at Sasha. "What's that, about two ounces?" Sasha nodded half-heartedly. I turned back to Casey and pretended not to know its exact worth. "That's like, I don't know, four or five hundred bucks. Free money."

"More like two or three," the guy in the Broncos hat corrected. He was looking at me now, and I saw he was fine as hell. "Free money either way," I said to him. "And from here on out, nobody has to worry about Tyler getting to be a bigger asshole than he is."

Casey looked at Bronco boy, but he'd gone back to playing the game. Casey looked at Chuck, and Chuck shook his head. Finally Casey nodded, and then he leaned back and crossed his big leg over his knee and slid an arm around the back of the couch and took a drag and blew smoke in my face. "Why should I trust you?"

I waved it away. "Why shouldn't you?"

"Because I don't know that mother-fucker. He ain't done me no wrong. Besides, I know Rawls ain't done thinking about how I fucked him up. For all I know, we get to Tyler's, and him and Tyler and who knows who else jumps us. You think I'm stupid?"

"Rawls is a pussy," I said. "Ain't nobody jumping anybody but us jumping Tyler. And it ain't even jumping him either. It's just justice." I looked at them all, one by one. "And everybody in Oak Park will benefit."

After another look at Chuck, Casey pointed his cigarette back and forth between me and Sasha. "Alright," he said. "We'll do it for some ass."

"Fuck you," Sasha said, standing up. "C'mon, April. Let's go." Casey, Chuck, and the other guy were laughing, but I stayed put.

"Let's go," she said, grabbing my arm.

I stared back at Casey and shook my head. "I thought you were a bad-ass."

He laughed. "I am, bitch. Alright." He nodded. "Get on these nuts and I'll do it." He nodded at Sasha, then at me. "She can go, you stay."

I didn't say anything, I just stared at him.

"C'mon, April," Sasha insisted. She was pulling me.

"You're lucky," I finally said.

"Lucky?" said Casey.

"You're lucky you didn't get cut that day you jumped Rawls." I stood up and looked down at him. "That's the only reason your fat ass is still breathing. Luck. And one day it's gonna run out."

"YOU *ARE* CRAZY," SASHA SAID as we walked back to the car. I pulled out two cigarettes and lit them and passed one to her.

"This whole town is full of shit," I said.

By the time she dropped me off, we had resigned ourselves to never getting our weed back, and, in addition, to never having boyfriends for the rest of our lives, and, also, to being lonely old biddies watching soaps all day, and we'd laughed about that.

Then I told her I was sure that if we put our heads together, we'd find a way to get the money for her car payment. She said she could get me a job at Applebee's, and I nodded politely at the idea.

I watched her drive off, and then I checked to make sure no one at home had seen me come in. Dad was asleep on the couch in a shirt and his gross little pecker was poking out of his boxers. I threw a blanket on him and checked Rawls' room. A couple science books were scattered on his bed, including one big yellow one about becoming an electrician. The beers I brought in the other day were unopened on the dresser where I'd left them. I don't know what I thought about that. I guess I was impressed. But mostly I was happy that he wasn't home so he wouldn't see me grab the butcher knife and strike out.

IT WAS A LONGER WALK to Tyler's than I thought, and by the time I got to the end of Oak Park and turned onto the highway I was covered in dust and had second guessed my plan so many times I wasn't even sure if I had one. I don't know what drove me, but I just couldn't have sat at home doing what, watching TV? Studying? Fuck that. I'd never studied a day in my life, and it was too late to start now. Plus I couldn't have sat still for ten seconds knowing some asshole from out of town had fucked me and Sasha out of what was ours. And made her cry. And made me waste my whole afternoon high. And changed my biggest problem in life from mosquito bites to a car payment that wasn't even mine.

A few cars drove past while I was walking down the highway, and it made me hope nobody I knew saw me. I passed a weedy cotton field and another field with a hay barn where some fat old cows looked at me, then a white church, and then I turned down the dirt drive that led to Tyler's falling-apart-ass green-ass house. It was a two-story but the roof was slouched, and a bunch of half-dead pecans were reaching over it like the Devil's hand. Tyler drove a red Prelude and I looked at my reflection in the window as I passed it and decided that even if I did look like shit, at least I didn't look scared. I made sure the knife was covered by my shirt and tight in the back of my shorts, then I knocked on the door.

When Tyler Maddux answered the door, I'd forgotten how fine he was. His eyes weren't cold, they were actually watery-looking, like they were full of light and tears, and he was barefoot in blue jeans and wore a half-unbuttoned red-and-black button-up shirt. He looked like a model playing a lumberjack on a TV show. The only thing wrong with him was his teeth, which were all kinds of crooked on the bottom row. He looked like one of them fish who lived under the sea with a light bulb hanging over his forehead and a mouth full of razor blades. I thought he was beautiful though, and I got insecure again as to what I must've looked like to him.

He raised an eyebrow and scratched the back of his neck while looking me up and down.

"Hi, I'm April," I said.

He didn't blink. "Nice to meet you," he said sarcastically. He looked out at the yard, then down at my gross legs and feet. "Where'd you walk here from?"

"I'm friends with Sasha," I said. Then I added like a question, "She was over here today?"

All his slyness vanished. He shrugged. "So?"

"Look, I don't know if she told you, but that weed she tried to sell you wasn't hers."

"Oh yeah?"

I nodded. "Now, I understand. In your shoes, I would've done the same. But the thing is, you didn't know who she was representing, and I think if you did, you might have paid her what was due."

He smiled, crooked teeth on full display. "What're you, the repo man?"

"Cute," I said. I cleared my throat. I blinked a bunch of times, trying to calm my nerves. "You're cute-looking too," I added, stepping forward. I reached out to touch his shirt.

He threw my arm back at me. "Get the fuck off!" He stepped back. "Who the fuck are you? Get the fuck out of here, girl."

"Fine," I said, clutching my arm like he'd hurt it. "But can I just ask you one more question?"

He looked completely confused as to why I hadn't left yet. "You got ten seconds," he said. "I don't know you. You don't know me. You need to leave."

I looked down as if ashamed, and I was, although more for what I was about to do than anything I'd done. I took a deep breath. I looked back up at him. I tried to look helpless. I tried to look cute. I tried everything I could to keep his attention and drag out the moment.

"Sasha said you told her you'd let her have it back if she, you know." I paused. "But she's got a boyfriend, so…"

"So?"

"So what about me," I finally said with perhaps more pride than I intended.

He looked at me like I was bat-shit. I tried to show off my hips, but I guess in a clowning way because we both knew I didn't have any, and he almost seemed to smile. Maybe that was my game, I thought, making fun of myself. So I played it up and did a hand gesture.

He squinted at me, like I was something in the distance, and for a second he really looked like he was a movie star, then his squint broke into loud laughter. When he didn't stop laughing, I stepped back. I put my hand on the porch post and picked off some paint and flicked it at him. He stopped and looked at me with something like surprise. He shook his head and turned around. He walked inside and left the front door open. Then he said over his shoulder, "Come on in then."

I felt more alive and afraid than I'd ever felt, and when I took the next step forward, I wondered not for the first time if being really afraid was all living ever really was. The first thing I saw was our weed on his kitchen table. I knew it was ours because it had a camouflage twist tie at the top of the bag, and nobody did that but Reggie. Next to the bag was a tin full of a shitload of other bags, and a little cigar box that had pills in compartments, and beside the cigar box was a gun. Tyler saw me eyeing it. Somehow without me knowing it, he'd stepped behind me and closed the door. Then he walked toward me, and I walked backward, deeper into the kitchen. I glanced down a hall and realized how big the house actually was. My heart was pounding. Half from fear, half from wondering what it would be like if we had sex. When I realized I was acting like I was afraid, I stopped.

"So what now?" I said, hoping he didn't hear the fear.

"You tell me, girl. What's your name?"

"April," I said. "And I already told you." I tried smiling.

He seemed unamused. "April what?"

"Cousins," I said.

He frowned like he was thinking. I glanced under the table and saw some grocery bags full of what might've been bricks of weed, and he had another plastic bag spilling over with different-sized baggies—I guess everything you might need to start selling a bunch of shit to a bunch of dumb-asses like me and everybody I knew. Mine and Sasha's sad $600 bag suddenly seemed like nothing compared to the hoard he was fixing to unload.

"Cousins," Tyler said finally. "I used to know a drunk named, um, Nick Cousins down at Smithy Sheetrock. Y'all related?"

I looked up from looking at his stash. There was a long pause. "He's my daddy," I said.

He looked me over again, then nodded knowingly and sadly and said, "I see it."

"How long you worked at Shitty Shit-rock?" I said, smiling again. "That's what we used to call it."

"Yeah," he said flatly. "I've heard that one."

"How long ago did you work with him?"

"I said I knew him, not worked with him."

I nodded. I began to imagine a younger version of Tyler, maybe even younger than me, selling my mom and dad drugs when I was still in junior high, maybe even middle school.

"How long ago?"

He scrunched up his face. "I don't know."

"I thought you were from Florida."

"I started up here."

"You started?"

"That's what I said, girl."

I felt like I'd hit a nerve, so I tried to be friendly again. "How long you been back in town?"

He took a step toward me. "Just a little bit."

I stepped backward, into the hallway, looking behind me into the dark.

"How old are you?" I asked.

He seemed offended. "How the fuck old are you?" His eyebrows shot up as if he'd made some brilliant point. I made sure to picture exactly where the butcher knife was against my back, and then I took a step toward him.

WHEN I LEFT TYLER'S HOUSE, what was left of mine and Sasha's weed was in a baggie swinging from my hand, as light as it was heavy. My knees were jelly, and my heart was pumping like it was gonna pop. My legs were moving as fast as they could without running.

I'd had to show Tyler the knife and explain I'd only brought it in case there was drama, and he'd only nodded.

It wasn't bad, I guess. It just wasn't what I'd stupidly hoped. I'd only been with a couple other guys, and none of them had been anything worth mentioning. All Chucks, to be honest. I thought that it might be different with Tyler because he was old and fine and a bad-ass, I guess. But maybe there was something about getting down with someone that sucked all the mystery out of them. It'd definitely turned everyone I'd ever done it with into ten times the asshole they were before, and Tyler was no exception.

Afterward we were lying on his giant mattress staring up at the fan, the breeze evaporating our sweat, and like every dumb girl ever, I couldn't help but wonder if he actually liked me, like maybe I'd been good enough to make him want me to come back on the sly. If I could somehow get him to be my boyfriend, then maybe I'd even be a bad-ass, the crazy-ass girlfriend of the hot shady guy who drove a Prelude and had his own house.

The only reason I thought any of this was because it had been so hot in his room that I'd asked if we could open the window, and instead of just saying yeah, he went over to it and opened it. It was hard, but he finally got it open.

"I don't usually open it because it gets stuck," he said, returning to the bed and sliding his arm under my head.

He'd done me a favor, and I was drunk on the romance of it.

"Can I ask another favor?"

"What."

But then the words sounded stupid in my head, and I didn't want to say them.

"Nevermind."

"What?" he said. "It can't hurt to ask."

"Oh," I said, genuinely surprised by his encouragement. I rolled onto my elbow and looked at him. "Can it be that we did it... just because?"

He rolled onto his elbow too, mildly amused.

I took a breath. The words were hard to get out. "I mean, can it be just because... we liked... you liked me?" I swallowed. "And not that other thing?"

He smirked. "You don't want your weed back, Miss Cousins?"

"No, I mean, it's mine. It's ours. I want it back." I closed my eyes and tried to believe in something like God for the first time in my life. "But can't you just give it to me?"

He laughed.

"You don't wanna have to've ho'ed for it?"

My eyes flew open, blazing in anger. He looked smug, still awaiting an answer. I looked away. I looked at the busted blinds on his open window and somehow calmed myself down enough to form words through clenched teeth. "Something like that," I said.

He laughed more. He sat up and lit a cigarette, still snickering like he knew some special secret I didn't. I felt more naked and put my shirt back on. He offered me a cigarette, which I took. He tried to light it, but I took the lighter out of his fist and lit it myself and threw it back at him. It bounced off his chest and he glanced at where it landed on the floor.

Then he leaned back, blew smoke over my head, and pointed at me with his cigarette. "You want to be girlfriend-boyfriend?" He laughed again, like he'd been thinking of that one awhile. Then he shook his head like he was trying to stop, but couldn't help himself. He knew it was pissing me off.

"Shut the fuck up," I said. "You're a piece of shit."

"I'm sorry, do you know me?" He was angry.

I felt humiliated. I got up off the bed.

"I wanted to ask a simple question. You're a goddamn asshole." I put my pants on. "How big a piece of shit do you have to be to steal something just to get some anyway?" I stepped into my shoes. "I'd rather be anything than something that pathetic."

I walked out of his room.

"Hey!" He ran around the bed and came after me.

I ran through the kitchen and grabbed our weed off his table. He let me get the weed, but he grabbed my knife off the counter before I could get to it. "Drop it," he said, pointing the knife at the bag.

"It's mine, mother-fucker!" I shouted.

"You think I wanted you in my bed, you skinny piece of shit? You're dumber than you look." He stepped forward, calm now, pointing the knife blade at his own chest. "I'm the only one moving anything around here from now on. You and that girl Sasha push more than a fucking nickel, I'm gonna hear about it, and I'm gonna get it again, you got me? And then you're gonna have a lot more dick to suck than what you just done to dig your way outta that."

I almost exploded. I almost ran at him. I almost shoved the knife in his neck. Instead, I looked at the gun on the table. Tyler saw me look, and then he laughed.

"Do it," he said. "I would fucking love to have a reason."

"Fuck you," I said, and I turned the doorknob.

Before it opened though, Tyler pushed the kitchen table across the room and pinned me against the door with it. I couldn't open it or move. Then he pulled the table back and grabbed my wrist and held it over my head. I tried to push him back, but he was too strong. Then the knife was at my throat, and I thought my life was over again, just like when I'd seen Rawls with the same damn knife in his side. My whole shitty little life flashed before my eyes. There was one good memory of me and Rawls and Mom and Dad at the beach, then the rest was mom's face all fucked up from drugs, and the time I stole dad's car and crashed it, and the summer I spent at Grandma's where she tried to beat Jesus into me, and then this, and that was it.

"Drop it," Tyler said.

I let go of our $600 worth of marijuana, and Tyler turned me around. With my back against the door, he poked the tip of the knife into my chest and reached down and picked the bag up off the floor and then dumped it all out on the table until there was about two joints worth left in the bag. Then he wadded that up and stuffed it down the front of my pants. "For your trouble," he said. "Because that's about what you were worth." He raised an eyebrow. "Now you want anything else?"

"My knife back," I said.

He smirked and offered it handle first. He jerked it back when I reached for it and swung it point down into the table next to the gun, where it stuck.

"Get the fuck out and don't come back."

Had I been born larger, or older, or a man maybe, maybe I would've done something different than I did. Maybe I would've gone for the gun. Maybe I would've gone for the knife. Maybe I would've just beat his ass with my bare hands. Maybe I would've got my own ass beat, or died. But I wasn't born anyone but me.

I turned the doorknob in what felt like slow-motion. I opened the door and took one step out, then I stopped with my hand still on the doorknob and turned around and said, "You think you're a bad-ass, Tyler, but you ain't."

"And what're you? Think about that," he said, "when you're digging weed out your ass."

"You ain't shit," I said, letting myself cry. "As a matter of fact," I wiped my eyes, "the only bad-ass around here is Casey

Bentley, and he ain't gonna like it too much when he hears how you done me and Sasha."

"Two dumb hookers? I don't even know who he is, but I don't think he'll give a shit."

"Casey Bentley and I go way back," I said. "I tried to tell him you was gonna come in here and fuck up his game, but he didn't listen."

"His game?"

"You don't know nothing, do you. Tell you what. Go back to Florida, Mad Dog. That's right. I know who you are. Everybody in Oak Park does, because I told them, and they already don't like you. In fact, I'm gonna come back by here in the morning, and if you're gone, with your little BB gun and your even littler dick, then I'll keep my mouth shut and won't tell Casey Bentley what you done to Sasha—that's his girlfriend—and what you done to me too."

He busted out laughing. "You think I give a fuck about Casey Bentley? I never even heard of him."

"Well, he's heard of you, trust me." I pointed at his supply. "And he's got ten times that in his fucking glovebox. He's been moving weight since he was fourteen. By the way, I didn't see no money around here neither. Casey Bentley's got a money-counting machine on his coffee table you can hear from the street, and it don't ever turn off. He's a bad-ass for real, and he's coming for you. Just you wait." I glared at him like I'd just cast a hex, then I slammed the door.

I walked quickly but resisted the urge to pull the bag out of my drawers until after I got to the highway because I didn't want to give Tyler the satisfaction if he was still watching. I was past the church before any kind of normal feeling came back to me.

I didn't know what would happen with Casey and Tyler, and I didn't care. I hoped whatever might happen would end up bad for both of them. The rest of the walk home, all of that seemed to pass from my mind, and instead what I kept circling around was what story I was telling myself about why I'd slept with Tyler and whether it mattered. By the time I got home I decided it didn't, just like everything else didn't. Daddy's car was gone and Rawls was in his room booming his stereo and studying probably. I wanted to hang out with somebody but I didn't want to bother him. I took a shower and got high on the rest of me and Sasha's weed on the front porch and thought about Momma.

I GOT SUSPENDED FROM SCHOOL the next day. I had been pretty much failing algebra because I couldn't see how it mattered, when old-ass Mrs. Randall told me to stay after school. She was a churchmouse and had been trying all year to make me see why algebra was so important. I think she wanted to talk to me about Jesus—they all did—but she was a coward so all she could talk about was math. I felt bad for her, like she wanted to fix me because she couldn't fix her own sad life. Algebra wasn't about numbers and math, she said, it was about solving problems, and if you could learn the formulas of algebra and follow them to solve the problems, you were teaching yourself discipline to solve the problems of life. I looked her dead in the eye and said, "That's bullshit, Mrs. Randall, I'm sorry." She jumped back like I'd slapped her. "Life ain't got no solution. All problems do is grow, and then one day you're dead. All you can do is roll with them. That's why I know math is dumb as hell." I crossed my arms, which were all bitten up by mosquitoes and which I knew seeing would make her squirm. When she started to tear up, I said, "I'm sorry, but it just is." Then she left the room, and I told myself I wasn't being a brat, I was saving her from wasting her time. It was Mr. Woodson, the vice-principal, who came back in and asked me if I'd cussed her out. "Sure as hell did," I said. That's what actually got me suspended. I think they wanted to cut me some slack, but I was tired of pretending to be somebody I wasn't. Rawls was pissed at me too. I could tell he thought I was circling the same slow drain as Momma, only a hell of a lot faster, and he couldn't do nothing about it. I wasn't worried, though, because Momma had been twenty-nine when she left, so the way I saw it I had like eleven or twelve years before that. An eternity. I asked Rawls what he was studying.

"I'm gonna be an electrician," he said. "You know they make fifty an hour?"

"An hour?"

He nodded. "All it is is math," he said, "and tools. That's the only thing you gotta pay for. But if you can get on a good crew, you can use theirs and learn on the job. Only thing is, you gotta get that Associates."

"You going back to school?"

"Luther Tech. I'm getting my GED at the vocational fair they're having next week at the Chamber of Commerce, then I'm cleared to enroll. I'm gonna be making bank here shortly, April. We won't even have to live here no more."

"You wanna leave?"

"Hell yeah, I wanna leave! Don't you?"

I looked out the window at the rutted driveway and the bicycles flat on the ground and the power lines through the pines and the shit-ass ugly sky.

"I guess," I said. "But where would we go?"

"Anywhere. We could go across town, or we could go down to Tampa where Momma's folks are, or anywhere else. Florida's big. The point is, you need to stay in school and quit fuckin up so when we do leave, you ain't in trouble. And you ain't caught up in nothing. And I don't want you smoking weed or selling it."

"Don't tell me what to do, Rawls."

"I ain't telling you, April, I'm begging. I love you, and I don't want to see you get drowned by this place."

"What happened to you? You used to be a bad-ass. All you do now is talk like a goddamn preacher."

"You know what happened to me. Casey Bentley happened to me."

"Casey Bentley ain't shit, Rawls. He's a pussy."

"You don't know what you're talking about, April, as usual."

"I know more than you think I do."

"You almost killed me," Rawls said after a pause.

"I was trying to help."

"You could've killed him! You know what would've happened? Jail. You think school sucks? Jail's worse. You don't come back the same, and I'd have probably gone too. You see what I'm saying?" He pinched his fingers. "We were this close to this family getting split up."

"I was protecting my brother," I said defiantly.

"That's the point, April. You can't protect me, and I can't protect you. You think Momma and Daddy didn't try to protect each other? You think Casey Bentley wasn't trying to protect something? Everybody's trying to protect everything and that's what fucks us up. It's a setup. The deck's stacked. That's why we gotta get out."

Suddenly there was a knock at the door, and we both spun around.

"RAWLS! Get the FUCK out here!"

Casey Bentley's voice. Rawls looked at me. I shrugged.

Rawls looked out the window, then instead of going outside, he went to his room. When he came out a minute later, he didn't even look at me, he just walked past. Then he answered the door. I stood at his side. Casey was on the porch with a hat pulled low over his face.

"I just got fuckin jacked," Casey said. He was wheezing and looked like he was trying not to be seen.

"Sounds like a personal problem," said Rawls.

"Look," Casey said, "I know me and you got beef, but I come to ask you a favor. Dude named Tyler. Lives down the way. Mother-fucker thinks he's a bad-ass," Casey said. "Just got through waving a gun in my face. Took half my fucking stash." Casey lifted his cap and his forehead had a large gash, and everything around his left eye was red and swollen.

"Damn, son," Rawls said. "At your place?"

"Yeah." Casey glared at me while he lit a cigarette, then he pointed it at me. "And I'm gonna leave it up to her to explain how she's in the middle of this shit because I ain't trying to get a fucking knife swung at me again." He looked at Rawls. "But right now we need to talk in private."

Rawls looked at me. I didn't do anything. I didn't know what I was going to say. He looked back at Casey and lifted his shirt. I could see from the side the black handle of a gun in Rawls' waistline. "Just so you don't pull some shit," Rawls said. "If you're cool with that, we can talk in my room, and I ain't gonna fuck with you."

Casey looked around the yard, then back at Rawls and nodded. Rawls walked down the hall to his room, leaving the door open. Casey flicked the cigarette he'd just lit into the yard, came in, and shut the door. When he passed me, he said, "I know exactly what you fucking did." He held me with his eyes for a second, then went in Rawls' room and they shut the door. I tried to listen, but they turned up the music. I went back to the couch in the living room and stared down the hall. I got worried for Rawls. I wondered if it was a setup to get him back for what I'd brought on Casey, so I went to the window and looked out at the neighborhood. Nobody else came. I watched it get dark.

Casey and Rawls came out of Rawls' room in a cloud of smoke, and for one absurd second I was worried what Daddy would do if he smelled it.

TEN MINUTES LATER RAWLS WAS in basketball clothes and eating a bowl of cereal.

"Where you going," I said.

"Nowhere," he said. "And you ain't coming."

"Rawls, talk to me."

"You talked enough," he said. Then he just scooped mouthful after mouthful. His silent treatment was almost too much to bear, and I felt guiltier and guiltier.

"What'd y'all talk about in there? What're y'all gonna do?"

He slammed a fist on the table, and milk jumped out the bowl. "What the fuck are you over at Casey Bentley's for?

That mother-fucker is dirty. Always has been." He clutched his own head. "I don't know why I have to explain this to you! You were there when he beat my ass. And then you went over there? I don't know who you are anymore."

"Rawls."

He got up and threw the cereal bowl in the sink, re-tucked the gun in his waistline, and walked out.

I caught up to him in the yard and reached for him, but he grabbed my arm and slung me around and my butt skidded across the dirt, and I got sand all up my ass. I almost cried, but I fought it off. "I know where you're going," I said. "Why don't you just let Casey go. Why you gotta get in the middle now?"

"Because your dumb-ass stirred up a fuckin hornet's nest." He bit his lip and shook his head and jerked me up off the ground and pulled me close, and I could still smell the cereal. "You know what Casey told me in there?"

I shook my head.

"That you went over there and fucked Tyler."

He twisted my arm and I squirmed, but then I said, "So?"

"So it's true." He looked down. "I knew it was. I guess I didn't want to believe my own sister… was…"

"Was what, Rawls."

He shook his head. Without looking up, he wiped his eyes. "I love you, girl," he said, "but right now I can't stand to look at you."

I was crying now, too, and I hated it. I wiped my face. "Stop," I said to myself out loud.

"You got two whole years til you're done with school, April. Two years. That's a long-ass time. There ain't no way I can watch out for you for two whole years. If Casey's after you, he's gonna get you."

"But Casey ain't after me."

"Until yesterday he wasn't," Rawls said. "He had a little theory that you went over there to start a fight between him and Tyler, and then he told me that if I didn't help him take Tyler down, he was coming for you. That's why I'm going over there. I'm gonna end this shit tonight. For you."

"I don't need you to protect me," I wanted to say, but I didn't. My brother was the only person who had ever loved me, and I knew I couldn't stop him.

"Go back inside," he said, and he started to walk away.

"His bedroom window sticks," I said. He paused but didn't turn around. "It's low enough to climb in, and it's probably still open. It's a big house and if he's in the kitchen he might not hear you."

Rawls stood there, facing away, for a long time. Then he shook his head and walked on.

WHEN RAWLS WAS OUT OF sight, I paged Sasha and asked her to come pick me up when she called back. She said she had a test in the morning and needed to study. I let myself cry all the tears I'd held back from Rawls.

"I'll be there in a minute," she said.

When she arrived, I asked her to take me to the Dixie Stop. She did. I gave her some money and asked her to go in and get cigarettes. "Fine," she said, "but then you're gonna tell me what's got you so upset."

She left the car running and walked inside. I slid over into the driver's seat and threw it in reverse and left her. I drove down the highway past the fertilizer plant and dead stores and the payday loan and the daycare I went to one year and the reservoir and the river until I was back at Oak Park. I drove Sasha's Corolla past Casey Bentley's trailer and checked that nobody was home. I parked behind a phone pole covered in weeds and turned off the lights but left it running. Then I jumped a fence of Casey's neighbor's and passed a dog chained to a tree, got lucky it didn't bark, then jumped the fence again into Casey's yard and went in the back door of his trailer.

In the living room I stuck my arm under the couch and pulled out the box I saw Chuck kick underneath it the day before. I opened it and saw more money than I'd ever seen. For a second I wondered if God was real. Meaning would I be punished any more if I took it all, or should I just stick to our $600? And did it matter that Casey wasn't the one who owed it to us? Did it matter who you got even off of as long as you got even? I had all these other thoughts in my head too. Bigger thoughts almost like algebra but with people. I knew one problem was nobody respected or gave a damn about me except Rawls, but even he didn't respect me. So that was a problem. If nobody respects you, and only one person loves you, you don't get shit. You don't get to live. I might as well be that dog chained to that tree in that yard, not even barking at what's in front of it because it's been whipped so bad. So how the hell do you solve that problem? Maybe it was to never let anybody see you coming, not even yourself. Nobody thought I would go see Tyler, not even me, until I did it, and I'd survived just fine. And nobody'd think I'd rip-off Casey Bentley, not even me, not tonight, and so here I was, and doing it felt right. It was like finally the world had a map. As long as you keep surprising yourself, maybe you were going the right way.

Plus I never forgave that bastard for putting my brother in the
hospital and racking us up all those medical bills. Just because
it was over for Rawls didn't mean it was over with me. I still
felt like shit for stabbing him, and that was all Casey Bentley's
fault. Then I had this idea that losing is better than winning,
because when you lose, nobody respects you, and when no
one respects you, that just makes it easier to get them back
because nobody ever sees anyone they don't respect coming
until it's too late. In fact, if I was Rawls, I would've gone over
there to Tyler's and sent Casey Bentley to knock on the front
door while I snuck in the back, then shot Tyler in the back
while he was jawing with Casey Bentley in the doorway. Then
I would've shot Casey Bentley and left the gun on Tyler, and
left. Part of me was hoping Rawls would know this and do it. I
knew he'd be thinking it because he was smarter than both of
them put together, and I hoped he hadn't lost that that instinct
that says to keep ahead of everything or you die. If you're
always ahead, all anybody can do is try to catch up. And not
even the Devil and all of hell can catch anybody who's ahead
of themselves.

WHEN I GOT BACK TO the Dixie Stop Sasha was talking to
some boys from somewhere else. They saw me first and then
she turned and her smile vanished. She walked over and
opened the door and pulled me out of the driver's seat and
started hitting me upside the head. She called me all kinds of
things and I apologized and tried to get her to chill but I knew
she had to exhaust herself so I let her. I was on the ground and
she ended it by flicking her cigarette at me. I blocked it with

my hand, but the coals scattered and burnt holes all over my shirt. I tapped them out and then just looked at her with no real expression on my face. She helped me get up. I walked around to the passenger seat, and pulled out $600 exactly and handed it to her.

"The fuck is that?"

"I found our weed," I said, "and then I sold it."

"You stole that," she said, "just like you stole my car, April! You can't be doing that shit. I don't want this!"

"I'll just leave it here then," I said, and I put it in the console between two CDs.

We drove to the McDonald's and got French fries and ice cream.

"I slept with Tyler," I said. We were sitting at the outside tables in front of the plastic playground.

"Oh my God," she said with a mouth full of ice cream. Then she swallowed it. "Are you serious?"

"It wasn't that bad," I said. "It was actually kind of sweet."

"Really?"

"Yeah," I lied. "He was nice."

She looked confused. "But he stole our weed."

"I know," I said. "He even tried to give it back, but," I shrugged, "I told him I didn't want it."

"What? Why not?"

"Because... I didn't want it to be about that. I just wanted it to be what it was."

She looked as confused as anybody who'd ever met me or Tyler would've been. "You really like him?" she asked.

I nodded. "Kinda. He's cute."

"He's so mean."

"He is," I said reluctantly. "But I am too." I tried to look apologetic.

Sasha stared back, then shook her head and picked up our last couple of fries. She dragged them through the ketchup as if gathering her thoughts. "You're not mean, April," she finally said. She pointed the bloody fries at me and paused. "You're a bad-ass."

We held eyes for a second before she folded them into her mouth and smiled. I smiled back. Then she crumpled the fry box.

I got up and ordered us another to split. While we were eating it, I told her how Tyler had busted in on Casey and robbed him and how Casey blamed me and came over and asked Rawls to help him get back at Tyler. Then I told her that Rawls told him to fuck off and had stayed in his room, so Casey went alone. Then I went back to the truth, sort of, and told her since I knew Casey would be gone, I'd decided use her car to get our money back from him in case I had to make a quick getaway.

"Jesus Christ, April."

"Don't worry," I said. "I parked it in a hiding spot. Nobody saw your car."

"Fuck me," she said, tapping out two cigarettes.

"I'm telling you it's fine."

We smoked and talked some more until some assistant manager banged on the window and mouthed that we couldn't smoke in the playground. Sasha and I shot her a bird and got up and walked to the car. Instead of getting in, I walked her to her door and told her I was grateful for her. She was my best friend. She asked me what we were gonna do now, and I told her I was gonna walk home.

"By yourself? That's like an hour."

"I know."

"It's late."

"I'll be fine."

She frowned. "You going to school tomorrow?"

"Yeah," I lied. I hadn't told her about the suspension. "I'll be fine. I just need some time to think."

She still looked confused, but then she nodded and we hugged, and I bummed half the pack for the walk. Then I surprised both of us by kissing her on the cheek.

"What's that for?" she smiled. We never did shit like that.

"I don't know," I said.

DADDY'S CAR WAS BACK WHEN I got home, and it was parked all crooked, so I knew he was passed out in his room. Rawls was on the couch, alive but drunk. He was clutching a fifth of what looked to be gin and watching a weird TV show on mute. He looked at me when I walked in, took a long sip and returned his eyes to the TV where a guy in a suit was sitting in a chair in a room with a black and white floor and red curtains for walls. I walked over to him and stood in front of it.

"Is Tyler dead," I whispered.

He stopped drinking for a second, then he continued drinking.

"And Casey?"

He lowered the bottle and looked at me, surprised, "How'd you know?"

I held out my hand. He looked at it, then passed me the bottle. I took a sip. It was gin, and I coughed. I wiped my mouth with my arm.

"Because if he threatened me, I knew you'd never trust him again even if y'all did take care of Tyler. Plus, there's one thing I know about you, Rawls, even if you don't yourself. Or if you forgot."

"Yeah?" he said like he was dead inside. "What's that."

"That you're a bad-ass." I passed the gin back to him. "Always have been. Always will be." I nodded at him, and I meant it.

He stared at me, then suddenly blew air out of his nose, a near-laugh. He sat up on the couch and pulled out a butcher knife and held it dangling from the handle. "This ours?"

"Shit," I said. "I guess I forgot it."

He looked at it, then looked at me.

"What were you gonna do, try to kill him? Or was this just in case he tried to hurt you?"

"I didn't know what I was gonna do," I said, "until I did it."

That's when I reached into my shorts and pulled a handful of cash out of each pocket—all the money I'd stolen from Casey Bentley—and I dropped it on the cushion beside him. Piled up, it was around $3K.

An hour later we were driving south out of town in Daddy's car. We'd left $500 for him and a note, but that was it. We were going about 90 when we passed a cop parked behind a billboard for Disney World, and my heart skipped a beat.

We drove slow after that.

21 EXTREMELY BAD BREAKUPS

21

Two COLOSSALLY IDIOTIC PEOPLE WHO have been dating for years finally get sick of each other, so they decide to break up, but they're also afraid that if they do, they won't be able to find anyone better, so they make a pact to have unprotected sex every day for a month. If they get pregnant during that period, they'll stay together for the kid. If they remain unpregnant, they'll take it as a sign that they need to break up. On the penultimate day of the month, they're fighting about nothing—screaming, slamming doors, deliberately sabotaging each other's self-esteem, dragging old arguments out of the past, etc.—but they still haven't gotten pregnant. So they have sex one last time to fulfill the terms of the pact. Afterward, awaiting the results of a pregnancy test together, they almost bond in their shared terror of either outcome. When the results are positive—it's a pregnancy—they heave a sigh of momentary relief. At least the decision to stay together has been made for them. But then the more enduring fear of having to be parents together hits them both like a speeding school bus destroying a pedestrian who has walked out into the street while looking at their phone. Both feel this metaphorical school bus of relationship-based dread slam into them for hours, then days, then years. Only after many, many years, when their child is an adolescent, does the school bus become a cloud, a numbness, an all-enveloping void with which the couple is only able to cope by medicating themselves with alcohol and continual exposure to violent entertainment. So, it's not even a real breakup, it's an anti-breakup, which is worse than all the real breakups to come put together.

20

A YOUNG COUPLE HAS TO break up because the man gets drafted to go to war and the woman wins a lottery where you have to be a nun to win. They are torn because they both love each other, but the man doesn't want to be imprisoned for draft-dodging, and the woman wants the money enough to become a nun. In the end, they hatch a plan to do long-distance while he's at war and she pretends to be a nun to get the money. Once she has the money she'll leave the nunnery and write him and tell him where she is, at which point he'll desert the army and they'll finance their life on the run with her lottery money.

The woman holds up her end of the bargain. She leaves the nunnery the second she gets the money, and she writes the man, but a reply to her letter from the man's commanding officer informs her the man was killed by mortar fire while fighting in the trenches, so the woman goes back to the nunnery with the money in hand, and they let her back in because this order of nuns is all about forgiveness. In fact, the woman's return confirms for the nun in charge that fate is ultimately benevolent, and even if you let people rip you off, eventually they'll change their ways and do right by you.

The woman settles into a routine at the nunnery then, telling herself she's only there until she figures out what she really wants to do with her life, but the longer she's a nun, the more she gets into it, and she probably would have remained a nun forever had the war not eventually ended.

Two weeks after the superpowers sign the armistice, the man shows up at the nunnery in uniform with his full accompaniment of arms and asks the head nun if the woman is around. She is, and she comes out, and when she sees her former lover's face she nearly faints. He's literally shell-shocked from the war and metaphorically shell-shocked from seeing her after all these years, and through heaving sobs he asks her why she never wrote him. He says he would've deserted in an instant if only she'd sent word. Instead, he remained in the trenches and was there exposed to levels of slaughter so extreme that his basic ability to live a normal life thereafter had been permanently undermined. Worst of all, he became a slaughterer himself, and at the end of most of his days in the combat zone, he actually begged God to let him be killed, if only because it would free him from the torment of life in the trenches, a thing he thought that death could not be worse than. As he speaks to her, his skin hangs beneath his eyes as if everything he's seen has somehow made his face a little bit melty.

Shocked that he's even alive, the nun explains that she did write him but received a reply from his commander saying he was dead. She darts back into the nunnery and returns with the letter, hands shaking. As the soldier reads it, his expression of confusion becomes one of profound regret and faint relief. He points at his name in the letter and explains that he and another soldier in his battalion who died on the first day of fighting shared the same name, and that the commander must have mistakenly believed it had been addressed to his dead brother in arms. The ghosts haunting the soldier's countenance seem to momentarily depart, and he looks at the nun excitedly. She looks sad, but then she embraces him. The soldier suggests that they leave the nunnery immediately. Then he looks over her shoulder into the foyer of the nunnery, and, seeing no one, whispers, "Do you still have the money?"

The nun then explains that she's not sure if she can leave. The soldier looks at her, confused. She says she actually doesn't mind being a nun. She says you never have to worry about the complexities of romantic entanglement, for one, since you and God can never break up because God loves you no matter what you do, what you think, or how you feel or act. Even if you hate God, she explains with a smile, God still loves you. The soldier is looking at her like she's lost her mind. As if addressing his unease, she adds that you can even forget about God when you want to imagine loving someone else. It's like God just becomes whatever you want your partner to be, omnipresent or never present at all, overbearing and demanding everything you have or absolutely indifferent and willing to let you do anything you want without ever asking for anything in return, and that makes it so easy to feel God's love and to love God back at your own convenience. The soldier, even more wounded and confused than before, starts to bash the whole idea of God and explain how the love of God isn't real, or at least isn't a satisfactory substitute for what they had, and could have again, so easily... but he stops himself before very much of it comes out of his mouth. He can see in the nun's smile and in her eyes how happy her faith in God has made her, no matter how ludicrous it seems to him, or ruinous it is to his own happiness, or how self-serving her idea of religious devotion is in general. He asks her if she's truly certain that remaining a nun is what she wants. She thinks about it for a moment, then nods slightly, wiping tears. He nods commandingly, the consummate soldier. He wishes her the best and salutes her, then turns on his heels and marches stiffly away, but halfway to the road his stiff march slackens, until he's just walking sadly. Seeing him walking so sadly away, she re-falls in love with him. She says a quick prayer to God asking God to say nothing if it would be okay to leave the nunnery. After one second of hearing no response, she praises God for giving her permission and rushes after the soldier, calling his name just as he has stepped into the street. He turns around in the middle of the street—smiling—only to be smacked into by an empty school bus going full speed.

The nun staggers backward, horrified. The soldier is just a clump of bloody flesh in the road—contorted, bleeding, bent, and moaning in an inhuman shape. She watches the bus disappear down the road, running stoplights and not hitting anything else, but causing other cars to crash as they try to avoid hitting it, or being hit by it.

Assuming the soldier is dead, or soon to be, and unable to bear seeing the man she loved, who'd been so brave in the war, and so devoted to her through the years, and so honorable and selfless in the ways of love just now despite his irreligious convictions, so indecorously mangled and bashed-in, she runs back inside the nunnery, devastated. There the head nun yanks her by the habit and spins her around and slaps her lightly across the cheek and says, "I've been watching you out the window and I could hear your whole conversation. This makes it twice you've intended to leave God's fold. With the money. For a man. You're clearly not cut out for nunning around up in here. Get out, and yes, we're keeping the money. We'll give it to someone who can take the vows of religious living more seriously." The head nun then yanks the habit off the woman's head and throws it across the room where it lands in a hamper.

The ex-nun staggers out of the nunnery, defrocked, destitute, hair freed from the habit, and broken-hearted. With all her beautiful long dark hair freely blowing in the summer wind, she even questions God, since what kind of God could allow a consummate soldier noble in the ways of love to be hit by a bus like that, let alone allow the war that slaughtered so many people in such gruesome events she'd heard about second-hand. Numbed by loss, hair amazing, she walks over to her would-have-been lover's corpse and forces herself to behold it in all its manglement. The crispness of his uniform contrasts sharply with how twisted and dead-looking he is in it. Then, her eyes shining with a Hollywood-esque, half-baked epiphany, the ex-nun seizes the soldier's sidearm and wrests it from its holster. "Let's see how merciful you really are," she mutters Godward, and then with a shaking hand she points the barrel at her own chest and pulls the trigger. The blast spins her around twice and she falls crossways over the soldier, gushing blood all over his body from the hole on her heart. The impact of her fall, however, startles the soldier out of his grisly coma. He sees the nun's beneficent face tilted just above his. Her eyes widen, glimmering with the recognition that he's still alive—while simultaneously dimming with the reckoning of her own impending demise. He tries to mouth something, but he can't because she's crushing his lungs. She tries to roll off of him, but she's lost so much blood that she's too weak to roll more than a few inches. The wound on her heart is now bathing his face, and he's blinking and choking on her blood while trying to show the same heroic resolve in the face of tragedy for which he was known in the trenches.

"We should have just broken up," the soldier says ruefully, coughing and spitting between gulps of blood. "Before the war."

"I know," the ex-nun agrees.

There's a terrible silence as both imagine the lives they might have lived had they not tried to stay together during the war.

"You know what?" she mutters weakly. "Let's break up now."

"What? Why? We're about to die."

"I know, but it'll be more meaningful if we break up on our own terms and not have Death do our dirty work for us."

The man is silent.

"Don't you see how dying's a cop out?" she asks, annoyed at his silence.

"Who cares!" he says. "We're dying!"

She can't believe that he can't understand why they shouldn't break up before they die to assert their agency in the face of imminent mortality, and he can't see why they shouldn't forget about that and meet death together, perhaps in discord about what it might mean, but at least defiantly allied. They go back and forth several more times, hashing out their various arguments, but they slip simultaneously into separate unconsciousnesses before their tiff is resolved.

19

THE IDIOTS WHOSE ANTI-BREAKUP RESULTED in a child are now in their fifties, and they tell the child, who is now an adult, that they're finally considering breaking up because of irreconcilable differences, but first they'd like input from him because he knows them better than anyone.

Their son doesn't understand why, given how long they've been together, their differences are suddenly so irreconcilable. His parents then awkwardly reveal the circumstances of his conception. It takes them several hours to describe their fears, why the pregnancy pact seemed like a smart move at the time, and how they've been unhappy ever since. The son is confused for a long time, but once he possesses a full understanding of the situation, he explodes in anger. "You should've just broken up!"

"But then you wouldn't have been born," they say.

"I wouldn't know that," the son says. "There wouldn't even be a problem."

The parents look down at the ground, then at each other, imagining the lives they could've lived if they'd broken up

earlier. The son looks from one to the other. They say they
see the wisdom in what he has said. Then, with great regret
for their original decision not to, they finally break up right
there in front of him, only it's much harder than it would
have been earlier, because now they've been together for thirty
more years and their adult child is standing there. Watching
the breakup play out in almost surreal slow-motion, the son
clings to the hope that knowing what he now knows about his
bizarre, almost preposterous origin will somehow invigorate
rather than incapacitate his own ability to capably navigate
his own romantic dilemmas.

18

THE CHILD OF THE IDIOTS is a surgeon trying to save the lives
of the soldier and ex-nun who are both lying comatose on
adjacent operating tables and who have just been helicoptered
in… while also breaking up with the only other person in the
O.R., a nurse with whom the surgeon has been having a secret
affair because the hospital prohibits employees from dating.
The double surgery lasts 79 hours and has to be done simultaneously because too much of the nun's blood is still mixed
with the soldier's, which requires a bunch of other little surgeries to be done to stabilize him before it can be pumped out,
and the son of the idiots is the only person believed capable
of pulling this surgery off. In fact, he is considered by many
in the surgical community to be the preeminent surgeon of
the age.

   While moving back and forth between the two near-
corpses, trying to repair their wounds in reverse order—her

blood loss, his drowning in her blood, her gunshot to the chest, his bus accident trauma—the nurse he has been dating is unable to focus on passing him the clamps because the surgeon is also saying things like, "I think we should see other people," in between things like, "Clamps!" The nurse's hands are wet from tears, and the nurse keeps dropping the instruments on the floor and having to rewash them. The surgeon orders the nurse to go home because there is too much at stake for the nurse to be so emotional. The nurse calls the surgeon cold-blooded and asks why the surgeon chose now to break up. The surgeon shouts that he has to concentrate and he can't when he's living a lie by having an unsanctioned workplace relationship. If it were up to him he'd break up at one of their houses or at a restaurant and have a real conversation about it, but these two people's lives are at stake, and he knows that if he can just break up with the nurse right now, they will probably be saved. The nurse shouts that that is unfair! Just then the machines both patients are hooked up to start beeping like crazy, and the surgeon roars toward the nurse, "Out of my O.R.!" then dives back into the soldier's chest cavity with three different types of medical instruments in each hand. The nurse steps backward through the flappy doors. Then the surgeon looks up at the nurse with burgeoning remorse. He promises they'll continue the discussion later. "And," the surgeon adds, "I'll listen to everything you have to say, and think about it, too." The nurse nods, faintly hopeful, as the doors flap shut between them.

While changing from scrubs to street clothes in the locker room, the nurse reflects that by postponing their conversation, some change in circumstance could intervene in the surgeon's life—i.e., the surgeon might get sad—and that might keep the door open for the nurse and him to be together. At this thought, he smiles while tying his shoes, then goes down to the lobby. Through the sliding doors at the entrance to the hospital, the nurse sees it's pouring rain. The nurse checks his bag for an umbrella, but realizes that in his haste to prepare for the double surgery earlier that day, he'd forgotten to check the weather. As he steps out into the rain with his coat thrown over his head—the sound of the rain on it like a hundred tiny drums as he runs to his car—he realizes that what just transpired was probably the last conversation he and the surgeon will ever actually have about the relationship. His shoes and socks get soaked as he runs, speculating that if he ever tries to reinitiate the uncomfortable discussion, the surgeon will probably repropose postponement, endlessly insisting on the urgency of some emergency that conveniently renders every conceivable difficult discussion temporarily unhaveable. The nurse reaches his car, drenched, squishy, and cold, and falls into the driver's seat and slams the door and starts the car and sits there with rain dripping down his face into his lap.

17

THE NURSE DRIVES HOME IN the downpour, veering wildly around other cars, enraged one second, bereft the next, disgusted with himself for being such a pushover, furious with the surgeon for prioritizing professional excellence over personal relationships, then veering into admiration for the surgeon for being so good at saving so many hard-to-save lives, then being upset at himself for admiring that quality more than he admires his own self-worth, then being furious with himself for carrying on an unsanctioned workplace relationship. *Dating a coworker is so fucking stupid*, he thinks. *What the fuck are you doing with yourself? Why can't you just get it together? Just be happy and find someone who's also happy and who you make happy and who makes you happy and just be happy with them, fuck!*

At home the nurse calms down by scrolling the internet. One of his friends from school has just posted a music video by his favorite band, which has just released a new album. The fact that he hadn't even known that his favorite band had come out with a new album strikes him as particularly significant. He watches the video several times. It's epic. It does everything that that band has always done well... times ten. It makes him weep. He pours a glass of wine and replays the video. He turns it up. He finds the song on his phone and puts in his earbuds and walks, invigorated, through the now-just-misty rain, down the street to his favorite bar, blasting the song. It's the sort of bar the surgeon wouldn't be caught dead in, but where the nurse likes to watch sports sometimes and relax. As he walks into the bar, his mood is more than high, it's bordering on dangerously manic. *God it feels good to step out of the rain into somewhere familiar!* Besides that, there's an awesome song from the nineties that's just started on the jukebox. Not one by his favorite band, but still a great song. He pulls out his earbuds and basks in it like entrance music. This is who he is. This. This moment. This place. Right now. This is love. This is life. This song. He's not some over-devoted neurotic second-fiddle to some stuck-up workaholic Christ-complex-having mother-fucker. He's an everyman. He's normal. He's a decent human being doing the best he can, and right now he's in tune with the music of the universe. As soon as he thinks this, he orders a shot and sees a cute man at a nearby table who looks woefully lonesome. The nurse walks right up to him, and they instantly click because the nurse is in possession of that perfect balance of recklessness and confidence that only comes in the wake of one's life being upended, and the other guy is self-deprecating and ironic and deadpan about his own recent romantic mishaps. The nurse asks what the other guy does, and the other guy says, "Hopefully... you later." Then he turns red and covers his face and says he's a freelance blogger and editor for a bunch of terrible websites, and he's literally never been that forward.

"Awesome," the nurse says. "I fucking love the internet."

"Really?"

"Love-hate."

"Me too."

"Obviously."

They look at each other. Fast forward an hour and they're practically attacking each other back at the freelance blogger's surprisingly well-appointed apartment. The love-making is as epic as his favorite band's recently released music video. It's also serendipitous and lasts as long as both want it to. In its throes, the nurse feels like all his blood has been replaced by the notes in that brand new song. But when they're done, the nurse is surprised to find his mind flooded with longing for the surgeon again, and he succumbs to a post-climax vortex of futile nostalgia that stirs in his soul a sadness tracing all the way back to the emotional errors of adolescence. The blogger is not blind. He reluctantly asks the nurse what's on his mind. The nurse, trembling, overwhelmed to a level he hadn't even felt on his harrowing drive from the hospital, chronicles through tears his breakup with the surgeon. The blogger isn't overjoyed to be used in this way, but the experience helps the blogger realize how much he might actually like the nurse. That he's willing to listen to the nurse talk about someone else strikes the blogger as an indicator of chemistry for which it might be worth sacrificing a small amount of emotional labor. The blogger realizes what just happened between him and the nurse wasn't mere meaningless fun. As long as it didn't get out of hand, he might actually develop enduring feelings for this person. Suppressing the fears that he's just a rebound, the blogger allows the nurse to curl up in his lap, at which point the nurse starts sobbing like a child. When the nurse is all cried out, a deadness different than any he's ever felt creeps through his emotions like tentacles touching the farthest reaches of his being, and he stands. He tells the blogger he feels much better, and also much worse. The blogger asks what this means. The nurse says he's sorry, but he needs to leave. The blogger asks when the nurse might want to hang out again. The nurse says nothing. The blogger starts to cry and says, "I guess I understand what you're going through." Then the blogger adds, "Not that you've asked one question about how I'm dealing with my own heartache." The nurse's feelings return, and he sits back down and asks the blogger to tell him about his situation. The blogger shakes his head and tells the nurse that it's obvious he wants to leave, and so he should. The nurse is paralyzed with indecision, torn between his pity for the blogger and his genuine desire to be alone with his own pain. He finally stands and leaves. He walks home in a cold fog that has replaced the mist.

Back at home, he opens his laptop without thinking, and the song that inspired him to go out blasts into his house. He mutes it. He doesn't want to hear it. He looks up the blogger's work online. He finds a piece the blogger wrote about how we're all living in a materialist dystopia, and the only cure for loneliness might be to give up our belongings and serve the poor, the sick, and the dying. Into this thesis the blogger interweaves references to societies of pre-sapiens humans who lived in present-day Guinea, the changing conception of the atom in the physical sciences, the growing problem of income inequality, and the disappearance of the honey bee. It's a remarkable piece of general-interest advocacy, not to mention a monumental and adroit exercise in unexpected synthesis, and it has over seventy-five thousand shares, and although the nurse can see that it's the most objectively beautifully written piece of long-form journalism he's ever read, it makes him feel nothing.

These eight lines by Christina Rossetti, spoken from the perspective of someone who is dead, vividly evoke, to me, the consciousness of the nurse at this moment:

> I shall not see the shadows,
> I shall not feel the rain;
> I shall not hear the nightingale
> Sing on, as if in pain:
> And dreaming through the twilight
> That doth not rise nor set,
> Haply I may remember,
> And haply may forget.

16

WITHOUT THE NURSE IN HIS O.R., the surgeon works through the night and is able to save the ex-nun from her gunshot wound, and even the soldier from drowning in her blood, but he fails to save the soldier from the trauma he suffered when struck by the bus. The surgeon feels so guilty for not having saved the woman's lover that he stays by her bedside during her recovery, refusing even to perform any other surgeries. When his coworkers suggest he go into counseling because he's clearly just transposing some other emotional wound onto this woman and her loss, he snarls, "None of you will ever understand the pressure of being the world's greatest surgeon!" His coworkers back slowly out of the room. After missing several surgeries in a row, however, during which every patient dies because he isn't there to work what are, effectively, his surgical miracles, he is fired from the staff at the hospital, but they let him stay in the ex-nun's room out of respect for his record. He practically lives there, growing a huge gross beard, refusing food, and even stealing pills from the hospital pharmacy and drugging himself into nightly stupors to pass the time until she wakes or until he dies, whichever comes first.

When she does wake, his heart soars, and he brushes to the floor the crushed pills he was about to snort and rushes to her side. The ex-nun blinks dreamily at his haggard countenance. He clutches her hand and welcomes her enthusiastically back. Feeble but able to speak, she tells him that she could sense his presence while in her coma. He looks surprised. She knew he was her doctor, she explains, and then her guardian angel, and in her dreams the two of them became lovers. In fact, she says, to her, she and he have already spent a lifetime together, a blissful one. They lived in a shack on a remote beach, and every morning he cooked her breakfast from eggs he foraged from wild pheasants who nested in the dunes, and every evening she cooked him a fish that she caught from the sea with her hands.

She says that once she's physically recovered, nothing would shorten what is sure to be her long psychological recovery more than to run away with him and find that shack on that beach they shared in her mind and make it their own in the world. The surgeon is so moved by her innocence, and still so wracked with guilt over having not saved the soldier, that he can't bear to inform her that she's not really his type and that he stayed by her side not out of amorousness but self-reproach.

They go on a road trip to find the beach they lived in in her anesthetized delirium, and although they don't find it, they find one similar and inexpensive enough to rent, several hours up the coast. It's still summer, too, so they're able to enjoy walking the sand and trying out their new-to-him but old-to-her relationship. The surgeon keeps his lack of attraction to her a secret, and finds other people to be with when he wants to, and the deception is easy because the ex-nun is neither suspicious nor jealous. *She might even be okay with it if I told her*, the surgeon thinks. Maybe he will tell her. He realizes he might even actually be close to being happy. Since he knows he doesn't want to be with her, ironically, being with her as a sham is actually kind of easy. He gets all the benefits of platonic companionship without ever having to confront any real emotions—except for living a lie, of course, but living a lie isn't really an emotion, it's a skill, and it's in matters of skill that the surgeon excels. He even makes enough money working as a surgeon in the local hospital—mostly patching up the minor injuries of fishers and vacationers—to finance their upper-middle class lifestyle. After a couple months in their beach house, however, it's the ex-nun, not the surgeon, who realizes that they're ill-fit, and the reality of living with him doesn't live up to the fantasy she experienced during her recovery, so she breaks up with him one crying morning over some pancakes he's made her.

As the surgeon drives back to the city alone, he weeps tears of unexpected relief—finally freed from his self-imposed debt of guilt to her, and the cognitive burden of constant rationalization that is the price of living a lie, a price he didn't realize the size of until he was no longer paying it. He's so happy about all the beautiful possibilities of a wide-open future, he's paying hardly any attention to the cars around him, and a school bus with no children in it broadsides him, and his car is spun into a concrete embankment where the force of the bus crumples it like a tin can. The bus hardly slows, glancing off the embankment, wobbling twice, and then smoothly reentering traffic. No one sees its plates or gets a description of the driver. The authorities use the jaws of life to free the surgeon from his vehicle, and, finding his I.D. from the hospital at which he used to work, they helicopter him there and call his ex, the ex-nun. She rents a speedboat and comes down the coast and arrives at the surgeon's bedside just as he's pronounced dead by the nurse who once loved him, who still works at the hospital, and whom the ex-nun watches try everything possible to save the surgeon before giving up. She looks at the nurse as he walks sadly away from the body—not unlike the soldier had once walked away from her and into the street. The nurse looks back at her, too, as he exits the O.R., and both of their puffy, tear-filled eyes bespeak a hundred shared and unshared sadnesses.

It's one of those classic "ships that pass in the night" moments. Here's the full metaphor in its original context, an 1874 Longfellow poem called "The Theologian's Tale":

> Ships that pass in the night, and speak each other
>   in passing,
> Only a signal shown and a distant voice in the
>   darkness;
> So on the ocean of life we pass and speak one
>   another,
> Only a look and a voice, then darkness again and
>   a silence.

15

AFTER THE NURSE WAS DUMPED by the surgeon, but before the surgeon moved to the coast with the ex-nun, the nurse was on a barstool in the dive where he met the blogger, and he happened to overhear a couple breaking up two barstools down, so he leaned over and eavesdropped as the couple catalogued everything they hated about one another. This was weeks after his fling with the blogger, but he was still so reeling from being dumped by the surgeon that he apologetically interrupted the two women, then told them that they should think twice before breaking up. Breaking up, he said, always seems like the right move when you're feeling sad and happen to be in a relationship, but you always underestimate the sadness you're going to experience on the other side. This argument was somewhat specious, of course, and partially motivated by wish-fulfillment, since the nurse was adopting the posture of someone who'd broken up with someone only to regret it, when, in reality, he had been broken up with by the surgeon, and he had no idea whether the surgeon had regretted it. The women to whom he was speaking didn't know any of this, however, so his argument appeared sincere.

The nurse then went on and on—drunkenly, abstractly, the way the heartbroken do—about how being in a relationship is so much work that freedom will always seem more appealing, but that freedom itself is two-faced: seen from afar as heaven, but experienced from within as hell.

"What if we could be like glue?" he pleaded. "What if we could always just stick to who we were with? Wouldn't that be much simpler than all this cancerous choice? This whole consumerist conception of intimacy?" Here he found himself channeling, unconsciously or not, the blogger's article. "Then this whole anxiety would be nullified, and our souls could spread wings instead of shrivel!" He pounded the bar with his fist, and some of the tears shaking in his eyes fell out.

The women didn't know him and were very much annoyed, not to mention unmoved, by his bellowing. They said something polite and turned back around, but the nurse got off his barstool and walked between them so that he was facing one of them at a time, turning from one to the other as he articulated *ad absurdum* his anti-breakup treatise. He blamed all the world's calamities on the casualness with which people broke up and the gamesmanship with which they approached desire, consciously or not. The women looked at each other, silently communicating many things the way only people who have been together for a very long time can do. Then one of them told him to get the fuck out of their faces, they were trying to have a private conversation. The other one said with searing sarcasm, "But thanks for your opinion,

Jack." The nurse looked shocked, as if suddenly aware that it might be annoying to have someone you don't know at all tell you everything they thought about love. The nurse apologized profusely, returning to his barstool, but his former audience just shook their heads at him and left the bar.

On the sidewalk, one of them lit a cigarette. The other one watched her light it. Then they both laughed at the ridiculousness of what had just happened. They had a little moment, then—almost bonding, smiling in each other's eyes, both thinking the same thing—that although alone they made each other miserable, whenever it was them against some outside adversary, they felt like they fit into each other like perfect puzzle pieces. At this, they both got, or seemed to get, extremely sad again. The nurse was watching them through the window of the bar and seemed to be trying to read their lips. The women shook their heads, remembering. They'd had this conversation before. They knew they had to break up. It was just hard to do so on the heels of the solidarity they'd shared in the face of that heartbroken blowhard. Now it was going to be harder than it would have been if they had just done it angry like they'd been about to before he so clumsily interposed. They cursed the nurse, and then they broke up, quickly and bitterly, and both of them turned away from one another and walked in opposite directions.

After a few steps, the one who lit the cigarette turned back around and watched the non-smoker, who just kept walking. The smoker then shouted down the street, "Wait!" The non-smoker turned. "What if we just got married?" the smoker asked, flicking her cigarette away. Sparks burst as the butt struck the wing mirror of a parked school bus partially bathed in sinister lamplight. The smoker stepped through the shower of sparks, unblinking, staring at her almost-ex, awaiting her response. The proposed-to non-smoker finally replied, "Are you insane?" "Maybe!" the smoker blurted. "Ugh. I don't know! I'm just saying, what if that crazy guy wasn't actually crazy?" The non-smoker considered it, then looked back at the bar. She could see the nurse in the window, hands on the glass, transfixed like a child who wants to believe that Santa or the Tooth Fairy is real. She sighed and turned back to the smoker. "Well?" the smoker asked. The proposed-to non-smoker bit her lip, shook her head, twisted one hand in the other, and said she just didn't know. Seeing the way she was playing with her hands, the smoker got an idea. "What about rock, paper, scissors?" "What?" "Rock, paper, scissors." The smoker stepped forward striking her palm with her fist. "If I win, we get married. If you win, we break up." The proposed-to compressed her lips for a moment in thought, then said, "I guess... it is a little easier to bear if we don't decide ourselves." "Exactly. It's not up to us. It's up to fate." The proposed-to thought about it some more, then said, "Two out of three?" "Of course," the smoker said. So they bounced their hands in their palms three times and then—the smoker picked scissors, and the proposed-to picked rock. Then they did it again. The proposed-to picked rock again, but the smoker picked paper. "Fuck," said the proposed-to. "What?" said the smoker. "You won." "I know," said the proposed-to. "I was trying to lose, though." "Now you *want* to get married?" "I don't know! In that moment I did!" "This is stupid!" said the smoker, waving her hands in the air. "This isn't the way to decide anything. This is a mockery of intimacy!" "Fuck intimacy," said the proposed-to. "Where did intimacy ever get us? Talking about our relationship for the millionth time in some dive bar?" "God, you're right. We're pathetic." "No! We're not! Not if we follow through, just this once, on something." The proposed-to held her fist above her palm. "It's tied. Let's *do* this. Let's *finish* it." The smoker seemed afraid. "And," the proposed-to added, "let's up the stakes. If you win, we still get married." The smoker nodded, listening. "But if I win," the proposed-to said, "we kill ourselves." "Whoa. Why?" "I know it's extreme, but I've been thinking about what that total loser just said in the bar. If we break up we'll just second-guess why we broke up, maybe forever, and whatever we feel about it will fuck up the dynamic of us and whoever we meet next, if we're even lucky enough to meet anyone. I'm sick of it. I'm forty-six. You're thirty-seven. What more could we possibly learn or get out of life that we haven't already? What are we waiting for? Old age? Where there's even more past to mourn? Sharper anxiety about dying? Marriage, ludicrous as it is, is the only stage we've never taken it to. State-sanctioned, public, permanent commitment. I'm not even that big of a fan of it, frankly, but that's almost what makes it perversely alluring. To do the opposite! And not knowing what it would actually be like… that's the only thing keeping me interested. Other than that, I'm basically ready to check out. The long goodbye. Six feet under. Now. How about you?" The smoker thought about it for a long moment, then nodded heartily. "Fuck it." "Hell yeah. Are you sure?" "Yeah. Let's do this." "Awesome. Ready?" The smoker nodded. They pounded their fists in their palms three times and then shot. They tied twice again, both rocks and then both scissors, before the proposed-to finally won with her rock crushing the smoker's scissors, sealing their suicide pact. There was a tearful moment of recognition that this was the end of their lives, but they decided to hurry up and carry it out before they changed their minds again, so the proposed-to ran back into the bar and came back with a steak knife from the kitchen, and they stabbed each other repeatedly, passing it back and forth, until they both fell over as the nurse in the window pounded on the glass in horror.

"Oh my God!" he shouted, turning around to see if anyone else had seen what he'd just seen, but all the other patrons were drinking and watching sports on the screens above the bar, cheering for their teams and talking shit about the opposing teams.

14

WATCHING THEIR BODIES DYE THE moonlit sidewalk the color of blood, the nurse gravely fathomed the macabre consequences of his boneheaded meddling. *They were going to break up already, but, God, not like this. If only I hadn't... oh God what unspeakable chain reaction did I initiate...* His face withered and he bit his tongue and put his cheeks in his hands and wept. He pounded his forehead against the glass, rattling it, and causing a frat boy eating a buffalo wing to glare at him. He clawed the grimy wood of the window sill. Because he was a nurse, he knew it was too late for him to do anything, but out of posterity he dialed 911 anyway. Behind the dead bodies, the lamplit and now also moonlit school bus shined with double menace. While the phone rang, the nurse vaguely recalled that a bus of a similar description had hit the soldier who the surgeon he'd once been in love with had tried to save while breaking up with him, and later a similar bus had hit the surgeon. Interrupting this thought, the 911 operator inquired as to the nature of his emergency. The nurse replied breathlessly that he'd just watched two people stab themselves outside the… and he was about to name the bar when the smoker got up off the sidewalk. The nurse almost dropped the phone. The smoker was standing, wiping herself off. He watched then as she helped the proposed-to get up too. Both then looked at him through the window, then at each other, and then walked into the bar, squeezing blood out of the fronts of their shirts.

"Hello??" the 911 operator asked. "Where was the stabbing? Hello, sir?"

The couple stood before the dumbfounded nurse, and the proposed-to held up a tube of fake blood. The smoker held up the steak knife, and she pushed it into her hand. The blade vanished into the handle with a springing sound. It was a trick knife.

"Nevermind," the nurse said quietly to the operator. "False alarm."

The smoker raised an eyebrow, then stabbed the nurse in the crotch with the fake blade. He jumped back on instinct, but his jeans just pushed the retractable blade back up into the handle, and the two women laughed. Then the smoker explained that that whole scene was a piece of performance art designed to teach him not to meddle in the breakups of others. The proposed-to stepped forward, adding, "When you try to stop a breakup, you may end up making it worse. You may cause a thousand breakups, or a double suicide." "We're still breaking up," the smoker added, "but hopefully you've gained a deeper appreciation of the danger of butting into total strangers' dramas." The nurse's tears were dry by this point. He asked stutteringly how they'd planned the whole thing. They explained that back at the bar they'd passed notes on cocktail napkins while he waxed obnoxious about how everyone should stay together. "Any more questions?" the smoker asked. The nurse shook his head. "Good," the proposed-to said. "Now watch this."

She turned to the smoker and said, "I break up with you." The smoker bowed and said, "And I with you." Then after a perfunctory hug they walked out of the bar through different exits. The nurse stood there in stunned silence staring at his own empty hands. The bartender shouted at him, "Hey, pal! You want another?" The nurse nodded and went back to his original barstool.

He wished the women hadn't left so he could buy them a drink to thank them for the lengths they'd gone to to help him understand something they'd had no responsibility to teach him, but which he otherwise might never have learned about love, and also to apologize for interposing himself into their private concerns. He vowed to show them his appreciation if he ever saw them again, but after a few more drinks, he forgot this vow. He spent the rest of the night wondering if he was truly over the surgeon, or, if he wasn't, when he would be. The drunker he got, the more over the surgeon he believed he was. Then he got so drunk that he started watching the sports on the screens and getting really into it. It was actually quite beautiful, he thought. The athleticism, the drama, the pageantry! The blistering humanity. The mysticism of fandom. It all rather pleasantly overwhelmed him. He spent $80 that night on drinks and appetizers and didn't even remember coming home.

13-10

TWO PEOPLE UNRELATED TO ANYONE in the preceding narratives think they're in love, but they are also in relationships
with other people, so in order to be together, they break up
with their original partners. At first they experience bliss
together, but then learn that being together is actually worse
than being with who they used to be with, and they agree to
try to get their exes back.

The exes, ironically, have started dating too, and they
seem quite happy, so the new, unhappy couple who initiated
the original breakups decides to remain together to antago-
nize their exes, going out as much as possible wherever their
exes are likeliest to be, and at those places, faking like they're
having a blast, hoping to sew in their exes' relationship seeds
of envy and, ultimately, make the exes miss their former partners, too.

Unfortunately, they never see their exes at any of their
old haunts. The scheming couple then realizes that their old
partners are so content that they only spend time at home.
So, with the apartment keys they each still have, they break
into their respective exes' apartments. The first one is empty,
so they go to the other, where they burst in on their old partners having sex. The malcontent couple begs for their old
relationships back. The seemingly happy couple doesn't stop
having sex, but does say that they would consider getting back
together with their old partners, because although their sex
lives have improved, their relationship is dissatisfying in other
ways. In fact, what the couple still having sex misses about
their respective ex-partners is everything but the sex. But, the
sex-having couple adds, if the other couple wants their old
relationships back, they'll have to break up first, right there,

right then, and they have only five seconds to do so. The more trusting member of the malcontent couple shrugs and says, "Okay, let's break up." The other one, however, looks skeptical. "What if we break up, and then they don't? Then we'll be single and won't have our old relationships back." "We'll just get back together," the trusting one says.

"Oh no," interjects a member of the couple still having sex. "Breaking up is a mind-fuck. We're not going through that unless you guys are breaking up for real. If you can't do it right now, you're not committed to the breakup." "Yeah," says the other member of the couple having sex. "But how do we know you'll honor your end of the bargain?" asks the skeptical member of the malcontent couple. "We don't," says the more trusting one in a hushed tone. "Exactly," says one of the ones having sex. "Maybe you should have thought about this before breaking up with us." "Fuck you!" says the skeptical member of the malcontent couple, "this is exactly the kind of hardball negotiating I broke up with you for." "Well, then, why do you want me back?" answers the one who had been called a hardball negotiator. "Because... because...," the skeptical one looks at the more trusting one for support, then at the hardball negotiator, "Because you're a beautiful person? I don't know. Other than hardball negotiating all the time, you're the most beautiful person I've ever met, and we click. I didn't know that before. When we're together, yeah, it's not always sunshine and rainbows, but it works. It's like a good car. It gets you from A to B. And yeah, sometimes you want a new car. Everybody does. I want a new car all the time. Especially when I was driving you. But actually, shopping for a new car sucks, and half the new cars today break down as soon as you drive them off the lot, but you never broke down, as long as I did basic maintenance. I just didn't know how valuable that was until now." The conclusion of the speech is met with silence. The skeptical person looks around, frightened, then shatters the awkwardness by adding, "I love you! Is that so stupid! Is it so crazy to love someone and not realize how much until you break up? Is that a fucking crime in this country?"

"So," the more trusting member of the malcontent couple says to the skeptical one, "is this really the end? For us, I mean? I guess I hadn't thought about how much I actually do respect you. This was all your plan, dating to spite them, coming over here, trying to get our soulmates back. You just… go for what you want. You're so bold, even though you're skeptical. That's a rare combination, and I would've never gotten this close to getting my ex back without you." The more trusting member of the malcontent couple starts softly weeping. "I'm hopeless… I'm a follower. I might… I might love you too much to let you go. Oh God…"

At this point, one of the members of the couple who had been having sex climbs out of the limbs of the other—the hardball negotiator—and says to the self-described follower while wiping off, "But I've always loved you for being who you are, and you're not a follower, you're emotionally open. In fact, you're the only one here who actually knows how to love, how to give themselves completely to another person." Then this person points at the bold, skeptical person. "Even though I don't know you, I'm just guessing, based on the speech you just made, that you don't know how to love. It's not much of a judgment, since it's true of me, too. I mean, I'm sure you're nice, but you don't strike me as particularly emotionally open, at least not as open as your current partner and my ex." The emotionally open follower weeps even harder. The bold skeptic frowns. The former partner of the emotionally open follower looks back at the hardball negotiator and asks, "Does that make me a fuck up? That I love this other person for being weak, for having the strength to be weak, I mean? Instead of flexing and striding and barking orders and hardball negotiating all the time, even though I was unhappy when I was with them? And I'm happy with you, but I don't love you? And at the end of the day I choose love over happiness? I mean, that's what I'm asking. Can that even be? Or am I missing something important that I don't understand? I'm happy all the time with you, but I still don't love you, because what I really love is someone who knows how to love, how to believe in someone else, because that's what I lack." This breaks the hardball negotiator into tears. Then the trusting, vulnerable follower's ex suddenly kneels and starts kissing their feet, declaring their adoration of the vulnerable follower over and over in such exaggerated terms that it sort of embarrasses the vulnerable follower. The hardball negotiator stops crying to look up at the bold skeptic and says, "Maybe we should all just break up. Maybe… we should all just become single and wipe the slate clean. A hard reboot." The hardball negotiator looks at all of them. "I love everybody in this room now. I love you because of how self-abasingly you love them and how good our sex life is, and I love you because of what we had that *did* work, *in* public. And I love *you* because we hardly know each other and it seems unlikely that you'd be half as crazy as these two are, and maybe it is beautiful that you love so vulnerably. I'm not sure what that means, but I'll tell you this. I'd like to find out. Maybe we have more in common because we're the only two people in the world who know these two in the same way. Maybe that's not love either, but like I said, if we were to get together for a drink, or coffee, just the two of us, who knows what we might discover about love that we don't know already." "Really?" says the follower. "Hey!" interjects the bold skeptic. "You already have someone kissing your feet. Hardball negotiator's mine." The bold skeptic faces the hardball negotiator. "I want you back. And I want you to want me back. And you do because you just said you did. So just act on it. It can be like it was." The bold skeptic looks at all of them and says panickedly, "Let's just keep it simple!"

"You're not listening," the hardball negotiator says, "you're just being bold and skeptical, as usual. We should all break up. Clear the air. Just for an hour, just to take some time to think. If we all broke up, and I mean *really* broke up, and banned anyone from getting back together for an hour, we might give ourselves the emotional space we need to realize who we really want to be with."

The follower is the first to nod. Then the one kissing the follower's feet stops and stands and says, "I don't know what's going to happen, but I think the hardball negotiator is right." The foot-kisser then turns to the follower. "And if you don't want to get back together, it's okay. I've learned from you that that's what love means."

"Hey! Stop that," says the hardball negotiator.

"What? I just agreed with you."

"No, you're setting it up so you and the follower can get together when the moratorium lapses."

The foot-kisser looks offended. "I'm sure I have no idea what you're talking about."

"You do so! You're gaming the system!"

"Not everybody's as hardball as you. It's obviously made you paranoid."

"That's exactly what I would say if I was gaming the system! You're not a foot-kisser, you're a gamer of systems."

"Both of you stop," the bold skeptic cuts in. "Look, we just have to do it. No more caviling. Four-way split. Plain and simple." The bold one looks straight at the hardball negotiator. "Everyone ready?"

"Thank you," says the hardball negotiator to the bold skeptic, fairly surprised at the bold skeptic's change of mind.

The bold skeptic bows and offers a smoldering look.

"But no smoldering looks," adds the hardball negotiator, pretending to be addressing everyone. "And no seductive posing."

The bold skeptic frowns, hurt.

"No moving," the vulnerable follower adds diplomatically. "If we're statues, our minds will be free to examine our hearts without interference."

"You're making a lot of sense right now," says the foot-kisser smoothly.

The hardball negotiator elbows the foot-kisser in the torso. "Ow!"

"You're doing it again."

"Jeez." The foot-kisser rubs their torso tenderly. "Sorry."

The bold skeptic tries to smile at the hardball negotiator, but the hardball negotiator is gazing at the vulnerable follower.

"So, that's it? We're broken up?" asks the foot-kisser, still massaging their torso.

The foursome nods in a circle, then stands extremely still.

After a quarter of an hour without incident, the bold skeptic whispers to the room, "This is really good, guys. I think I'm really getting somewhere."

"Shhh," says the hardball negotiator, whose eyes are closed.

"Yeah," agrees the vulnerable follower. "No one can concentrate with you talking."

"All you do is agree with everyone," the bold skeptic snaps.

The vulnerable follower looks hurt, then glances at the hardball negotiator for support. The hardball negotiator winks, then goes back to meditating.

The foot-kisser sees this and whispers to the bold skeptic, "You saw that, right?"

The bold skeptic nods and announces to the group, "Guys, we have a problem. Me and the foot-kisser don't even like each other. So it's not fair if you two get together. We'll only have each other to choose from." The hardball negotiator and the vulnerable follower ignore the announcement. "Hey!" the bold skeptic shouts. "I'm talking here. This is a real issue. We need to talk about it."

"Please," pleads the vulnerable follower. "We still have three-quarters of an hour left in which to reflect. Who knows what might happen if you allow peaceful contemplation to work its mellowing effects on your addled psyche. Can't you just trust the system?"

Tears are running down the bold skeptic's cheeks. "No! How can you all trust the system so easily? Especially when we've got a system-gamer right here?" The bold skeptic gestures to the foot-kisser and says to the hardball negotiator, "Your words. Not mine."

"Hey," replies the foot-kisser to the bold skeptic. "How would you like it if I accused you of being a system-gamer?"

"Don't listen to them," the vulnerable follower says to the foot-kisser. "You're a foot-kisser. The bold skeptic is just lashing out in pain." The vulnerable follower then touches the bold skeptic's cheek and says tenderly, "It's the only system we've got. That's why we believe in it." The vulnerable follower gestures at the foot-kisser. "You might even find that you're able to love certain people more than you once thought possible. If only you'd try."

The bold skeptic looks the foot-kisser up and down, and, with great resignation, sighs and wipes away tears and resumes standing still.

A minute later, everyone appears to be thinking about what they genuinely want, what they genuinely don't want, what they genuinely might want someday, and what they genuinely believe they once wanted, and how those past wants might influence the desires to which they'll be subject once the moratorium on binding romantic decision-making expires. Fragments of an enormous, vaguely school bus-shaped asteroid, however, strike planet Earth and end all life before the forty-five minutes elapse.

9

Two wriggling-tentacled aliens whose only job is to observe Earth and ensure that it isn't destroyed by an asteroid, and who have been doing that successfully since their first fuckup annihilated the dinosaurs, are currently fighting, at least on the surface, about whether they should put in for a promotion that would enable them to observe a more interesting planet. The green alien is angry at the purple one for being dishonest about their motivation for the promotion. The green one has accused the purple one of wanting to abandon Earth not because it's dull, but because it's politically unimportant. The purple alien rejects this accusation and insults the green alien's lineage and intelligence, but the green alien is relentless in the accusation, and the purple alien reluctantly confesses that its desire to observe a different planet indeed hinges on that planet's importance. The purple alien then makes a passionate appeal for the green alien to assist in the attainment of this promotion. If they could observe a more important planet, the purple alien urges, they'll be paid more, the craft in which they live and from which they observe whatever planet they're assigned will be more deluxe, and the new challenges and change of scenery might rejuvenate their partnership.

The green alien shakes its sixty heads and says sadly that it has no desire to abandon Earth. The purple alien gently counters, "What if we found a planet that was more interesting *and* more important? Then we could both be happy." The green alien shakes its sixty heads again and confesses that it never wanted to leave Earth at all, not even to find a more interesting place, and it was only pretending to consider that to please the purple alien, whom it loves. The purple alien looks sad and says it loves the green alien too, but it has to leave. There's no way that it could ever be happy here behind this lifeless moon, watching this dusty, stupid, self-destructive, squabbling little ball of repetitive trauma and melodrama burn itself out for the rest of its limited millennia. The purple alien would always wonder what would've happened if it had tried to climb higher in the Galactic Bureau of Planetary Observation. The green alien's sixty eyes glimmer with fluid and it says that it knows this about the purple alien. Then, the green alien says, as if saying something extremely difficult to say, that perhaps if they broke up, the Galactic Bureau of Planetary Observation would send it a new romantic and professional partner, and the purple alien could get a promotion to wherever it wanted, or no, *needed* to go. The purple alien's sixty eyes look into each of the green alien's sixty eyes, and both aliens instantly understand that, in order to truly show their love for one another, they must split up, since it would be torture for the green one to know the purple one didn't want to be there, and it would be torture for the purple one to stay, knowing that the green one knew that, not to mention the disappointment of never pursuing its own dreams of rising through the Galactic Bureau of Planetary Observation to become a famous and powerful protector of the galaxy's most important civilizations. As the gaze between them climaxes in terms of an interpersonal reckoning, an asteroid slips past them in the background. A few moments later, while the couple is quietly and gently negotiating how they're going to split up sections of the craft so that they don't constantly run into each other until the purple one's transfer request goes through, a million alarms go off. Both aliens turn and rush to the cockpit of their craft and see the vaguely school-bus-shaped asteroid as enormous as Madagascar hurtling violently along a vector to impact Earth somewhere in the middle of the Pacific. All one-hundred-and-twenty of their eyes go wide. They leap to the controls and initiate the deployment of an elaborate array of enormous lasers mounted on the hull of their craft. The purple one's one-hundred-and-twenty tentacles rapidly type coordinates onto a screen while the green one looks back and forth between another screen and the window shouting out numbers to adjust the aim of the lasers. Their gray rock-colored camouflage craft drifts out from behind the moon where it's been hidden, and in the silence of space the laser array unfolds like a scorpion's tail whose stinger is trained on the Madagascary asteroid. Then helixes of bright green anti-matter coil from the base and around the stinger until the point is glowing with a ball of green and gray light. The ball suddenly lengthens into a beam and cleaves the asteroid into several smaller pieces. Some glance off Earth's atmosphere like pebbles skipped across a pond's surface and speed off into the void of space, but two slivers do make earthfall, one as big as Manhattan and another as big as Puerto Rico. The one as big as Manhattan lands in Wyoming, where it disturbs the supervolcano beneath Yosemite that had been dormant for 174 millennia, triggering a cataclysmic eruption. The fragment shaped like Puerto Rico lands in Kazakhstan, obliterating the Eurasian steppe like a thrown brick hitting a wedding cake. As the North American supervolcano gushes material from the mantle into the atmosphere, its shockwave combines with the shockwave from the Russian impact, and all of Earth except part of Antarctica is engulfed in a succession of mile-high moving walls of thousand-degree nickel, silicone, and iron. "Fuck," mutters the purple alien. "Fuck," the green one echoes. They both close their one-hundred-and-twenty eyes. "We're fucked," the purple one says. There's a red phone-like device on the wall of the cockpit with a sign above it that says Headquarters for the Galactic Bureau of Planetary Observation, and it starts to flash like a strobe. The pair of aliens stares at Earth through the annoying flashing lights. The once blue and green marble is now all but a fireball, waves of molten air and liquid rock washing endlessly around it like clouds once did. The aliens look back at the strobing phone, then resignedly at each other.

It all just reminds me of a famous epithalamic fragment by Sappho. Originally only three lines in Greek, my maximalist and admittedly self-indulgent translation is meant to emphasize the height of the branch and the weight of the misapprehension:

> The final apple
> redder than yesterday
>
> hanging from the tip
> of the highest branch
>
> of the tallest tree
> miraculously overlooked
>
> by those who picked clean
> the rest of the orchard.
>
> Wait, nevermind.
> Not overlooked.
>
> Just out of reach.

8-6

Many years before the performance artists taught the nurse not to meddle in the breakups of strangers, they are practically strangers to each other, having just met at a performance art show that had been very bad, and at which they'd made each other laugh by making fun of the artist whose show it was, and after that laughter had decided to go home together, and now being on the subway sitting side-by-side and unselfconsciously making out because there's no one else on the train.

They stop at the next stop when a mother and father with a young boy and girl enter the car and sit directly across from them. The young girl starts to cry from something, perhaps the noise of the train or perhaps the late hour. Neither member of the couple smokes at this point, but the one who would go on to become a smoker starts making faces at the girl, and for whatever reason this relieves the girl's unease. The girl playfully sticks her tongue out at the future smoker. The one who would eventually be proposed to looks on admiringly at the future smoker's rapport with the child, and scoots an inch closer to her.

The father of the girl then sees his daughter with her tongue out and calls her name. The girl's mother, who had been looking dead-eyed at the row of advertisements above the heads of the future performance artists snaps out of her trance and shouts the name even louder. The girl, chastised, climbs out of her seat and waddles to the mother, who holds her in her lap until the family exits the subway car two stops later. At this point, the couple starts making out again. Then they stop. They talk about the family they just saw. They talk about what happened with the daughter and how mean the parents seemed. Both are relieved to find out that this conversation is as good as their conversation at the art party was, and they both comment on this, congratulating each other on their apparent chemistry. They don't make out for the rest of the ride because they have too much to say. They agree on many things, and the things they disagree on are interesting rather than worrisome. They both agree that chili is an extremely economical and healthy food to build a diet around, for example, but they disagree on which ingredients make the best chili. During this discussion, in which many other topics are covered beyond chili, several people get on and off the train, but all of them go unnoticed by the couple. Eventually the train emerges from the earth to travel aboveground for several stops, and everyone on the train except for the couple checks their phones. Out the window, every light on in every window of the city's many buildings seems so quaint in the crisp winter evening air that it quiets even the couple, who stare breathlessly at the almost model-like cityscape, fathoming all the innumerable narratives it wordlessly evokes.

A year and six weeks later, they break up. Two weeks after that, they get back together. A full year after that is another breakup, and that's followed by a reunion three months afterward. A third breakup occurs at the six-year mark, and it lasts an entire year before the couple reunites once more. As far as breakups go, all of them are bad, but only extremely so when weighed against the relative serendipity and sweeping innocence of this moment, with the dark, magisterial city scintillating before them as they gently travel through it on a fixed but rickety track.

When the train goes back underground, the couple is laughing about the performance art they saw again, and they're crying from laughter when they walk up the steps of the subway platform and lock elbows and zip up their coats and throw on their hoods as they enter the neighborhood where the future proposed-to person lives. On the way to her house, the future smoker gives a beggar a whole twenty-dollar bill, and after they are out of earshot, the proposed-to asks why the future smoker gave so much money away. "I don't know," the generous future smoker says. "It's cold, and they looked hungry." The skeptical future proposed-to person scrutinizes the character of the generous future smoker for the first time. The generous future smoker, a little too drunk, excited, and happy to care about feeling scrutinized at all, keeps walking into the street just as a school bus, driverless, with all the windows down, with the cold air whistling through the windows, speeds toward the generous future smoker, who has just thought of something else funny about that night and is laughing while turning around to face the scrutinous one and tell her. The scrutinous one sees the bus in time enough to jerk her future lover forward by the fur of her coat as the school bus barrels down the avenue, throwing up paper trash, shaking and veering, obeying no traffic signals, striking a recycling bin that had been blown into the street by the wind, and shattering it. While the wind from the bus is still blowing on them, the generous one gratefully beholds the scrutinous one and says, "I think you just saved my life." The scrutinous one glances premonitiously down the street and watches the bus as it skids around a corner. At this moment, the generous one tilts the premonitious one's face toward her and kisses her. This specific kiss instantly erases from the other's mind both the fear of the mysterious bus and the issue of the kisser's profligate generosity.

In the proposed-to's house the two have sex that surprises them both in its satisfaction relative to how drunk they are. Afterward they talk about their past. Every story the future smoker tells resounds thematically with the future proposed-to's own mental autobiography, and equivalent portions of the stories told by the future proposed-to resound with the future smoker. Both have an enormous feeling that for the first time in their lives, everything about the person before them fits what is missing in their theory of themselves. When they finally sleep, they don't wake up for nine hours. The generous future smoker has an epic, happy dream. The scrutinous future proposee, however, has many fragmentary and frightening dreams. All their dreams are forgotten, however, when they see each other the next morning. A ray of sunlight has reached through the window and warmed a yellow parallelogram on the floor of the bedroom that the generous one steps directly into when getting up to go to the bathroom. The scrutinous one observes this footstep from the sheets with no small measure of joy. Alone in the room, the scrutinous one thinks generous thoughts about the generous one. The scrutinous one feels herself floating through these thoughts as if though a palace of comforting clouds, the bed underneath a kind of enchanted chariot, her own bedroom a kind of endless sky. This is also the first time the scrutinous one considers becoming a performance artist, but this ambition will be withheld from the more generous future performance artist for several weeks.

This reminds me of a poem by a 14th century French priest. His name is unknown, and it's only presumed that he's a he, or that he's a priest. That profile is, however, unlikely to be incorrect, since male priests would've been the only people likely to have scribbled anything in the margins of the transcribed pages of the sort of dense, ecumenical histories in which this Old French poem was found. It's my own translation, and an incredibly loose one:

> What if love is Eden
> and we but Adam and Eve
>
> all just desperate not to err
> so badly we're bidden to leave?
>
> But the scripture is written already.
> The fall to come foregone.
>
> So exiled by language we'll never be ready
> to read, we must let go and love on.

For what may or may not be obvious reasons, but which I have no desire to go into, I've decided to keep this final, semi-autobiographical vignette rather brief. I'd also like to add that I in no way consider it anti-breakup propaganda. Unlike the nurse in his interaction with the performance artists, I know that dissuading others from breaking up is at best futile, and at worst invites calamity by forestalling the inevitable.

5-1

A COUPLE KEPT BREAKING UP, but first they had to get together, which they did. Then they broke up. But then, after breaking up, they got back together. Then things were fine for a while. Then they broke up. They decided not to get back together, but once they decided that, they did. Then they were happy, but they broke up again for other reasons. Then, when they least expected it, they got back together another time. Then, just as suddenly, broke up. Now, when either tried to remember a time when they were neither together nor broken up, they couldn't. They decided this meant they should get back together, and they stayed together after that, until late in middle age when they happened to break up again, and this time they didn't get back together. Through the end of middle age, both regretted not getting back together. Then, in early old age, one of them stopped regretting it, but not the other.

UNDER THE SEA

THE WORDS HAD NOT SEEMED REAL.

"One day?" I asked.

The doctor nodded. He looked guilty, as if the diagnosis was somehow his fault, which was not reassuring.

"What do you mean *one day*?"

He blinked, and his professionalism seemed to kick back in. He pulled off a glove, put his hand on my knee, and said, "I'm sorry. But yes. It's not long."

"How can you even know that?"

"Diagnostic techniques advance every day. Better data, finer instruments. It's all algorithms now. In a few years, we'll know to the minute, maybe to the second, how long people have. Some places in China can do it already."

"There's nothing I can do?"

The doctor shook his head. "It's too advanced."

"But I feel fine!"

"It's that type of disease. You feel fine right up until the end. You're lucky."

THE CLINIC'S DOORS SLID OPEN, and when the hot, wet wall of humid air hit my body, it felt like an alien planet. There was its sun. There was its sky. There was a parking lot. There were some cars, my own somewhere among them. I saw fast food trash in the pinestraw. I saw a strip of bushes and a strip of traffic past that. I saw a saggy stoplight, saggy power lines, puffy white clouds. My heart was pounding in my ears like I was alone at the bottom of the ocean, and all of this was the ruins of Atlantis.

The doors whooshed closed behind me, cutting the cool air from the clinic off from my back, and the wet afternoon enveloped me. My legs felt like they were spinning inside my pants.

I guess I crossed the parking lot and walked into the street. I didn't even know I'd ended up there until a car slammed on its brakes. I looked all the way back at the clinic and felt like I'd teleported.

More cars zoomed around me. I raised my hands. A semi stopped screechingly. Through the glare of the windshield, the trucker was only an outline. The road was hot on my feet. I was barefoot, I realized. I looked back and saw my shoes a few feet apart from each other in the parking lot of the clinic. A white van rolled over them without touching them.

The trucker honked, and I crouched and held up my hands and apologized. I stopped traffic in the other lane, staggered to the other side of the street, and stepped through a hedge into the parking lot of a rundown shopping center.

The pinestraw in the hedgerow had pricked the bottoms of my feet, and now the parking lot asphalt was pricking them in the exact same places, only with heat. I closed my eyes and stood there letting it soak up through my heels. My legs felt like little elevators, lifting the energy of the earth up into my body. I realized how cold it had been in the clinic. I stood there a moment more, hoping to wake, but it wasn't a dream, and when I opened my eyes again, a headache I had not even known I'd had had gone.

In the shopping center was a huge shuttered drug store, an open deli, a closed bar, a used clothing emporium, and a decrepit arcade. I realized I was clutching my phone as tightly as if it was a fingerhold on a cliff keeping me from falling into a chasm. I was supposed to be calling my husband, I realized. Looking at my sad little phone made me dizzy. It was like a shard of dark matter—a hundred times lighter or heavier than expected. Around it my hand already looked skeletal. My skin waxy, my fingers like someone else's. I looked back up at the puffy white clouds. I don't know what they looked like, but it was something. I don't know why I was looking at them. I pulled the phone up to my ear like I was a doll made to do make this one motion, and nothing else.

I gazed down at the stains in the parking lot as it rang. Thousands of black dots marred the asphalt, ancient remnants of dropped gum and infinite spills. I couldn't understand how there had ever been so many people chewing gum and spilling beverages all over this irrelevant half-acre. The call went to voicemail. I left no message. I texted him and used his first name so he'd know it was urgent. I refrained from disclosing that I only had one day to live. He'd have assumed I was joking, or worse, being dramatic, and that would've made him take even longer to reply. That I had used his name but not mentioned why was the most effective way to communicate the urgency with which I desired to speak with my husband without having to say something I couldn't even yet comprehend. Besides, my fingers were sweaty, and every single letter had taken monumental effort to input. Every breath I took left me feeling more delicate. Every speckle of asphalt prickling the soles of my feet as I staggered toward the arcade, I guess to await his call, and I guess because its door was open and was closer than the deli or the store.

An air conditioner hanging from the ceiling of the arcade was dumping cold air straight down and right out of the open entrance, where it was instantly absorbed by the sweltering heat. When I walked through the doorway, I paused in the bath of this weirdly cold, estuarial column and for a moment felt as if coated in magical fog.

Near the back of the arcade, three young men were blasting pink plastic shotguns at a two-paneled screen. Then they seemed to get into an argument over who got to shoot next because there were only two guns. Everything on both screens was on fire. Only the tall one glanced over at me.

He was kind of punk-looking with a chiseled jawline. They all were tattooed and pierced, and handsome, to be honest, but only the tall one's eyes sparkled with anything like kindness or intelligence. Immediately, I had a vision of seducing him as the final, crazy act of my otherwise not very spectacular life, but it passed as quickly as it came. Then I glanced at him again and wondered why not. What else was I going to do, lie down and cry in the parking lot? The word *seduce* suddenly came to life in the weird little theater between my ears. I saw a small, cute snake biting a piece of wet fruit. *Seduce.* I saw a face chewing ice in a dark hotel room. *Seduce.* I saw another face without eyes whose mouth had a glacier for a tongue. *Seduce this dude*, it said.

I felt like Eve almost, but old instead of young, and in the dumb, violent dump at the end of time instead of a golden

Garden at the beginning. The thought of seducing him passed again, but in a strangely persistent way, like a holiday bell-ringer you ignore on the way into the supermarket knowing you'll have to ignore it—or not—at least once more.

I glanced around the arcade again, looking for something to look at. It took a conscious effort not to fall down, and somehow looking was helping. The arcade's oversized door-mat was littered with cigarettes, like the boys had attempted to flick them outside from all the way back by the gun game, but the falling column of air-conditioned air had knocked their cigarette butts down into the doormat. The smell nauseated me and, simultaneously, reminded me pleasantly of college. I leaned on a candy machine for balance, which made a noise and caused all three of them to turn from the game. I fumbled, pretending I was buying candy. It was an old-fashioned plastic bin half-full of dust-coated M&M's, a collection of tiny ugly worlds. I suddenly realized I should drive home, but then I couldn't imagine walking back across the street and into the clinic parking lot. It felt like walking right into hell through my own open grave. I hadn't had any M&M's in years and would've bought some, but didn't want my last mouthful of candy on Earth to taste how they looked.

I tried to exchange a dollar for tokens but found I couldn't hold the bill still. George Washington's eat-shit smirk, his ridiculous cravat, the boxy patterns, the flourished borders, the inscrutable numerical sequences, the fucking tint of the ink... it was all just preposterous. All of history. My throat leathered up. I could've been knocked over by a shhhh. I wanted to be. I wished the trucker would've hit the gas instead of the brakes. Suddenly my thoughts didn't feel like mine. The dollar fell from my fingers. I was a statue watching a smaller artifact from the same culture that had fashioned her fall to the floor.

When the dollar bill started spinning in the flow of the air conditioner, I felt relief, its own motion permitting mine. Reaching down and picking it back up felt wonderful, oddly, so I knelt even slower than I would've. It was a mini-vacation, picking up paper money, a small, perfect action, quasi-religious. And when I stood back up with the dollar in my hand, I understood all of history, all of economics, all of politics, all of love, and all of art, or felt like I did. But I couldn't have explained it to anyone who wasn't also already dead and still walking.

I faced the token exchanger like it was my nemesis and fed George Washington confidently into its lips. It took it without hesitation. Behind its eyeless face, the brain of the machine grinded emptily for ten seconds, then vomited four light-colored copper tokens. They were light in my palm. Ms. Pac-Man was closest, but the screen was directly in the sun coming in through the doorway, so you couldn't even see the game. Just outside the sunlight, however, was a pinball machine that looked twenty years old or more and was themed on a roller coaster. I walked to it and touched the glass covering the game, and the glass was cold, and the coldness soothed me.

The vertical panel of the game showed a blonde head stretched back and screaming as she gripped the crossbar in her cart, eyes wide in joy and terror. My knees crumpled, and I pressed my palm against the glass to hold myself up, but my sweaty hand squeaked on its surface. I felt the boys look. They must have thought I was drunk. Then I remembered I was barefoot and thought that they must have thought I was crazy. I inserted a token but it took two, so I added another. A dark, miniature amusement park behind the glass blinked creepily to life. I wanted it to possess me. I wanted the pinball machine to be haunted like in a movie. I wanted it to suck my soul into its machinery so I could live inside it. I could be the blonde on top, gaping at braindead teenagers forever, feeling their grubby fingers on my dusty red buttons, sucking their parents' money from them, dead and immortal.

I looked at the young men, bragging and smoking and joking and blowing up scenery. The tall one's backwards hat was pointed toward me, and it showed the Denver Broncos' logo, which is my husband's favorite team because he grew up in Colorado despite being born in Ohio. For a moment, at least, the hat seemed to portend my seduction of its wearer, but I shook the notion from my mind. This was my last desperate act, not that. This would be the most beautiful round of pinball anyone ever played. Three silver balls, Scheherazade-style, this was the method through which I would hold back death.

Knowing as long as a ball was in motion I'd still be alive, I plucked the plunger, and ball number one looped up and disappeared into a panel of mushroom bumpers. Then it bounced off a little shield-shaped thing and hit an unforgiving pole. The ball, spinless, slid toward me like an anvil on a doomed trajectory. I pounded the side buttons, but the ball was going to split the flippers. I pushed the whole machine left and knocked the ball off its path at the last second and attacked the left flipper, but by then the buttons were all dead. Nothing was flipping. The marquee beneath the blonde flashed *TILT*, buzzed once, and the game went black.

My reflection in the dark glass panicked me. I checked my phone, but he hadn't gotten back. Dizzier, I touched my navel and tried to focus on breathing. I wondered if dizziness was a symptom or if I was wasting time by panicking about whether it was or wasn't. My diaphragm tightened and receded. I was able to not think of anything. A dozen breaths later I was standing with a hand on the pinball machine as a crutch. The machine lit back up, and I remembered I still had two tokens. I put them in and pulled back on the plunger.

I watched my ball get caught in the mushroom-shaped bouncers for a surprisingly long time, loudly racking up points, but somehow this triumph felt empty, like when you try to go back to sleep after waking up from a good dream too soon, and when you return to it, the world is the same but a crucial emotion is missing. I was about to leave the rest of my balls for the universe to do with as it saw fit when I felt someone's presence beside me.

"Yo, lady," said a male voice. "You okay?"

I knew it was the one in the Broncos hat without looking.

"Excuse me," I said without thinking, either. "I'm playing a game here."

The ball was still pounding around in the mushrooms. When it finally fell, I waited until the last second, then slammed the right flipper button with perfect timing. The ball flew through a hanging flap and zipped up a curled white ramp.

"Oh," he said, backing away. "My bad."

One of his friends buzzed his lips. He shot his friend a bird while walking back toward them, and then they laughed at him. Something shot my ball up another ramp and the scoreboard went crazy with sounds and bells. When my ball got stuck in some kind of bonus cage, I glanced back and saw he was watching. He looked away and grabbed a pink gun out of his friend's hand, which his friend protested. In my game, the cage had opened and two balls had come out where there had been one. They followed one another lazily, like pals, drifting toward the limp left flipper. I don't know why I didn't hit the button. I watched the balls glance off it and fall into the hole in ignominious succession. Letting them die felt good somehow. When the next ball popped up I fired it into the mushrooms and watched it suicide too. With *GAME OVER* blinking on the marquee behind me like an explosion in an action movie—or so I imagined—I walked over to the boys and their guns and said to the tall one, "I lost."

All three stared at me. After a moment, the tall one frowned at me like he thought I was about to ask them for money.

"Any other games in here worth the tokens?" I asked coquettishly. He still looked clueless.

I looked at his torso, then back up at his eyes. I thought I was being enormously clear, but I saw on his face an almost unplaceable lostness, so I took the plastic gun out of his hands and pointed it at him and said, "I'd play this one, but I hate guns." I handed it back to him, held it against his body, then let it go.

A moment later he handed the gun to his friend.

HIS APARTMENT WAS ABOVE THE bar, where I thought he was leading me at first, but then we walked around it and up an outdoor stair. I regretted coming on to him the whole walk over, yet also felt the terror of an upcoming eternity of nothingness distorting my decisions and sucking me forward like an enormous vortex. I kept telling myself the second my phone rang, the suction would reverse and blow me back, toward the clinic, toward my car, toward my husband, toward my home, toward my grave, toward the world moving on. But the phone hadn't rung, and then it began to seem like it never would, and that made me feel like I'd been granted a second method by which I might live forever.

I sat on his couch in front of a coffee table covered in ashtrays, magazines, and unwashed dishes. He sat on a folding chair he'd pulled from behind a door and opened next to me. I got the feeling I had sat in his normal spot and he'd neither wanted to correct me by asking me to move nor presume to sit beside me. By the time the young man and I had finished smoking two bowls of weed whose pedigree he tediously and endlessly extolled, I'd halfway forgotten my diagnosis and slipped back into something like normal time. At one point I had the very high thought that I was just a fraying strand in the elaborate tapestry of history. It must have been good weed after all. When I remembered death again, instead of feeling like I was dying, I felt above it, like a goddess trying as hard as she could to seem mortal—like my whole life I had been temporarily waylaid by this petty body in this petty reality and soon again would resume my proper position in the pantheon.

Imagining my breath as one of the four winds, I slowly asked the young man what he did. He said not much, just hang out. When he saw his answer didn't impress me, he added that he'd worked at the hospital for a while. I asked if he was a doctor. He said no, and I was disappointed that he didn't get my joke. He then reported that he'd brought the food cart around to the inpatient rooms. "But I got fired," he concluded, as if that was the end of his entire life's story.

When I asked why, he shook his head as if such a question was existentially unanswerable. He asked if I was high, and I said yes. He asked how high I was, and I said I didn't know, pretty up there. Then I said it was the highest I'd been in as long as I could remember. He asked if I wanted to get higher. I said I didn't need to, but the way I said it left it open. He produced something from a tin box that looked like brown sugar but glossier, then he said, "Because we could get seriously tilted."

"What is it?"

He smiled at the utter innocence of my question, then looked at me like he wanted me to guess.

"Meth?"

He drew some out on a piece of plastic that looked like it had once been a gift card.

"Heroin?" I didn't know anything about drugs.

"You'll be fucking plastered to that sofa," he said aggressively. Something about his confidence made him sadly repulsive, and I was prevented from walking out right then only by my fear of moving a muscle.

He tapped some of the crystals into the end of the same pipe we'd used for the marijuana. He was grinning, too, like he was getting away with something. Now I didn't want to leave, but I did feel like correcting him.

"Is that even yours?"

He looked at me, offended. "Hell yeah, it's mine."

"Sorry," I said.

"What do you care?"

"I don't. I don't know why I asked."

He shook his head and went back to packing the pipe. It was my least favorite thing about myself—a kneejerk suspicion that came out when I was on edge. My husband had borne the brunt of it graciously for our entire marriage. I was about to apologize again when he grinned at me with desire. I felt like forbidden fruit suddenly, or a trophy of some sort, and I didn't know how I felt about feeling that way. I wanted to touch him, then I didn't, then I did again. More than anything, I wanted to not think about anything to do with myself. I decided not to smoke whatever he was putting in the pipe because I was afraid it might make me think about myself even more. Marijuana was plenty, I thought, and then, as soon as I had thought that, even marijuana was too much. I wanted to run screaming outside. I saw myself do it in my head. I ran so fast, though, I tripped and bounced down the stairs and rolled out into the alley, head cracked open, blood gleaming in the sun. I saw myself explode through a hole in his apartment wall as if fired from a cannon. I saw a giant eagle crash through the window and pluck me from the couch and race screaming with me in its talons into the afternoon sky.

In reality the couch was simply too cushiony to move from. And if I moved I knew I would die. If I moved my pinkie even a centimeter from its position on the armrest, that would begin the chain reaction that would inevitably lead to me calling my husband and telling him what I'd been told and watching him watch me while I lost all my dignity. Sitting on this disgusting couch was holding back a tidal wave of eternity.

Showing the same concern he'd shown in the arcade, my host asked if I was okay. My eyes were closed. Slowly, as if I could forestall the future with the pace of my pronunciation, I asked him his name. When he answered I didn't understand what he'd said.

"Caleb?"

"No, *K*… *Lo*. Like Sweet'N Low… except *K* instead of sweet, and no 'and'."

I crushed my eyelids, trying to think about what he'd just said.

"What's your real name?"

"K-lo. I just said it."

"That's not a real name."

"Yo," he barked. "It's what I go by."

"What's it's from?"

"What do you mean?"

"How'd you get that name."

"Fucking… childhood. Look, you want to hit this or not?"

He was lying. He'd given it to himself. I shook my head. I didn't want to hit it.

I hadn't opened my eyes yet, and in the dark I heard the lighter spark and something crackle. Then I heard him sucking air through the sides of his teeth. I expected it to smell but it didn't. I heard him put the pipe on the table. He offered a beer, his voice wavering. He breathed in again through his teeth. I sensed in him something of the host who'd realized he'd failed to entertain his guest before entertaining himself, and I felt sorry for him. I nodded and whispered, "Yes to the beer." I heard him rise. I still hadn't moved or opened my eyes. I felt like a space traveler. My husband and I used to watch *Star Trek*, and I felt like the captain, the bald guy, the fabric of time flowing around my aerodynamic scalp. K-lo shuffled back over and opened the can so close that I felt the fizz on my forearm, and I opened my eyes.

He'd taken off his Broncos hat. There was a red line pressing his bleached hair to his temples. He was backlit by a window with a sheet over it. There was a TV under the window, and in the reflection of the screen he looked like an angel in one of those engravings by Dürer, or whoever it was that did those.

"Yo," K-lo said slowly, trying to push the beer can into my fingers.

It was the coldest thing I'd ever touched. I tried to sip it, but my lips were too weak, I couldn't even purse them. I set the can on a magazine on the coffee table and leaned over in K-lo's direction and curled up on the couch and started crying and staring into the rippled denim wall of his jeans.

"Yo. Damn. Are you okay? Hey. What's wrong?"

I remembered my mother and father, both long dead, wondering if they were here with me, watching over me like real angels, and I knew they were not. I rolled off the couch and lay in the gutter between the couch and coffee table— with a plop. Springing into action, and, after some straining, he got me up. He walked me to the kitchen and got me water. I tried to drink it, but the water tasted so good that I burst into tears and had to set it down or drop the glass. To lie on the floor. That was all I'd wanted, I realized, since talking to the doctor. No, actually, I wanted to lie on the asphalt in the sun and be baked into the sky, to become a lump of cloud, leaving behind an anonymous skeleton, but that seemed impossible. I got on my knees and put my forehead flush to the grimy lino-leum. I rolled my forehead side to side. I clawed the tiling. In my head, it peeled back to reveal a new plane of reality, like the whole world was just a bunch of cheap props with outer space behind it, and I was dismantling the stage. K-lo knelt and stroked my arm, then put a hand under my head. He smoothed my hair. He told me it would be okay. His fingers were clammy on my body, but they felt so good. He asked me if he could take me somewhere. I couldn't stop crying. He said he had a car. I said I had a husband. "Oh…" he said. Then he added, "That's cool." He said he would take me to him. "You'll be aight," he said confidently. Stillness and peace washed over me, and I tried to say, "Please say that again," but I just spat mucous, so I stopped trying to speak. I pictured K-lo, determined, turning down our street in a beat up whatever he drove, parking in our driveway, walking me up the steps, delivering me—ghoulish, but unadulterous—to my home and husband on the doorstep. I found the notion of a hand-off perversely pleasant. It meant that at no point I'd be alone. It felt like a good little boring ending before the cosmic one, and I surrendered to it in my mind.

But when I finally was able to stand, K-lo put his hand on the small of my back, and something ancient leapt through me. Frog's blood is what I'm calling it. Something shooting out of my heart to the ends of my fingertips. I turned him around and looked at his face. I held it with my hands like my mother used to do, like I was about to dab a napkin in water and aggressively wipe something away. He smiled awkwardly and I saw his front tooth was chipped. I felt like a reptile, like a wooden carving come to life in a story. A mermaid, but less cute. Lovecraftian. Pitiless. All-pitying. Beyond pity. Medusa. I put his other hand around me. I felt resistance in his elbow, but I held his palm on my back. His eyes were wide in fright. I told him I didn't want to go.

"You sure?" he asked incredulously.

I nodded. "Sorry, I'm a mess. I'm not used to smoking."

"You feel better?"

I let go of his arms to wipe snot-wet hair from my face. He took the opportunity to step back.

"What do you think about me and you," I said. I swallowed hard and looked at him. "Right now." I looked down the hall. "You got a room?"

He looked at me impatiently.

"Yeah, I got a room."

"Where?"

"In there, but—"

"It's okay," I said, holding up a finger to pause our conversation. I glanced around for paper towels. Miraculously there were some. "It's not a big deal," I said quickly, grabbing and tearing one off. I blew my nose in it. I took another and wiped my face and looked at him. His lips were curled in perplexity. I looked around for the trash. He nodded, and I found it beside a shelf with an ancient microwave on it. The garbage was overflowing the receptacle. I wanted to smash it down but didn't for fear of seeming imperious and instead gently lay the paper towels on top of a box of takeout. I took the glass of water off his table and took a sip. I smiled, pretending everything that had just happened hadn't, and for a moment it worked. For a moment, I was a mutant whose indifference to anything remotely resembling a reasonable perspective on her own situation was her ineluctable power.

"We could hook up," I said. "That's what I'm saying. I like you."

He looked like a pet when you try to speak to them, stuck in simple incomprehension.

"If you don't want to, that's fine."

"I didn't say that," he said.

"Well, do you?"

"I don't know."

"Why'd you bring me here then?"

"I don't know," he said.

I cleared my throat and walked toward him, trying to unbutton my top button at the same time, but my fingers were too shaky, so I stopped.

"You want me to leave, don't you."

He didn't do anything, then he shook his head.

So I went back to working the button. When I got it undone, I tried the second one down, but it was even harder.

I finally lowered my hands and stared at him. "Little help?"

He was a statue.

I frowned. I pulled my shirt apart. Some buttons bounced on the floor. We both heard them roll somewhere.

Standing there facing him, I imagined my blouse like petals of a giant rare flower, and I felt like a crazy forest spirit in human disguise, trying to be plucked, and he was a dumb, illiterate farmer who still somehow knew better than to tangle with a goddess.

"I'm serious," I said gently.

"I would," he finally said. "I mean, I would, is what I'm saying."

I lifted my eyebrows impatiently.

"But you were crying."

"C'mon," I said. "You never fucked somebody who was sad before?"

"Jesus."

"I'm sorry. That came out wrong. Everyone's sad. That's all I meant." I sighed. "Look, I had a rough day, and I'm kind of in a hurry. Do you want to or not?"

"Do *you*?"

"Yes!"

My voice seemed to startle him. He glanced back at the door.

"What?" I said.

"Nothing."

"Are you expecting someone?"

He shook his head.

"Then what's the deal?"

"What about your husband?"

"He's fine."

"Does he know where you are?"

"No."

He still didn't seem satisfied.

"We have an open relationship," I lied.

He frowned. "What is that?"

"Nevermind." I stared at him as I took another sip of water. My hand wasn't shaking. I felt like a human. Maybe he could tell, too, because when I set the glass back down, it was like he'd teleported to me. Face to face, he finally looked at me liked he'd looked at me when I'd first walked in the arcade—like a hunter only with kindness and intelligence in his eyes. I felt a pang of guilt for what a different me might have considered sexual tourism, but then I felt that flame-licked, medieval feeling when you like the guilt, and then I felt the guilt return heat to my skin. We leapt into each other, hard and soft. Our teeth hit and everything felt like the past only plastic, like a bad vacation, like tedious poetry. Like we were both inhabiting minor roles in a fairy tale, people soon to be destroyed by the machinery of the plot. But it still felt blessed. If I was smashing into K-lo, how I could have mattered to anyone or anything. It was freedom from mattering. Then the freedom faded and I started to feel what I guess was something like love.

Like it was seeping through our ill-fitting skin. It was too passionate. It wasn't gross, it was tender, which made it even more
gross, which made it even more tender. I hated it and loved
it. It was impossible not to feel saved, for a moment, by the
bristle, by the hard, busy tongue. He tasted like failure. Kissing
him felt like falling off a cliff. It felt like wasting three wishes. It
felt like being in a hot air balloon being blown into power lines.

K-lo's room was so depressing that, walking into it, my
stomach turned. There were rags on the floor, and it smelled
of old fruit. A window unit pumping cold air seemed to
intensify the odor. I asked for the bathroom. He nodded
down a hall. I staggered off, holding myself up with a hand
on a completely empty bookshelf in the hall. I stopped short
when I heard him rifling for something in his room. I turned
and watched him searching desperately in the dim light. He
looked up and whisper-shouted that he didn't have a condom.
His unexpected conscientiousness was pathetically touching,
and I decided I didn't need to see the bathroom. My body felt
like a heap of fine sand tossed into the air, and the wind blew
me into his bed.

I'd rather it had gone on longer, since it was effectively distracting, but it was otherwise ineffective enough that I wasn't
terribly disappointed when it ended. I'd forgotten how awkward it can be when you don't know your partner and they
don't know you. Afterward, K-lo kept trying to kiss me, and I
kept turning away. He asked me why I'd come on to him, and I
said in a tone of attempted old-fashioned Hollywood glamour
that I was going through a divorce and he was a kind, handsome stranger. Although I wanted to be free of his company
at that point, I also didn't want to leave the bed, another piece
of furniture in the folds of which I could try to hide from time.

K-Lo kept pouting, so I told him he'd been wonderful, by the way, my most memorable roll in the hay in ages, and other corny lines like that. He got up and sat on the edge of the bed and hunched over and lit a cigarette. I suddenly had the fantasy that if I said the right thing right then—if I made up the right lie and then said it with total conviction—I could change the course of his life. Because we were strangers and we had already slept together and obviously never would again, in his mind, I imagined, there would be no incentive for me to lie to him, and he therefore might believe anything I said. Plus, he seemed like a genuinely good person. What if I told him that I was a prophet and I'd slept with him because I believed that he would go on to save the world? Why wouldn't he believe me? Why would I make something like that up? Would that make my life matter more, if he then went on to become, not even a messiah, but maybe just a better taxpayer? Or artist? Or father? Or inventor? Or teacher? Then he turned and puffed his cigarette and asked again if I wanted a ride home. I now understood that he wanted me gone. The shameful realization that I had been patronizing him the whole time, and he was tired of it, suddenly struck me. I checked my phone, again afraid I'd missed my husband's call, but I hadn't.

I covered my breasts with one hand and reached to him with the other, pointing at his cigarette pack. He got one out of the pack and put it in my mouth and then leaned over and lit it. I smoked it with my eyes closed and then blew the smoke at his head. It tasted good, better than sex or getting high. I had the thought that if I could do it all over again, upon leaving the clinic, I'd have simply gone to the nearest store and bought cigarettes and smoked a couple. When the cigarette was halfway finished, however, I felt nauseous and

remembered why I hated them. I got to my feet and picked up my clothes. I took one more drag and dropped it in a can of soda on his dresser.

"You leaving?"

I just looked at him while I got dressed, as if this question was stupid. He asked if I was sure I didn't want a ride. "I have a car," I said.

"Where?"

"Across the street."

With painful slowness, his confusion melted into recognition.

"You were at the clinic," he said, almost a question.

I nodded.

He squinted at me, as if reconsidering all my antics.

"I didn't want to drive home," I said.

"You okay?"

"I'll be fine," I almost said. But then I didn't. I don't know why. Maybe I didn't want to lie to him.

"You're a good guy, K-lo," I said. "I hope all your dreams come true."

It was cheesy, but I meant it, and I think he could tell.

IT HAD BEEN SO DARK and cold inside that leaving his apartment felt a bit like rebirth, moving from the netherworld into a world of too vivid color. Humidity immediately beaded all over me, and I was grateful for every droplet.

I was halfway across the speckled parking lot when my phone rang, startling me.

"What's up?" blurted my husband before I'd even said hello. "I was taking a power nap."

I said where I was.

"Oh, right," he said. "I thought you drove."

I told him I had.

"You cool to drive back?"

I told him to come get me.

"Is everything okay?"

"Just come," I said.

"What happened?"

I didn't say anything. Then I heard rustling and movement and footsteps.

"I'm on my way."

A JEEP PULLED UP IN front of the bar. A middle-aged man in sandals and dreadlocks got out, unlocked the bar, went inside, and a moment later the neon signs came on. I looked up at K-lo's bedroom window, still dark. I could tell it was his because I could see the back of the air conditioner wheezing in his window, dripping water, sucking air out of the world. Above the building, several intersecting power lines gave the impression of a big empty sail. From my angle, it made the building look like a kind of ghost ship, with K-lo in the captain's quarters and the dreadlocked sailor belowdecks in the galley. Even the wooden stairs I'd staggered up and then drifted back down evoked a kind of mildewed rigging. I turned away from the ship to face the comparatively shinier complex of medical offices across the street, floating forward more than walking.

Everything felt like it was still underwater, but no longer was I the stunned witness to the sad ruins of some other planet's or time's civilization. I was a monster who belonged here among such wreckage, invisible tentacles billowing all around me, touching and connecting everything, wondering nothing, unseen and all-seeing, marked for extinction like everything, and finding there a forbidden comfort uneasily bordering grace.

AVERN-Y6

RXGR-14 ENTERED AVERN-Y6 TOO EXHAUSTED TO think, aching from abdomen to antennae. Avern-Y6 was packed. The sucking sound of soldiers slurping athletically from generous puddles echoed around Rxgr-14 like white noise. As he negotiated the bodies and feelers of the other patrons, his own feelers felt like they were still digging, still pushing dirt forward, still pulling it back, still tamping it down, smoothing it out, and digging it out of the wall in front of his compound eyes. When he wasn't depressed, he called it tunneling. When he was, he called it moving dirt. Today was a moving dirt day.

There was always more to move, for one, and whether he moved it quickly or slowly, well or poorly, no one took notice. There were too many others just like him. Rxgr-14 wasn't sure how many workers there were, but he was certain it was more than he could imagine. He'd always been able to count pretty high, but somewhere up around a hundred his brain turned into fog. It was part of why he liked coming to Avern-Y6, a soldier's watering hole, despite the fact that those soldiers sometimes gave him shit. As a lowly worker, he felt unique among them.

Rxgr-14 chose an unoccupied divot in the far, uncrowded corner of Avern-Y6. His reflection shimmered in the puddle of golden liquid. He looked old. He wondered how long it would be before he died. In the mirrors of the lenses of his eyes, he observed tiny versions of himself, each looking up into him with the same grim curiosity.

Rxgr-14 looked around at the soldiers. How did they not go crazy worrying about dying while rushing into danger? Rxgr-14 reassured himself that they were probably as afraid as he was, they just knew how to conceal their fear from others, or from themselves. That's the real trick, Rxgr-14 thought. Maybe courage was a kind of camouflage behind which you hide the fearful part of you from the part that's brave. But how can the mind hide something from the mind? Dirt can't move itself.

Rxgr-14 appraised his reflection again. His exoskeleton was scuffed and matte. He'd once been so shiny he couldn't have hidden in the deepest blind alley in the colony. Now, however, his careworn carapace absorbed all available light. The tips of his antennae hung over his forehead, wilted, as if even the memories within them had given up on being remembered. One of those memories, an unexpectedly resilient one, suddenly came back to him—of being bulldozed on unsteady, newborn feelers out of the nursery into the loud wide bright central shaft linking every tunnel and compartment in the colony—the song of the queen exploding brilliantly into his unimprinted mind like a synesthetic symphony, his pliant antennae spasming to capture even a fraction of that zooming psychedelic melody.

Now, his antennae were bald, bent, and blunted, and the song of the queen was a background soundtrack hardly distinguishable from the susurrations of the slurping soldiers.

Rxgr-14 bent to the golden fluid and drew in a liberal sip. He closed his eyes, inclined his head toward the rotunda of Avern-Y6, and swallowed slowly. As the cold liquid rode down his esophagus, his thorax warmed, and then the warmth spread until he felt it creep up behind his eyes, and he opened them in pleasant surrender.

He looked down at himself in the liquid again. His mouth was open and grinning. His carapace didn't look dull; it was rugged. The many lenses of his eyes weren't chipped; they were distinguished. His antennae didn't dangle sadly; they swayed laconically. He wasn't debilitated by age; he was seasoned by experience, and he was at the peak of his powers. He was one of the most gifted tunnelers in the colony. Sure, he wished he was younger, but youth is its own prison too, he reflected with a nod. So is power. So is everything I want that I don't have, he thought on. And a fuzzy thesis formed in his mind about why one tended to magnify beyond all proportion the superficial deficiencies of one's own physique, but before it reached the point of clear articulation, the notion vanished into the same cognitive fog that high numbers did.

And the more he drank of the fluid made from the fermented ooze secreted by the sterile breeders of the royal caste in the capacious distilleries beneath the nursery, the less and less he minded his status as an exhausted laborer disgusted with the futility of existence.

A FOGGY NUMBER OF SIPS later, Rxgr-14 reflected happily that he still had several hours before going to sleep, and soon his friends Lnzt-16 and Tzara-9 would arrive, the latter of whom he was in love with, albeit unrequitedly. But was it not a gift to be in love at all? At least you knew what you were all about. Better to be subject to unfulfilled desires than to have the world at your feelers and falter in your will. Stacked as the odds of one-sided love are, thought Rxgr-14, aren't stacked odds the stuff of legends? He looked around. What were any of us but the legend we tell to the audience inside our own mind? So why not tell a bold one? Why not start at the bottom? A worker like him, a soldier like her, separated by both caste and, he admitted, his own towering cowardice? What a story!

Rxgr-14 drank excitedly, hoping Tzara-9 arrived first so they could conversate alone. Tzara-9 was flirtier when Lnzt-16 wasn't around, and Rxgr-14 reveled in her undivided attention and saucy personality. He liked Lnzt-16, too, but what he really wanted was to interlock mandibles with Tzara-9. He thought about it often, and he thought about it now as he plunged his mandibles into the amber liquid below him and slurped. A few moments later, a figure darkened the puddle. Rxgr-14 lifted his head partly, then stopped. He could tell it was Lnzt-16 from the extra-large shadow he cast.

"*Mon frère!*" Lnzt-16 bellowed. "You won't believe what I must tell you!"

Rxgr-14 regarded his friend's upside-down reflection in the amber liquid.

"Hey."

Lnzt-16's mandibles clicked excitedly. "Very big news indeed, *mon frère*."

Lnzt-16 was three times Rxgr-14's size, and his carapace was shinier by an order of ten. Beyond being an incredible physical specimen, Lnzt-16 was atypically conscientious, warm, and friendly for a member of the warrior class. To say that Rxgr-14 felt both envy and admiration for Lnzt-16 would be an understatement. Rxgr-14 lowered his head back down and slurped.

Lnzt-16 frowned at his friend's apparent glumness, then threw a monstrous, spiky feeler around him.

"My news is big, *mon frère*, but, eh… not urgent. What's wrong?"

"I had a bad day," Rxgr-14 said flatly. "So I guess I got drunk."

Lnzt-16 smiled brightly. "But that's what drinking is for, *mon frère!*"

Rxgr-14 inclined his head at Lnzt-16's reflection. "That was yesterday. Today, I was hungover, which made today a bad day too, so all I wanted to do all day was drink even more, so when I got off work, that's what I did, and now I'm drunk again. It's like a damn curse."

"Oh," Lnzt-16 said. "Well, what did you get up to last night?" He wriggled his feelers. "Nothing lifts the spirits like a sordid tale of woe and excess!"

"There's no tale. You weren't there. Tzara-9 wasn't either. So I was drinking alone, thinking about how lonely I was. And am. Then some of your brethren started calling me 'bug,' so I left. It was humiliating. But, whatever."

Lnzt-16's head swiveled. "Who called you… that?" He reared on his feelers to get a better view of the others.

"Settle down," Rxgr-14 said. "I deserved it. I was being a jerk."

"What'd you do?"

"The big bronze dude? What's his name?"

"Eybv-99?"

Rxg-14 nodded. "Yeah. He shit on one of the workers when they over-filled his divot. Literally covered him, abdomen to antennae, in hot, liquid shit."

"Who?"

"Some worker. I don't know his name."

"And you stood up for him?" Lnzt-16 asked, impressed.

"Not really. I just told Eybv-99 he shouldn't waste waste." Rxgr-14 inclined his head toward the ceiling. "You see that?"

Lnzt-16 squinted up at the rotunda.

"See how cracked and dry it is? If everybody who drank here just did what they were supposed to do, this place would last forever. It's just typical of… you know what? Nevermind. I don't want to talk about it. I was hammered. I called him out. He called me 'bug.' I left before it got ugly."

Lnzt-16 frowned. "And then you went home?" Lnzt-16 asked with a frown.

"No, I went to G2, and, uh, actually, ended up over at Z9."

"Yeesh."

Rxgr-14 shook his head. "I know."

"Z9 is nothing but burnouts and… the laziest of workers, *mon frère*. No offense."

Rxgr-14's antennae swiveled. "I said I know," he said sharply.

Lnzt-16 looked down, chastised.

Rxgr-14 shrugged. "It's not all that bad, actually."

"Oh?" Lnzt-16 lifted his head back up, then nodded amiably. "I suppose I've never been to Z9. I only know what I hear."

"There's a worker there I might have a thing for."

"Oh yeah?"

"A minor thing. She's a brilliant tunneler."

"Did you two speak?"

Rxgr-14 shook his head. "No."

"Why not?"

"I don't know. I don't know the scene there. They know I hang with you guys. I don't even know why I went. I felt like a creep."

"That's why you should only drink here, *mon frère*." Lnzt-16 glanced around. "Avern-Y6 for life!" Then Lnzt-16 seemed to get an idea. "Maybe you should invite her here. What's her name?"

Rxgr-14 dismissed the idea with a wave of his feeler. "You don't know her. Besides, this place is an acquired taste."

Lnzt-16 shrugged, letting it go. Then he frowned at his friend and leaned in. "Look, you know I have your back. Eybv-99 knows it too. You'll always be safe here, as long as I'm around."

"I know." Rxgr-14 smiled at his friend reluctantly. "I appreciate it."

Lnzt-16 looked at him hopefully.

"Besides," Rxgr-14 said with a smirk, "you guys do have the best booze."

Lnzt-16 smiled.

Rxgr-14 bent down and took a sip. Then, coming back up, he wiped a long feeler appreciatively across his mandibles and said, "Down in Z9, it's literally like drinking mud."

They both gazed appreciatively at the clear golden liquid in their puddle.

"Anyway," Rxgr-14 said, "you guys were gone last night. So I just ended up drowning in it."

Rxgr-14 lowered his head to sip again, but Lnzt-16 stopped him with his feeler.

"No need to drown again, *mon frère*. I'm here! And I'm certain Tzara-9 is en route." Lnzt-16 wriggled his bright, pliant antennae in a clumsy attempt at irony. "You're not lonely anymore."

Rxgr-14 pushed Lnzt-16's feeler away. "Loneliness was last night's reason. Tonight, it's social anxiety."

Lnzt-16 frowned. "And if you ever relax, you'll be drunk because you're happy. If reasons to drink were reasons to live, *mon frère*, why, you'd be a prophet!"

"Would you please stop saying *mon frère*?"

Lnzt-16 looked at him, surprised. "You don't like it?"

"You don't even know what it means."

"It's… an expression."

"Of what?"

Lnzt-16 lifted his head. His weaponlike mandibles danced for a moment as he thought. "Of friendship," he finally said. He looked at Rxgr-14 melodramatically. "Or so I thought. Maybe I just don't have your way with words."

Rxgr-14 looked down. "No, no. I'm sorry. I'm just… I'm off tonight."

"I don't like you like this, *m*—my friend. If there's anything I can do to lift your spirits, will you tell me?"

Rxgr-14 looked at Lnzt-16's reflection. "I'll be fine." Then he looked up at the real him. "Where were you last night anyway?"

"Right!" Lnzt-16's eyes suddenly lit up. "My big news! I had a date."

Rxgr-14 threw up his feelers. "Wow. That is news. That's huge. Who was it, your soul mate? Or just someone impossibly beautiful who only wants to interlock mandibles with no strings attached? Or something even better perhaps?"

Lnzt-16 scowled. "I have no desire to be cruel. I won't tell you about my life if it hurts you so much to hear about it."

"No, no. Goddammit, I'm being a jerk. It's just that you're always going on dates. No offense, but you're literally always going on dates."

"Not with a member of the royal caste, I'm not."

Rxgr-14 looked at Lnzt-16 with genuine surprise. "Wings?"

Lnzt-16 nodded, spreading wide his middle feelers and even fluttering them a little.

Rxgr-14 took a moment to imagine it, then said breathlessly, "Who?"

"Szafair-2."

Rxgr-14 thought, then shook his head. "Doesn't ring a bell." Then he said, "What'd you two do?"

"Had a drink," Lnzt-16 said. "Walked the long way around the reservoir. Showed her a few of your tunnels. She was impressed." Lnzt-16 tapped his head with his forward feeler. "Told her I knew more about tunneling than the average executioner." He smiled. "Due to the informal tutelage of my exceptionally talented drinking comrade. And then I told her your name."

Rxgr-14's eyes clicked in awe that Lnzt-16 would mention him. Then he shook his head incredulously. "Educated. Modest. Sincere. Comfortable mixing among classes. And you even managed work in that you liked to party. Well done, *mon frère*."

Lnzt-16 offered his friend a self-assured smile, practically basking in Rxgr-14's astute admiration. "Indeed," was all he said. Then he seemed to remember his point, and he leaned forward while casting a cautious glance across the other imbibers in Avern-Y6. "But it's what happened next that you've got to keep real, real quiet."

"You interlocked mandibles with a royal?"

"Shhhh, no. Not even I'm that uncouth, *mon frère*. Not on the first date. No, we did something even more dangerous, even more forbidden." He paused, then added, "Even more spectacular."

Rxgr-14 was rapt, and Lnzt-16 milked it.

"Well, spit it out," Rxgr-14 said. Then he glanced over Lnzt-16's shoulder and said in a lower voice, "Tzara-9 will be here any minute."

The expression on Lnzt-16's face changed from bemusement to concern, then he nodded curtly. It was an open secret that Tzara-9 was in love with Lnzt-16. Rxgr-14 suspected that Tzara-9 and Lnzt-16 had interlocked mandibles, but he'd never asked about it directly because he hadn't wanted to know.

"Before I tell you what we did," Lnzt-16 began conspiratorially, "I need to describe for you her wings."

Rxgr-14 leaned in.

"They were huge, but you wouldn't have known it. Unlike your typical aristocrat flaunting their flappers every chance they can to keep you supremely aware of who you are and who you are not, Szafair-2 had hers tucked in behind her back. I didn't even know she had royal blood at first. You know what I'm saying?"

"How do you know how big they were if they were tucked in behind her back?"

Lnzt-16 paused dramatically before he said, "Because she unfurled them for me when we flew."

Rxgr-14 stared at his friend for a moment. Then he said, "Yeah, right."

"I swear! She lifted me off the ground, and then we flew around, and I saw the world, the whole world, from a point of view that was far above it, my friend."

"Where?"

Lnzt-16 just stared at him.

Rxgr-14 thought about it, then seemed to figure it out. "The reservoir?" he asked disappointedly. "You don't even need wings to jump that thing."

Lnzt-16 shook his head, then inclined it.

Both of them gazed up at the ceiling again, but in his mind's eye, Rxgr-14 passed through the ceiling and imagined the tunnels directly above it. He didn't have to work very hard to visualize them, for in his mind was a map of every passageway in the colony, and he followed them all the way up as far as they went.

"You were outside," he said.

"And it was beautiful," Lnzt-16 confirmed.

"In the sky?" Rxgr-14 asked in disbelief.

Lnzt-16 nodded. Then he spread his feelers and closed his eyes and swayed slightly, speaking meditatively. "It was the purest feeling of freedom I've ever known. I've lived a life of great privilege, I don't have to tell you, but nothing has ever come close to the feeling of flying." He opened his eyes. "It made me wish I had wings, too." His compound eyes glimmered pensively. "Why, it made me feel like I was *meant* to fly, you know?" He looked around. "Like we all were. I don't know."

Rxgr-14 processed this.

Lnzt-16's deadly mandibles clenched and unclenched, then he stabbed the dirt with a feeler.

"I'd trade anything for wings. I'd trade anything not to…" his antennae wriggled awkwardly, indicating his whole body, "be this. I know that probably sounds crazy to a worker, no offense."

"None taken."

"But being held by her feelers as we flew through the air, and feeling the wind flow over my armor in the clear bright sun like that… it felt like I, I don't know, like I had become something that I… oh, you know what it was like… it was like…"

Rxgr-14 leaned forward eagerly.

"Ah," said Lnzt-16, giving up. "I don't know what it was like. Maybe there's no way to describe it."

"You weren't afraid?"

"Oh, I was." He pointed a feeler upward. "But she wasn't."

The words sank in. Rxgr-14 looked down at his reflection in the liquid. "They must fly all the goddamn time."

"Maybe. Maybe not. Who knows what royals really do, *mon frère*. Mere mortals, we, eh?"

Rxgr-14 nodded.

"I'll tell you this though," Lnzt-16 continued. "You don't realize how big the outside world is until you see it from up high. It's like the reservoir times a hundred, and whatever that is, times a hundred more, and probably again, too. There isn't a ceiling either."

Rxgr-14 had been leaning forward to take a sip, and he stopped. "What do you mean?"

"You know how if you keep digging down you hit rock?"

Rxgr-14 nodded.

"Well, if you keep flying… you don't hit anything. It just goes on. I kept waiting for Szafair-2 to crash into it, but no matter how high she went, she never did. I bet she could've gone higher. And you know what else?"

Rxgr-14 shook his head.

"The higher you get, the littler things are, and there's more of what is, not less, even though you're further. Can you believe that?"

Rxgr-14 tried to picture it.

"I saw the main gate," Lnzt-16 said. "You know how it's five bodies wide?"

"Actually, four-point-six body-widths is the optimal diameter for vertically presenting apertures—"

"Yeah, yeah, but, the point is, from up high, it looked, uh…" Lnzt-16 searched for a point of comparison, then saw a speck of sand that had fallen into the puddle from which they were drinking. He pointed at it. "It looked like that."

Rxgr-14's antennae curled back as he scrutinized the utterly miniscule speck.

"I used to think that up was bigger than down, but it's not, not really. Down and up are the same, they're just different. It's distance that changes a size, not depth or height. Crazy, huh?"

Rxgr-14 thought about it.

"That's what I'd do," Lnzt-16 said, looking up again. "If I had wings, I mean. I'd just go out there and go up and up and up until… until… I don't know what. Just to see how far it goes though. Just to be able to look back down and see how small the whole world got."

"You'd probably hit rock eventually. There must a ceiling. Nothing goes on in any direction forever."

Lnzt-16 shrugged. "Maybe. But we'll never know, will we? We're just... you know... what we are."

"It doesn't matter," Rxgr-14 said, looking at Lnzt-16 with blazing admiration. "What you did was amazing. You're the first soldier to ever fly, probably. And she's insane. What's her name again?"

"Szafair-2."

"Just to be able to lift you," Rxgr-14 said, indicating his friend's physique with a tilt of his head. "Her wings must've been enormous."

Lnzt-16 nodded seriously. Then he glanced around. Avern-Y6 had gotten busier. Lnzt-16 spoke in a lower volume. "It made me want to do more than hunt down bugs in abandoned tunnels for the rest of my life. It made me want to, I don't know, live different. Even without wings. I mean, doesn't this seem redundant? Life, I mean. Doesn't it seem like we're just going through the motions? Carrying out these pre-programmed routines? I mean, when there's a world out there? With a whole damn sky with no ceiling?" Rxgr-14 saw himself in the obsidian mirrors of Lnzt-16's eyes. "What're we *doing* down here?"

Rxgr-14 shushed him with a nudge of his feeler. Across the room, another soldier with a rust-colored carapace was watching. Both of the soldier's antennae were pointing straight up, as if trying to isolate an aberration in the signal.

Rxgr-14 looked gravely at his friend and said, "You better keep thoughts like that to a minimum."

Lnzt-16 checked over his shoulder. The warrior with a rust-colored carapace had returned to slurp from his divot. His antennae had returned to the passive position.

Rxgr-14 looked at the reflection of his friend in their own puddle and muttered, "You're not crazy though Just don't tell anyone. If the royal guard knew you went outside, with a princess no less. Hell, commiserating with a—"

"You don't have to tell me, *mon frère*." Lnzt-16 pointed at himself with his feelers. "I'm the one they send in to decapitate commiserators, remember?"

Rxgr-14 looked at him. "Even saying it is dangerous."

Lnzt-16 nodded.

Rxgr-14 wriggled his right antennae and whispered, "Even thinking it."

They both lowered their heads and drank.

When Rxgr-14 lifted his head back up, the rust-colored soldier had turned his back to them.

"How'd you two even meet?"

"Szafair-2?"

Rxgr-14 nodded, then glanced across Avern-Y6 and added, "Just leave out the revolutionary rhetoric."

Lnzt-16 leaned in. "Last week, our squad got an award for killing a shit-ton of millipedes."

Rxgr-14 frowned. "How many?"

"A bunch, but, they would've died anyway." Lnzt-16 shook his head. "Don't worry about it. That's not the point. The point is, Szafair-2 was mistress of ceremonies. During the ceremony, I noticed her wings folded back. I was like, I like that. She's not wagging them in our fucking faces like these other fucking breeders. I mean half these ceremonies supposedly held in *our* honor are just excuses for them to lord their fucking wings over us, you know what I'm saying?"

"I said take it easy."

"Sorry." Lnzt-16 shook his large head as if to free it of resentment. "So anyway, I ask her what her name is. She asks mine. We get separated. Then some more ceremonial stuff, speeches by the commander, songs to the queen. I completely forget about her. Then later, out of nowhere, she pulls me aside and asks me what I'm most proud of. Just like that. What are you most proud of? Like a test or something. I thought she was joking. I was like, this girl's crazy. Who does that?"

"Jesus. You don't think she's an informant, do you?"

"Informant?"

"For the royal guard, dumbass. You know they have spies in every Avern. That's part of their job. To act all, you know, un-fascist. So they can root out trouble-makers. Like you."

"No, no, no," Lnzt-16 said. "I thought of that. She's not like that. She was sincere."

Rxtr-14 looked at Lnzt-16 skeptically for a long time, then he nodded. "So what'd you tell her you were proud of?"

"I told her I'd have to think about it. And to be honest, at that point, all I was thinking was, do I actually have a shot with her? But she just gives me this disappointed look and walks away. Like, what, she's not interested because I can't answer a complicated question like that in two seconds? So I stop her from leaving and say, a little pissed-off, I'm proudest of my mother."

"Nice."

"Not the queen, the soldier who reared me."

"I know."

"She saved sixty eggs during the great flood by relocating seventeen loads of dirt all by herself from an old nursery to reinforce the wall in the main nursery, the one between it and the reservoir."

Rxgr-14 rolled his eyes. "I *know*. You've told me. And everyone else. A hundred times."

"Before my mother, soldiers were useless in disasters." He twittered his antennae. "The signal to kill is so overwhelming. You workers don't understand. But she fought it off and thought like you. One of you, I mean. And it saved lives. Worker lives."

"You were reared by a progressive heroine of the highest order. I know."

"You're not impressed?"

"It's great. Congratulations. Transcending our programming is possible, blah blah blah. But what's going to happen to workers like me when the queen realizes you guys are better at tunneling than we are?"

"Tunneling?" Lnzt-16 shook his head. "All she did was move some dirt."

"It's the same thing!"

"We'll never be better than you. You guys are artists. It's just that, during emergencies, we could contribute a little bit more. That's all."

"Are you kidding? With those mandibles? I'm telling you. This is how evolution works. All it's going to take is one soldier with half a brain—no offense—and the connections to sell it to the breeders. And then one morning me and all the other workers are going to wake up with a new order in our heads: go dig your own graves."

Lnzt-16 snorted. "That's ridiculous. The queen would never... could never... there's too many of you. You're irreplaceable."

"She could, and she would, and you know what the truth is? I wouldn't even blame her. If I was queen, I'd do the same thing. Your mandibles. They're bigger. There's no way around it. We only invented the techniques we have now because we had to compensate for our smaller ones. But once that dam breaks, and you guys know what we know, there's no reason to keep us around, to keep feeding us, to keep getting us drunk. And our numbers? That's a liability, not an asset. You know what happened to the foragers."

Lnzt-16 huffed. "That's a myth."

"You think it's a myth because it scares you to think about what it means. But think about it. They used to call us tunnelers, now we're called workers *and* we forage. Foragers were fast, but they ate half of everything they brought back. Now, back when we were surrounded by a shit-ton of bugs, foragers *had* to be fast. But now there's no bugs. You guys killed them all off or chased them away. Without bugs to pick them off, the queen realized she could send some slow-ass tunnelers to bring back whatever she needed, and tunnelers, being slow, don't eat *near* as much of it. When she figured that out, that's when she got rid of the foragers."

"I've heard all that nonsense before. She couldn't have killed them though. A queen wouldn't kill her own. We're her children. All of us are. We're in this together."

"Stop thinking like a soldier. Think like a queen. She doesn't need to kill us. She controls the means of reproduction. If she wants to get rid of a whole class, all she has to do is stop *making* us. One day, eggs that would've been foragers are fertilized by tunnelers. Then over time, as the foragers die of old age or get picked off by the remaining bugs, she changes the name of tunnelers to workers in the colony song. Now, work? That could mean anything. Next thing you know some workers are foraging, some are tunneling." Rxgr-14 pointed at himself. "And here we are."

Lnzt-16 laughed. "You're paranoid."

"I'm telling you," Rxgr-14 said, "the first time one of you digs a tunnel in a pinch, then goes on to kill some shit, and the tunnel doesn't collapse, and the queen finds out about it, it's over. Worker culture, our values, our craftsmanship, our *bodies*, it's all gonna disappear."

"You don't even like other workers."

"That's not the point. I'm not even sure it should be different. Like I said, if I was the queen, that's what I'd do. I'm just saying, *your* version of history is totally fucking naïve."

Lnzt-16 frowned. "Whatever." He shook his head. "I don't even know what got us on politics."

After a sulking silence, Rxgr-14 said, "You were telling me about how you met, uh, Szafair-2."

Lnzt-16 brightened up. "Oh yeah. I almost forgot the best part, besides the flying."

Rxgr-14 looked at him curiously.

"I heard the queen sing," Lnzt-16 said. "In her real voice."

"When?"

"After my step-mom spiel, Szafair-2 said she wanted to show me something. I had no idea she was gonna take me flying, so I didn't think anything of it when we snuck *down* into the nursery."

"The nursery?"

"From the nursery, we got into the hatchery, which as you know borders the throne room. So, I couldn't see her, but I was close enough to hear her real voice."

Rgr-14 nodded. "The walls are thin down there so the larvae can hear the song and develop accordingly."

"Wow," said Lnzt-16 sarcastically. "Is that a fact? I never knew that."

Rxgr-14 rolled his compound eyes. "Whatever."

"You know," Lnzt-16 resumed contemplatively after a moment. "Come to think of it, she was singing the forager song."

Rxgr-14 looked up. "Really?"

Lnzt-16 nodded.

"See? They were real!"

Lnzt-16 shrugged. "Just because there's a song about something doesn't make it real."

Rxgr-14 threw up his feelers. "Where else would it come from?"

Lnzt-16 ignored the question. "Look, if she phased them out like you say, why would she be singing it?"

"Maybe she's bringing them back! Maybe she's sad! Maybe she loved them! Maybe she's singing their song because what she had to do broke her heart! Can't you imagine what it's like to be in charge? Me and you, we're expendable. She's got to keep the colony going. That means killing us off if it comes to it, or bringing us back if it comes to that. If she wasn't willing to do that, she wouldn't be queen. It explains everything."

Lnzt-16 shook his head. "Doesn't pass the smell test."

"What a cliché," Rxgr-14 said. "A privileged soldier who only thinks in black and white."

Lnzt-16 glared.

"I'm sorry but it's true."

"That's classist."

"You're right. It is. You get to have everything." Rxgr-14 gestured to himself. "Let me at least have this."

"Let you mock me? Let you lord your paranoia over me as if it were proof of your intellect and not just a difference of opinion? I would prefer not."

"Sorry," Rxgr-14 said bitterly. He took a sip from the divot, then tilted his head accusingly. "Wait a minute. If you were all the way down by the throne room, how'd you get all the way outside without getting seen?"

"There's a secret tunnel. A direct one."

Rxgr-14 pounded the ground with his feeler. "I knew it!"

"It was well-made, too. Like one you'd have made. Smooth walls, tightly packed, and perfectly surfaced so that it just holds the light. And straighter than a snitch's antenna."

"I sure wish more soldiers gave a shit about surfacing. We'd face a lot less tunnel collapse."

"I know. You've taught me that."

"I'm sorry I called you a cliché just now," Rxgr-14 said.

"It's okay." Lnzt-16 shrugged. "You know what? Maybe I am one."

"You're not."

Lnzt-16 looked at his friend and said sincerely, "Thank you."

"Are you going to see her again?"

"Szafair-2?"

Rxgr-14 nodded. "I mean, you can't, can you? If the royal guard found out, you'd…"

Lnzt-16 silenced him with a nod and said, "We're meeting tonight."

"Tonight?" Rxgr-14 looked around. "Where? Here?"

Lnzt-16 shook his head. "Up by the dump. Later." He smiled. "I've got to get hammered first."

Rxgr-14 laughed. "You're insane."

"I wish you could meet her. When I showed her your tunnels, she asked how well I knew you."

Rxgr-14's eyes clicked several times in succession. "Really?"

"She might want someone new to oversee the secret passage. I got the feeling she had all these plans or something, clandestine plans, but who knows what for. It was like she was recruiting me, and asking about my friends. Anyway, I hope it's okay that I mentioned you. Mainly your insights about the structure of the walls and stuff. She was into it. I'll ask her about it tonight if you want. Who knows, maybe she could get you a sweet-ass gig."

"Wow. Yes. That would be awesome."

"What would?"

Rxgr-14 and Lnzt-16 turned around. Tzara-9 was standing behind them.

She smiled at Rxgr-14, and the dazzling hues of emerald in her compound eyes all changed as they caught the light.

"What would be awesome?" she asked again, cocking her head as she walked between them. She stepped right through the liquid in the divot and took her place on the other side.

She was still staring curiously, waiting for an answer, when Rxgr-14 looked at Lnzt-16 and said, "Uh, nothing." He looked back at her. "Just work stuff. Boring, really."

Tzara-9's antennae twinged skeptically, then she shrugged and dropped her face into the trough of fluid she'd just walked through. Rxgr-14 watched the panels of her shiny, smoke-green exoskeleton shimmering and flexing as she swept the fermented unfertilized reproductive proteins into her mouth with greedy swishes of her bladelike mandibles. Tzara-9 drank with greater abandon than anyone Rxgr-14 had ever seen, and Rxgr-14's most successful conversations with Tzara-9 involved him and her riffing back and forth on the infinite merits of drunkenness and the inglorious insufficiencies of sobriety.

Mid-slurp, Tzara-9 lifted her head and shook the amber droplets off her mandibles and smiled at them both. "Seriously, you two. What would be awesome?"

"Nothing," said Lnzt-16 too quickly.

Tzara-9 furrowed her compound eyes at Lnzt-16. Now she knew something was up.

"Lnzt-16 got a promotion," Rxgr-14 blurted.

Lnzt-16 looked at him.

"Really?" Tzara-9 said. "That's amazing! Way to go, *friend*!" She grinned and clapped him on the back so hard that Lnzt-16 winced.

"Um, yeah," said Lnzt-16, recovering. "But it's really not that big a deal. It hasn't even gone through yet. Might not even get it." He lowered his head and added before he started slurping, "And I don't want to jinx it by talking about it."

Tzara-9 stared at him as if offended by the attempt to exclude her. Then she calmly lowered her aquiline head to the edge of the puddle and flicked the liquid vulgarly with the twin tips of her antennae, splashing Lnzt-16. Rxgr-14 practically gasped. Lnzt-16 looked up at her like she was a ghost. She smiled at him hard.

ONE'S ANTENNAE HOUSED ONE'S MEMORY and established a neural connection to every other consciousness in the colony. Every experience of every individual was encoded in coils of nerves within. This coiling, royal researchers had discovered, transmitted a two-way signal between every other member's antennae. The network meant an individual's private and social memories were unified in the psychology of the colony, but the network wasn't always easy to access. Generally speaking, only the queen could experience these memories, and, although she was typically too busy to snoop through private memories one by one, a general feeling—anxiety, conspiracy, lust, murderous rage—could be felt by anyone whose antennae were functioning properly. Colonial lore was replete, therefore, with villains who'd escaped the influence of or even gained influence over higher authorities by modifying or otherwise tampering with their antennae. Some cut them off to forget trauma, or to disconnect from the colony before doing works of great evil. In the past, antennae loss had been seen as a sure sign of moral degeneracy, if not intentional heresy; recent attitudes, however, had liberalized. A damaged antenna was less and less an emblem of wickedness and more and more simply a risk to public health. Thus the rationale for culling the antennaeless had become more humane even if the result was the same. Many opposed the policy of quarantining and incarcerating or executing the abnormally antennaed, of course, arguing such workers and soldiers were perfectly capable of living normal lives; however, because most of this opposition came from older members of the colony whose antennae had been degraded by labor or combat or the passage of time, antennae reform was often seen by the mainstream as a way for has-beens to hang on and unduly shape colonial policy long after their relevance had lapsed. Infrequently, some members of the colony were permitted to live on in a state of partial or complete antennae loss, if they knew the right royal member or were seen as feeble enough to simply disregard. Other amputees fled the colony to live beyond its walls. They were then considered "bugs," a catch-all slur usually reserved for rival species, particularly termites. But to put any antennae, even one's own, at risk—for any reason—generally made others uncomfortable. Because antennae were a network, whenever any antenna was knocked, twisted, crushed, or otherwise twanged, there was a chance that another nearby would sense it. That Tzara-9 would risk breaking this taboo to goad Lnzt-16 was, in the eyes of Rxgr-14, half her charm. She was a total maniac, and Rxgr-14 idolized her willingness to shred the expectations of those around her, even as it made him feel uncomfortable, not to mention cowardly by comparison. Outwardly, at least, Lnzt-16 seemed to regard Tzara-9 as a lazy and unvigilant soldier, and he often accused her of getting by on brashness alone, which he had characterized as "all well and good… during peacetime" in those exact words so many times that the phrase was as maddening to Tzara-9 as *mon frère* was to Rxgr-14. For all his amorous and political adventurousness, Lnzt-16 was inflexibly hawkish on defense. Tzara-9 had more than once accused him of being a thoughtless playboy who'd goose-step to anyone who fluttered their wings, but, mostly, Rxgr-14 knew that Tzara-9 was as eager for Lnzt-16's approval as she was likely to provoke him into sputtering defenses of the genteel machismo that was so obviously precious to him and so often preposterous to her and Rxgr-14. Rxgr-14 believed the three of them were friends because Lnzt-16 was too noble for his peers, Tzara-9 was too reckless and self-destructive for hers, and Rxgr-14 was too neurotic and arrogant for his. His infatuation with her, especially, made tragic sense. He would've done anything to be more like either of them, but Lnzt-16's chivalry, being so rooted in his warrior status, was unattainable for Rxgr-14. Tzara-9's general truculence, by contrast, was a perspective possible for him to adopt, if only he'd had the courage. Rxgr-14 had a hunch, too, that Tzara-9 was just as nettled by her own neuroses as he was, but instead of employing internalization to deal with it, she vented it by provoking the world.

LNZT-16 DELIBERATELY WIPED THE UNFERTILIZED fermented reproductive proteins off his face, still shocked that Tzara-9 had abused her antennae. Ignoring him, Tzara-9 launched into an extended complaint about her workday. A fellow soldier had apparently chided her for arriving late to duty, which had been to guard the chamber where excess royal waste was stored before workers came and picked it up and distributed it throughout the colony, smashing it into the weakest tunnel walls.

"The fucking litter box?" she said. "Picture this idiot, okay, this unfucked errand boy with antennae straight as splinters, lecturing me on security protocols. I was like, *Hello*. It's *piss*. Who's gonna steal it?" She looked at Rxgr-14 and Lnzt-16 for validation, then, as if their validation mattered not a whit, she face-splashed into the puddle and guzzled some more.

"Actually," Rxgr-14 said when she had resurfaced, "lots of soldiers don't appreciate how vital waste recirculation is to tunnel surfac—"

"Oh, spare me. I know it's important. I'm not saying it's not important. But no one's *stealing* it, got me?" She blinked at Rxgr-14. "So who cares if the solider *guarding* it is two seconds late. See what I'm saying?"

Rxgr-14 thought about it, then nodded. In a sense, she was right. "What'd you do?" he asked.

"Told him to fuck off," Tzara-9 said.

Lnzt-16 scowled.

"And that I hoped one day someone got bored enough to interlock mandibles with him so maybe, I don't know, he'd bend an antenna against a wall or something and have a free fucking thought for once in his life."

During this speech, Tzara-9 had curled her antennae into a semi-circle, evoking a halo—historically, an impolite gesture indicating that one considered oneself the equivalent of a queen, but which had slipped into general acceptance, signifying self-congratulation.

"You should still arrive for duty on time," Lnzt-16 said. "It makes us all look bad."

"Who, you and him?" She pointed at Lnzt-16 with one antenna and Rxgr-14 with the other. "Or what—you speak for all soldiers now? What're you, an ombudsman now?"

"You know what I mean," he said.

"Maybe I don't. Maybe you should to explain it to me. You're a bona fide hero, after all. I came to your award ceremony. It must feel nice to get recognized for murdering an entire litter of millipedes. I heard they were defenseless and asking for refuge, but, I'm sure that's just a rumor."

"Hey, I was following orders. And you weren't there. And what's your problem anyway?"

"You tell me. Or are you not an expert on all my flaws?"

Rxgr-14 was looking back and forth between them, confused and anxious. "C'mon," he said to Lnzt-16 in a conciliatory tone. "Maybe she's got a point. Remember what you were saying? Like how we all just, you know, follow the rules too much?"

"I don't remember what I was saying."

Tzara-9 looked at the two of them, suspicious again, but instead of prying, she lowered her head and silently drank.

Watching her drink, Rxgr-14 realized Tzara-9 had possibly played them. By deliberately flaunting her soldierly negligence, she'd provoked Lnzt-16, which had caused Rxgr-14 to blurt out something he might otherwise have kept private.

When she lifted her head, Rxgr-14 tried to steer the conversation back to safety.

"It's just crazy," he said with forced amiability, "how different we all are." He looked at them both. "You're nothing like him. And you're nothing like her. And neither of you is anything like that losery guard, or that bully, Eybv-99. Thank the queen, am I right? That we're all different." He laughed nervously. They both just stared at him. He looked around Avern-Y6. "There's probably as many opinions on how to be a good soldier as there are soldiers in here. Kinda beautiful if you think about it."

AVERN-Y6 WAS NOW WALL TO wall with shit-faced soldiers, some of whom were on top of the others, forming clusters of interlocked chaos around each divot and making it havoc for the workers who had to squeeze their way in between the bodies to refill the hole in the floor with fermented unfertilized reproductive protein. Beyond that, a low-grade restlessness pervaded the entire chamber. Rxgr-14 caught himself glancing at the ceiling, envisioning it caving in and killing everyone. He had no reason to believe a cave-in was imminent, but he couldn't shake the thought that some dreadful event was verging.

When Tzara-9 was serenaded by a throng of drunken veterans near the center of Avern-Y6, she checked Lnzt-16 for a reaction. Rxgr-14 watched worriedly. When Lnzt-16 didn't react, and the song increased in both compliment and insult, Tzara-9 encouraged the singers, seemingly tempted by the lewd buffet on offer. When the song ended, Tzara-9 said, "Hmm. Maybe I *should* go over there."

"Wait," Rxgr-14 blurted. "Don't leave us."

She looked at him pitifully. Then she stared at Lnzt-16—a dare of some sort.

Lnzt-16 met it. First, one of his antennae pointed to the group of soldiers, then his head swiveled to follow his antenna—an expression of sarcasm—as if his mind lagged behind his social awareness.

Finally, appraising her suitors with a scholarly countenance, Lnzt-16 declared, "Their mandibles look small enough."

Tzara-9 grinned at the insult. "What's that supposed to mean?"

"I guess it means go have fun with those small-mandibled bug-likers," he said. "No one here is trying to stop you."

"I am," Rxgr-14 said, offering a desperate smile. "I thought we were having a good time."

Tzara-9 frowned. "Sitting here talking about nothing?" She glanced over her shoulder. The other soldiers' song had re-begun, this time a chant, and now everyone else was watching. This sort of euphoric taunting was commonplace at this time of night, and Tzara-9 was utterly unphased. In fact, as the soldiers formed a line thrusting their heads in a grotesque dance that implied that Tzara-9 ought to interlock mandibles with all of them in a row, she only smirked.

"At least they're not afraid of a little fun," she said, directing it at Lnzt-16.

Lnzt-16 pinched his mandibles together, barely constraining rage, then lowered his head and slurped in stoic silence. He slurped until there was almost nothing left of their puddle. Rxgr-14 and Tzara-9 watched him clumsily chase the last drop of ooze across the indentation in the floor with his gargantuan mandibles. It was so small, and his mandibles were so large, it looked absurd.

While he hated their passive-aggressive jabbing, Rxgr-14 feared that if they addressed their real feelings, he'd learn something he didn't want to know.

His plan for the night had been to get drunk enough to unleash his wild side. Then he'd say something beautiful or funny and Tzara-9 would want to linger in his company when Avern-Y6 closed. By then, the booze would have muted his inhibitions. He'd be living the way she always seemed to, in the moment, and she'd finally appreciate their profound similarity. To the credit of the royals who brewed the intoxicating liquid from their unfermented reproductive proteins, Rxgr-14 genuinely believed this plan was wise even though it was the same plan he'd had every night for as long as he could remember, and it had never yielded a closer connection with Tzara-9.

Tzara-9 suddenly bent down and helped Lnzt-16 finish off the last droplet, surprising Rxgr-14. Then their mandibles touched, and Rxgr-14 became completely uncomfortable in his exoskeleton. There was nothing in the puddle anymore, but Lnzt-16 and Tzara-9 were both still scraping, sucking at nothing. Tzara-9 side-eyed Lnzt-16, but Lnzt-16's eyes were downcast. They seemed to both be pretending that they weren't doing what they were obviously doing. Rxgr-14 knew then his plan was stupid, and he felt nauseous. He couldn't name what he was feeling. Neither appreciated how lucky they were. They were both so beautiful and powerful and free, and he was trapped in his horrible little body with zero chance of happiness, ever. He'd never had a chance with Tzara-9. Not as long as she loved Lnzt-16, and Lnzt-16 seemed to have no love for her, yet he seemed adamant about shielding her from his dalliances. Why? It was a stalemate of innuendo and inaction, and a colossal waste of time and energy for all of them. Worst of all, Rxgr-14 was sick of feeling like a spectator in his own narrative.

The soldiers who'd bleated at Tzara-9 were bleating at everyone now and had climbed atop one other while rearing on their hindmost feelers, forming a tower four or five bodies high. Their collective figure resembled a giant soldier, wobbling, assembled from smaller ones. It was not uncommon for drunken, peacocking soldiers to work themselves into such formations. The *coup de grâce* was for two soldiers to hold onto the effigy's "head" with their hind feelers and mime being its mandibles with their entire bodies, sometimes smashing or terrifying an unlucky worker. These particular soldiers' efforts were, however, undermined by how drunk they were. Watching them thrusting and shouting while building up their rickety avatar, Rxgr-14 reflected bitterly on the arrogance and entitlement of soldiers in general, and what he believed would be their eventual takeover of the worker class. Then a bolt of insight shot through him. If soldiers could become workers, what if he tapped his own inner soldier. What could he do then?

"Tell us about your date with the royal," Rxgr-14 said boldly to Lnzt-16.

Both friends' sets of compound eyes beheld him, then Tzara-9 glanced at Lnzt-16.

Rxgr-14 looked at Lnzt-16, too, but with his right antenna he pointed at Tzara-9. "Maybe then we won't be boring her."

He smiled as if this was a private joke between him and Lnzt-16.

Lnzt-16 blinked at him, betrayed.

"What date?" Tzara-9 asked, clicking her eyes.

"Yeah, what date," Lnzt-16 repeated to Rxgr-14. He turned to Tzara-9. "It wasn't a date." He looked back at Rxgr-14. "And what date are you even talking about?"

"The one with big wings, remember?" Rxgr-14 held out his middle feelers, which were so small that it came off as sarcastic.

Lnzt-16 stared at him. Rxgr-14, surprised by his own self-assuredness, stared back.

"A princess?" said Tzara-9, looking down her nose at Lnzt-16. "Yeah, right. Like any of those broodmares would stoop to commiserate with you."

"We did more than commiserate," said Lnzt-16 acidly. He stood up and looked down at her. "We interlocked mandibles for more than half a minute."

Tzara-9 froze as if this information had utterly scandalized her.

"It was decadent," Lnzt-16 added. "Indecent, even."

Tzara-9's mandibles hung, slack.

Lnzt-16 leaned in. "And you know what else? Our antennae got all twisted up, too." Lnzt-16 pointed at Rxgr-14 with an antenna. "And he's right. Her wings were huge." Lznt-16's compound eyes blazed coldly as if he was looking right through her. Then he glanced behind Tzara-9 as if inspecting her wingless back, and he said, "Somebody's got a ways to go."

Rxgr-14 watched her antennae fall. He hadn't expected her feelings to be so easily hurt. She looked at the ground and said nothing. Lnzt-16 swiveled his head proudly. Rxgr-14 wanted to comfort Tzara-9. No one, winged or otherwise, was more clever or brave or worth spending time with in the entire colony, he wanted to tell her. When Tzara-9 lifted her face again, the emeralds in her compound eyes were the color of fury.

What had happened that they'd kept him in the dark about? Why had he felt the need to act like a warrior? He'd acted like a coward, and he'd stabbed his friend in the back and ended up hurting his other friend.

Tzara-9, having had time to compose herself, asked flatly, "What else."

Lnzt-16 had been trying to hail a worker to refill their divot, and at her question he stopped and faced her again.

"What do you mean what else?"

"What else," she repeated coolly. "What else happened on your illicit tryst?"

Lnzt-16 looked into Tzara-9's eyes as if to prove he could resist them.

"You don't want to know."

"Because you're lying," she said.

"No. I'm not."

"You are. You know how I know?"

He didn't answer.

"Because I know you," Tzara-9 said almost tenderly.

This appeared to make Lnzt-16 deeply uncomfortable. He looked away.

Rxgr-14 couldn't decide if he should intervene. Deep down he knew that Lnzt-16 had to reject Tzara-9 once and for all if Rxgr-14 wanted a chance with her. Who knows, he thought, if Lnzt-16 broke hear heart, he might even be able to swoop in and save her from her sadness. Then he was ashamed of himself for even thinking such a thing.

"Well?" Tzara-9 said, pressing her momentary leverage.

"Well what," Lnzt-16 snarled, his hardness returning. "Once you've interlocked mandibles with a royal, you never go back."

Tzara-9's own mandibles flexed, and for a moment Rxgr-14 actually thought she might attack him.

"I've never felt anything like it," Lnzt-16 added wistfully.

"How did it feel?" Tzara-9 said immediately. "Tell me."

Lnzt-16's antennae revolved. "It felt like... like..."

Tzara-9 extended her head as if awaiting her own decapitation.

"It felt like flying," Lnzt-16 finally said. Then he nodded at Rxgr-14.

Tzara-9's eyes dimmed. She bent to drink, but there was still nothing left. The worker who carried the sac had not yet made it to their divot.

Tzara-9 lay her head sideways in the trough, and then seemed to cough or heave in some sort of physical manifestation of disappointment.

Rxgr-14 glared at Lnzt-16. He'd gone too far.

Lnzt-16 glared at Rxgr-14. *He'd* gone too far.

"Yeah. It felt like flying," Lnzt-16 said again, casually trying to fill the silence, and perhaps trying to hurt Rxgr-14 by hurting Tzara-9 more. "It felt like I had left the colony behind with all its disappointments and complications. It was the purest, most liberating feeling I've ever had, and I'll never have it again, ever, with anyone else."

"How do you know?" Tzara-9 shouted from the floor. "You don't know what the future holds."

"I know what I want and what I don't."

"You're afraid of love."

"I'm not afraid of anything!"

"Are you sure!?" she shouted again.

"I'm quite sure!"

"But are you sure you're sure?" she said, getting up, getting right in his face, swinging her mandibles within inches of his. He took a step back. "See!" she said. "You are afraid." She closed her compound eyes and stomped and shouted with a quavering voice, "Admit it!"

RXGR-14 FELT LIKE HE'D INTENDED to dig a fleck of irregular silicate out of a wall only to find it was the tip of a massive quartz lode that would take a hundred tunnelers a dozen days to excavate. He briefly considered distracting them with an inane comment about the brittleness of the ceiling, the viscosity of the booze, or shifts of the idiom in the colony song that evening, but he knew it wouldn't work, and so he decided to leave. He lowered his head and backed slowly away from the trough, headed for the exit, trying to avoid the feelers of the hundreds of other rambunctious soldiers without looking up. As he made his way across the chamber and exited Avern-Y6, he thought he heard Tzara-9 cry out something like, "But the point of life isn't just to avoid pain!" but he couldn't be sure of her words, lost as they were in the cacophony.

Rxgr-14 stepped out into the main tunnel of the colony just as a new phalanx of soldiers was pouring in, and he had to dance a jig to avoid being trampled. When they had passed into Avern-Y6, the relative quiet of the outer tunnel becalmed him.

He looked up and down the primary shaft. Rising from below, and falling from above, murmurs of domestic complacency echoed from distant dens. He always forgot the majority of the colony didn't cram themselves into public places to plunge their faces into pools of oblivion every night. They lived quiet lives, and the sounds they produced in their pockets of isolation cohered into a comforting hum that permeated every tendril of the enormous underground labyrinth. For a moment the sound was soothing to Rxgr-14. Then it reminded him of the empty den where he'd soon be headed, and he was racked by frustration that he had never been able to find contentment in the simple life this hum—nay, hymn—evoked.

Rxgr-14 haltingly excreted a robust portion of the fermented fluid he'd been ingesting all evening, then used his feelers to spread, tamp, and smooth the excretion into the walls of the tunnel, moisturizing and sealing it against evaporation and the contact-erosion caused by its constant exposure to feeler traffic.

The less conscientious inhabitants of the colony did not spread, tamp, and smooth their waste, they just ejected it and moved on. Soldiers especially were derelict in this matter, but Rxgr-14 knew from a lifetime of study and practice that brittle walls were the harbingers of tunnel collapse, and collapses affected everyone, even soldiers. He felt superior for a moment, as another wave of waste erupted out of his anus. Tunnel maintenance was beautiful in itself, he insisted drunkenly. There was an art in *how* you spread your disjected waste, *how* you tamped it down, and *how* you smoothed it into the lining of these hallowed viaducts of history, culture, and commerce. For instance, which feelers to use? Most used their hind feelers because they were adjacent to the anus. Not a negligible insight. They were the most convenient to work with. But they were physically weaker than the penultimate set meant to power locomotion, and Rxgr-14 had learned that if you trained yourself to use your hind feelers to spread, backed up one step, and then used your penultimate feelers to tamp, then moved forward again, and used your hind feelers to smooth, you could achieve a more uniform distribution of waste, and more uniform thoroughfares meant smoother navigation for subsequent thoroughfare users, which might not seem like much in terms of combatting desedimentation, but when you considered that during rush hour these passages were packed with bodies of different masses grinding against each other at different speeds in different directions, all with different levels of care regarding the walls that held back the combined pressure of the known universe—well, the smoother the surface, the lesser the impact of all those attritional factors. A tiny overall decrease in commuter-tunnel friction applied colony-wide would not only boost structural resilience, it would lessen the ever-climbing commute times the colony seemed increasingly subject to in peacetime, potentially undermining political support for wars entered into cavalierly by members of the winged caste who, unconsciously or not, sought to curb the overpopulation of the underclasses with periodic bloodshed. If the strain on natural resources that fomented territorialism could be mitigated by the more efficient use of the resources the colony already had, i.e., their own waste, maybe war itself could be erased, or at least made as unnecessary as possible. It was not even far-fetched to imagine, Rxgr-14 thought, that in a world where violence was the thing that was scarce instead of material resources, the lowly worker might even be able to rise to a position of equality with, or even domination over, the soldier.

Rxgr-14's second wave of excretion finished with a dribble. He spread, tamped, and smoothed it just like the first. His prideful mindset, however, faltered back into melancholy when there was nothing to distract him from the quiet hum of the colony. What if he only cared about tunnel health and efficient infrastructure because he lacked anything better upon which to stake his identity? Soldiers were never lonely. They trained shoulder to shoulder, and even in combat, killed or died eye-to-eye with enemies whom they met as equals. All workers like Rxgr-14 had were the walls and the waste, which were to them the same thing.

The inner walls of the tunnel outside Avern-Y6 were dark and well worn. They widened moving down and narrowed moving up. They were mildly corrugated, light brown, two parts crystallized silica, one part uncrystallized clay, one-quarter part organic material. All in all, drier than they ought to be, but nothing to get particularly worried about. Then he saw something that was, in fact, of mild concern—a hairline fissure seven body lengths above his head, toward the direction of the heavily guarded aperture that led to the world above. He briefly entertained making a break for it, leaving everything, including his friends, behind. He'd either have to lie his way past the guards or run and hope they'd be too lazy to chase some shitbrained worker. Either way, Lnzt-16's words rang true. There simply had to be more to life than remaining below the surface repeatedly fulfilling the colony-assigned role until death. Remembering Lnzt-16, however, Rxgr-14 felt guilty, and he abandoned the fantasy of escape as quickly as it had come to him. With resignation, he excavated some of the mud he'd just made and worked it into a ball. Then he fed it under his middle and forward feelers, and began to bulldoze it upward to repair the mildly concerning fissure he'd observed.

He was tamping his waste into the miniature abyss, allowing the ritual of something he had done countless times to relieve his considerable ennui—when an alarm exploded into his mind, and his antennae twisted viciously back toward Avern-Y6. He turned his head to follow, and heard a ruckus erupt from the entrance—the unmistakable sound of clashing chitin. Dropping the half-recycled waste where he stood, Rxgr-14 sped back down and into the hole that linked the central shaft to Avern-Y6.

RXGR-14 REENTERED AVERN-Y6 TOO FRIGHTENED to think. He saw a wobbling column of soldiers' bodies reaching all the way up to nearly touch the rotunda. The tower swayed as if about to topple, bulging at the bottom and tapering at the top, where, like an ornament at its pinnacle, was Tzara-9, either screaming or laughing. Then he realized she wasn't

atop the column, she was clinging by her feelers to the ceiling. She must have climbed the side wall to escape the mass,
and the mass must've grown up after her. The puddles on the
floor were all deserted. The mass had drawn almost everyone
else in the chamber into itself. Some soldiers were spewing
booze down the sides of the tower, and others were excreting
waste in long shiny trails, like a kind of vulgar fountain, a
monument to gluttony. A smattering of others watched the
spectacle from the floor, transfixed, leaking excrement as
if some mechanism of mass hypnosis had overridden their
sphincters. The overwhelming song in Rxgr-14's mind was
strident and ambiguous, and the bedlam of bodies striking,
scraping, and crashing against one another as the mass veered
left and right obfuscated its meaning. It would not be long
before the queen heard the aberration in the colonial signal
and sent the royal guard in to restore order and expediently
dispense their version of justice. Rxgr-14 felt both repelled
by and summoned by the undulating motion and deafening
volume of his brethren. He noticed that his feelers were taking
him into them. Between him and the mass, a worker with a
sac of fermented fluid struggled to keep it from a zealous-eyed,
copper-toned soldier. The soldier hesitated, then eviscerated
the sac with one swipe of its mandible, and then on the return
stroke, hooked her other mandible right through the worker's
eye. The worker's tiny head popped off and rolled across the
floor, its mouth still trying to form enraged language. Rxgr-14
froze. He saw another worker who had seen this drop her sac
where she stood and join the fray with zombie-like submission.
Then, from somewhere near the top of the pyramidal mass
of thrashing carapaces, Rxgr-14 heard Tzara-9's voice shriek
something unintelligible. Then the tower, or the pyramid, or

whatever it was, shifted shape again, sliding across the chamber floor like a drunken colossus. Behind where it had been, Rxgr-14 saw Lnzt-16 on his back in the corner, wounded and fighting the air with his feelers. What had happened? Rxgr-14 fought the subconscious pull of the tower and moved toward Lnzt-16, then stopped when he saw his friend roll over. Beside Lnzt-16's head was a sac of the fermented unfertilized protein. Lnzt-16 wasn't hurt, he was drunk. He was wallowing. A breeze passed over Rxgr-14, and he looked up to see the mass of bodies bowing to and fro above his head. He couldn't see the ceiling. The noise was overwhelming. A plea from somewhere in the cyclone of faces and feelers above him pierced his mind—someone being crushed—then the plea was gone. The tower swayed away again, and Tzara-9 reappeared at its pinnacle, still grasping the ceiling, her desperate feelers clutching the loose silicate of the rotunda, causing sediment to shed. Then she lost her grip, and she fell into the fray and was immediately enveloped. Rxgr-14's heart spasmed like a separate animal inside him. He made a line for the tower, head down, trying to block the ambient signal to kill with sheer force of will. He heard something squishy, glanced up, and saw the colossus collapsing into a ball, now bowling slowly and unevenly around Avern-Y6. Three workers who'd attempted to evade its path had succeeded, but not their abdomens. They heaved their mandibles forward, hopelessly chewing air as a trail of guts behind them kept them glued to the same spot on the floor. The ball of bodies revolved and began to roll toward Rxgr-14. He crouched and waited until it rolled over him, and rather than let it crush him too, through a temporary fissure between two soldiers eating each other's faces, he leapt into it.

Then he was in darkness and splintered light. Sounds and sensations smashed together, spinning around. He smelled something. Was this an orgy? He'd heard soldiers had them. Then he realized his eyes were closed. He opened them. Pulled into the center by a hundred strangers' feelers, he saw how the mass cohered. The soldiers on the inside had interlocked mouths in a series of helixes. He tried to backpedal, but with his own feelers only half under his control, random mandibles gouged and scratched his exoskeleton. His only choice was to move forward and find a body somewhere in the vortex to which he could cling for long enough to survive it. Where was Lnzt-16? Rxgr-14's mouth opened instinctively as another feeler stabbed his face, and he bit into it. The taste of blood was shockingly bitter, and suddenly, he thirsted for more. For a moment he chewed at anything in front of him, engulfed in hollow rage. A hole opened in the flow of bodies, and briefly he could see back out into Avern-Y6. Lnzt-16 was in the corner of the chamber, looking upward. Then the hole closed. Rxgr-14 wriggled madly against the tumbling bodies until he found the edge of the mass and with one last push of his penultimate feelers, emerged. It took him a moment to realize he was high above the chamber floor, atop the sawing, crying, singing, stabbing boulder of soldierly bodies. He climbed higher, stepping on the faces of several soldiers, moving too fast for them to react—his tunneler's ability to instantly analyze and instinctively negotiate complex and shifting surfaces actually came in handy. He caught possible flashes of Tzara-9's dark green carapace ahead. If he could reach her, maybe they could help each other cling to the ceiling and crawl to safety. He knew where the ceiling was sturdiest. It all seemed like a good plan, and executable—until a feeler hooked around his throat and yanked him, choking, back into the heart of the maelstrom.

Twisted by and dashed against larger, harder bodies, he descended. Something clobbered his head. His thoughts halted. When they re-began, his eyes were flush against a gargantuan abdomen. It was bronze. It was Eybv-99. He was being vised between Eybv-99's rocklike thorax and the weight of bodies behind him. Then something bent his left antenna—casting a cold bolt through his being. He felt the crowd shudder around him. He heard Tzara-9 call Lnzt-16's name. Out of his control, Rxgr-14's swaying and whipping antennae suddenly straight-ened. His mandibles opened so wide they ached. He wanted to interlock mandibles now. Hurry. He searched for anyone with whom to connect—a cracked head struck his. Hot blood splashed his face. He was blind. A mandible hooked his. Alien saliva. A narcotic pulse. Nerves singing. Then the mandible snapped. Its owner screamed. A tinge of withdrawal. Spiritual agony. Eyes open. The wounded face he'd tasted sped away like an image in a dream woken up from. The vortex spun the other way. A curled pincher dripping green swept past his eye. The face of its soldier grinned in the dark and vanished. Rxgr-14 rose, or thought he was rising, until he hit real rock. He'd been falling. Now cheek-to-ground, impounded at the bottom of the pile, one of his middle feelers bent backward and snapped, spurting bright yellow fluid. A hairy appendage caught on his neck, and his abdomen and head were pulled in opposite directions. He looked down. Through the part-ing of his abdomen and thorax, he saw his own innards. The long green tubule of his heart stretched to twice his normal length. Some of the fibers that housed it snapped. This was it. He would die now. Unmeaningfully. Unexpectedly. Unable to mount even a semblance of a defense of his friends whom he'd imperiled. Worse than that guilt, however—what had anything mattered in his entire life?

Cutting short his mordant reverie, a random antenna jabbed Rxgr-14 in his compound eye. He felt its anonymous owner's mind quantum leap through his—their fears paralleling exactly—then the other mind vanished, and the body its antenna had been connected to plunged on. But it had given Rxgr-14 an idea. He looked for another antenna. One twittered just out of reach. He wrenched his neck with all his might to clutch it with his mandibles, but it slipped through. If he bit someone's antenna hard enough, the whole room would feel it. It might break the trance they were all in long enough for order to be restored. He'd surely be killed for doing it, but it might save Tzara-9. But antennae were so tensile— silken even—they were all but impossible to catch between one's fore-pincers. Another tendon in his lower back snapped, and again he felt his body breaking apart. His exoskeleton detached, and he felt the cold air of the colony tickling his unguarded heart. He had a final, even darker idea, and he acted immediately. He whipped his own antenna down into his mandibles and severed it cleanly. A psychological shockwave blew the others away from him in every direction, and it felt like much of his mind went traveling with them.

SPLITTING PAIN IN HIS BRAIN drove Rxgr-14 awake. He was lying on his back and felt like a cave-in was occurring inside him. Every thought a rock plummeting through darkness, clobbering the thoughts below. His left antenna hung by only a fiber above his compound eyes. He could see it dangling, swinging back and forth. Bodies around him were still scrambling outward like the walls of an impact crater. But an avalanche of imagery in his mind overwhelmed anything unfolding in the world: rivers flowed, rivers slowed, rivers sloshed, rivers froze, rivers reversed, rivers ran under rock, rivers glimmered in the sun, rivers cut through the snow. Mudslides, rainstorms, fleets of leaves, others like him shrieking, riding rough currents away from loved ones, drowning, succumbing to the flood, surfing the rapids, mastering whirlpools. Narratives, characters, faces, settings, flung themselves before his inner eye: sunsets, entrails, incursions by termites with globular eyes, hordes of wasps darkening skies, epic battles with beetles with horns, rodents sneering with blood-streaked fur ridden by armies of fleas. He saw others like him feasting on the whites of dead squirrels' eyes, biting the soft flesh in the inner ears of massacred rabbits, mass graves of aphids, silent invaders climbing vertical vines, devouring flowers, chased by spiders, suffocating in clouds of poisonous gas, dying of thirst mere moments before rain, digging out cave-ins, dancing drunkenly, flapping never-before-flown-with wings, washing ancient walls, shattering mandibles, clutching close familiar feelers, killing themselves, killing each other, dying alone, dying together, watching the light dim aperture-downward through the tunnels at the close of day, flying over landscapes he didn't even have words for, plumbing chambers of uncanny colors, rooms shot through with otherworldly roots, grizzled voices, forgotten songs, crystalline corridors, malodorous nectars, infinite cemeteries, dens of such unfathomable volume they contradicted every principle of architecture, realms of ruins, rooms of runes, winged ghosts, husks of royals mulched with husks of workers, soldiers swimming in seas of sugar, mountains of sugar, valleys of sugar, sugar in water, death in sugar, dreams in science, art in war, fortresses of quartz, thrones of bedrock, oceans of fire, battlefields of silence, a whisper of souls—all these fragments, not quite remembered, not quite invented, overthrew Rxgr-14's mind—and the world again went dark.

WHEN HE BLINKED BACK INTO consciousness a second time, he was lying on his side, and Tzara-9's blood-streaked green exoskeleton lay dead on the ground in front of him. Rxgr-14 ignored the searing pain spreading to the ends of his body and dragged himself toward her. When he got close enough, he learned that it wasn't her, but a stranger who happened to look like her from the side. With great effort, he turned his head toward the amassment of bodies, which had reformed in the far corner of the chamber. Rxgr-14 searched it for any sign of the real Tzara-9, but all he saw was the tower of gore churning around itself. Strangely, it seemed in no way spec-tacular. In fact, it looked quaint, almost meaningless, a puff of dust that hadn't yet settled, a shadow on a wall, a pass-ing feeling. He looked around for Lnzt-16, and his dangling antenna swung down in front of his eyes. Excruciation radi-ated to every nerve ending. On instinct, he swung the weakly attached nub into his mandibles and removed it with a twist of his neck. A new psychic wave threw him backward in agony. He twisted on the sand. The antenna tasted metallic, and he spat it out. Then, unexpectedly, he vomited so hard it rolled his body sideways three times. He thought he was dying again. Suddenly the chamber rumbled, and he forced his eyes open to watch from a low angle. In flashes of clashing exoskeleton,

Lnzt-16 marauded through the tottering cyclone of whorling soldiers, middle feelers wide and wild, massive mandibles scything others' limbs with impunity, and nothing seemed to touch him but the blood of those he mowed down.

Rxgr-14 wondered if his own self-immolation had somehow motivated Lnzt-16. He hoped it had, but his mind felt like it had a hole in it and was leaking, and even hope was hard to hold onto. He felt like he'd seen what lay below the hard rock that holds up the world, and emotions like hope or fear no longer made sense. Or rather, they did, but seemed more like choices, like up or down, or left or right, rather than unbidden energies that flooded one and drove one's actions. He tried to get off his back but couldn't. Then he realized he could use the wall to get up, so he rolled toward it. Arriving at the wall, he allowed his undamaged feelers to grapple and pull his body upright. He was so exhausted from this that he had to catch his breath. Then he limped to the divot around which he and his friends had been earlier. On his way, he heard a gargling cry. Glancing back, he saw the mass of bodies had mostly collapsed. Eybv-99 wobbled in front of its remnants, eyes wide, clutching his bulbed thorax, watching his own green heart slide out of his eviscerated body like he was dying while birthing a glowworm. Lnzt-16, having gutted him, was moving toward Rxgr-14, unblinking. It was then that Rxgr-14 saw Tzara-9 behind him, as if he'd cut her a path. As his two friends passed his own spat-out antenna fragment near the center of the chamber, Tzara-9 glanced at it like a religious relic, sacred and profane and terrifying.

Rxgr-14 closed his eyes to try to dull his headache only to succumb to a second deluge of alien memories. New terrains, vistas, fantastic events, and faces of his species that he'd never encountered all wheeled behind his compound eyes, and this time were accompanied by equally arresting ideas: What if one did run away from the colony? Did other colonies exist where workers subjugated soldiers? What if breeders were their slaves instead of their rulers? What if there were a society in which tunnel maintenance expertise trumped wing and mandible size in the competition for influence? Why shouldn't there be? What if the engineering mind, unburdened with the endless rearrangement of the environment, were free to grapple with questions of a purely aesthetic nature? Was there value in the consideration of beauty for its own sake? Or goodness? What was goodness? What if there were truths beyond those which justified the routines upon which colony prosperity depended? Or supposedly depended? What if the queen's will was incorrect? What if the colony itself was wrong, an aberration, an invasion, a blight, a sickness? What if the earth were alive and we merely its terrible parasites? What if I was a villain? What if we all were? What if there were protagonists in other tales to whom we were merely 'bugs'? Rxgr-14 opened his eyes. Now it was everything in Avern-Y6 that looked alien. Even his friends looked fake. They looked like they could be blinked away at will as they walked toward him. What if the queen wasn't even real? What if all the fermented proteins and dirt and the excrement and wings and feelers and even Tzara-9 and Lnzt-16 were just the outward, cosmetic features of a different kind of tunnel, a tunnel of dreams and madness, a tunnel of forms and desires, a narrative improvised by a consciousness too big for him to even imagine? What if that consciousness could be awoken into? Who would I be, Rxgr-14 thought, if I awoke into it? Would I wake from this dream only to discover I was dead? Or would I wake as a god?

Tzara-9 rushed around Lnzt-16 and arrived at Rxgr-14's body. She was talking rapidly. Lnzt-16 arrived behind her. Behind them both, the survivors of the frenzy reluctantly decoupled, limped woozily back to their respective divots, cleansed themselves, murmured reactions and rationalizations, and glanced in Rxgr-14's, Tzara-9's, and Lnzt-16's general direction. Rxgr-14 noticed how fast his heart was beating. The yellow fluid leaking out of his head had browned where it had dried against his exoskeleton, and the wound was redolent of the past. He looked into Tzara-9's eyes while she was talking, and, without knowing why, he psychically understood precisely what had happened when he'd briefly left Avern-Y6. Tzara-9 had asked Lnzt-16 why he couldn't admit he loved her, and after a long silence he'd said that he was afraid of the way in which she loved, which was reckless and thoughtless and furious and blind, and that he couldn't have handled the responsibility it would require to sustainably reciprocate. But since it was too painful to confront her pain at his inability to give her that what she wanted, he said they should stop spending time together at all in order to move on. She called him a fool and said she would prefer death to such timidity in matters of love, even though she was afraid too. He asked her why she simply couldn't be a more practical person. She told him she would never compromise herself. He asked why she even loved him, especially if she viewed him as some kind of inveterate compromiser. She told him because she knew him—she saw into him—and she was in love with who he could be so easily if only he chose to live—and love—without fear, with the same fearlessness with which he waged the queen's wars and murdered her enemies. He interpreted this as an insult to his honor and insulted her in return, calling her a frivolous soul with no respect for the responsibilities of genuine soldiery. Sneering at this, Tzara-9 turned around and began taunting the soldiers who'd been taunting her, hoping to drive Lnzt-16 mad with envy by playing right into his criticism, but then the soldiers, egged on by Eybv-99, suddenly attacked her, and then others had used her imperilment as an excuse to fight them, which had escalated into what Rxgr-14'd seen upon returning to the Avern. All the while Lnzt-16 just drank, face-down, until all the divots around him were empty. As he perceived all this in an instant, Rxgr-14 wondered if Lnzt-16's intention had been to get drunk in order to spite Tzara-9 in her moment of need, or in order to become so over-inebriated that he'd somehow insulate his subconscious against the hysteria, thereby enabling him to move through it and help her.

"Can you hear me?" said Tzara-9, her emerald eyes clicking above his. "Rxgr-14, are you okay?"

The tenderness in her voice caught him off-guard, and despite his detached perspective, it made him sad, and that brought him back to reality. His eyes clicked at her. He tried to nod but was unsure if he had, so he tried to speak, but the words wouldn't easily form. Lnzt-16, glossed with blood, glanced at the place where Rxgr-14's antenna was missing with solemn concern.

Rxgr-14 summoned the strength to smile, hoping to assuage his friend. As soon as he did, however, Rxgr-14 saw not Lnzt-16 standing over him, but the aperture at the top of the central shaft, four-point-six body-widths in diameter, but also impossibly tiny, because he was viewing it from above. Moving over it, the surrounding forest of grass a uniform green, almost like the surface of the water in the underground reservoir. Beyond the green sea was a strip of sand as thin as a feeler, and another forest, and another gray sea, and a place where there was brown, and a mountain of only straight lines, and a big black river that never moved but seemed to wobble in infernal heat. In the fringe of this montage, Rxgr-14 glimpsed the motion of broad wings that caught the light and broke it into different colors, gracefully lifting and lowering. He looked upward. Instead of the ceiling of Avern-Y6, he saw the tiny, useless mandibles of a pinched-faced breeder. It felt like a memory, only realer, and happening now. He looked back down at the world. He was flying, and he felt free. He even felt the wind entering his body through his petioles, and it blew against his heart, cool and invigorating, almost like he was a part of the sky he was moving through.

He blinked. Avern-Y6 was back. Lnzt-16 was still looking down at him, now even more concerned. Rxgr-14, however, relaxed in his thoughts and let Lnzt-16's memories flow through him again. He saw again the face of Szafair-2. He was sure it was her. Her milky quartz eyes blazed like a ghost's, and although she wasn't smiling, she looked contented, and certain of her almost holy purpose.

"Is he conscious?" Tzara-9 said.

"Hey," Lnzt-16 said. "Are you okay?"

Rxgr-14 blinked and managed to sputter, "I'm f... I'm... I'm f..."

Lnzt-16 nodded at Rxgr-14's head and said to Tzara-9, "It's *gone*." Then he looked into Rxgr-14's compound eyes. "You know it's gone, right?"

Tzara-9 pushed Lnzt-16 out of the way. "Would you relax? He'll be fine. I'm fine too, by the way."

Despite her taking an attitude with Lnzt-16, she looked down at Rxgr-14 beatifically. He appreciated her attempt to maneuver the discussion away from the fact that, without an antenna, and given the mayhem that had just occurred, he was doomed. When he returned her kind glance, he was instantly in her den. He could see her brittle, corrugated walls and the messy nest she spent sleepless nights in. He could see the stolen, drained, deflated sacs of fermented unfertilized reproductive proteins scattered around her mound of unrecycled excrement, all six of her feelers hugging an unfinished sac she continued to drink from, even in sleep. He even felt her drunkenness and peered into her dreams. Most of all, he felt a deep sadness and longing which made his own previous feelings of infatuation seem comparatively one-dimensional, if not juvenile. He was her... and this was just last night... until his eyes clicked again Avern-Y6 rematerialized.

"What?" Tzara-9 said. "What is it?"

"Noth..." Rxgr-14 coughed. "Nothing. Sorry for staring."

She smiled sadly. "I don't care."

Behind her, a blood-caked worker lugged two dead soldiers over divots toward the tunnel that led into the main shaft. Rxgr-14 was surprised to find that without counting he knew that exactly twenty-three soldiers and eleven workers were dead. Two other workers, who must have arrived recently because their carapaces were clean, labored to bowl Eybv-99's enormous body forward with their heads, but Eybv-99's body was stuck on another body that they couldn't see. Then there was the rumble of distant marching, and the three friends looked at each other.

"Goon squad," Tzara-9 said.

They glanced at the entrance of Avern-Y6 where the royal guard would soon pour in, flanked by soldiers who had not been drinking all night, whose loyalty to the queen was unquestioned, and whose judicial imaginations were undisposed to nuance.

"I won't let them kill you," Lnzt-16 said. "Not without a fight."

Rxgr-14 looked at him like he was stupid.

"I'm down for that," Tzara-9 added, nodding. She cracked her neck.

"No," Rxgr-14 said. He looked at his friends. "You'll be okay. Both of you."

Lnzt-16 frowned. "What about you?"

"Don't worry about me." Rxgr-14 wanted to tell them more, but his mind was still a tumbler of exotic and incongruous visions, some Lnzt-16's, some Tzara-9's, some of others around them, and some that were older, and some that he knew could only be visions of the future. He had to concentrate in order to keep them at bay. If he looked at Lnzt-16, he saw flying and killing. If he looked at Tzara-9, he saw drinking and wallowing.

With great concentration, he turned to Tzara-9 and said, "I loved you." Her eyes widened and she stopped moving completely. "I mean, I do love you," he corrected himself. He was able to stay in the present when he remembered his feelings. "I should have told you long ago, but I was afraid. I don't think it would have mattered, but I would have gotten past it, and we might've been realer friends, instead of the way I treated you, which was as a friend only so far as it might help me find a way to win you over. It was a coward's way to be a friend, and a dishonest one." He looked at them both. "But I'm not a coward anymore, and the truth is all I have left, which is more than enough." Tzara-9 glanced at Lnzt-16 with concern. "It's okay," Rxgr-14 soothed. He winced and coughed.

He'd forgotten he'd lost a feeler, too, the middle right one, in the chaos. He crouched over the broken limb awkwardly and looked back at Lnzt-16.

"Promise me that you'll—"

"Stop it!" Tzara-9 interjected. "Stop acting like this. You're going to be…" She looked around. "Look, what you did was good. You saved lives when you…" She looked at the wound on his head and trailed off. "It was a frenzy. It got out of hand. But you slowed it down, you gave us all a chance to…" Dirt began to shake from the rotunda above as the rumble of the approaching royal guard got louder. "… To think," she finished. Lnzt-16 looked back at Rxgr-14's antenna fragment in the center of the room. The workers cleaning things up had made a wide berth around it, and the soldiers were all still whispering and staring.

"I did it," Lnzt-16 offered. He nodded. "Accidentally." He looked at Tzara-9. "I was trying to help her, and I just…" He motioned with his mandible, "clipped it. Accidents happen. They think I walk on water, remember? I'm a hero. They'll believe me."

"They'll kill you," Rxgr-14 said. "We can lie all we want, but it won't erase the memory."

Tzara-9 and Lnzt-16 were silent. The marching got louder. Rxgr-14 stared into the empty divot where his reflection had shone in the unfertilized reproductive protein upon first coming in that evening, and where there was now only reflectionless dirt. He lowered his head into the hole, waiting for a moment, then turned up and looked at Lnzt-16 and told him what he wanted him to do without words.

Lnzt-16 shook his head.

"You have to," Rxgr-14 said.

"No," Lnzt-16 pleaded. "I can't."

Rxgr-14 said, "I'd rather it be you than them. And you'll be a hero... for slaying the upstart. For containing the problem. For enforcing the will of the queen. For taking bold action to protect the colony from the menace."

Lnzt-16 looked at Tzara-9, then at the tips of his own bladelike mandibles, then back at Rxgr-14. He took a step backward on shaky feelers. He finally shook his great head and said, "I can't do it."

Tzara-9 was watching Lnzt-16, her antennae curled back in fear and wonder.

"If you don't," Rxgr-14 said, "you'll both suffer. I can see it. I understand what will happen. They'll ask questions. They'll find out where you were last night. Then you really will be killed. And they'll blame her too." He looked at Tzara-9. "Somebody has to be sacrificed, don't you see? I'm gonna die either way. This way you get to be heroes." A new vision suddenly exploded into his mind, and he groaned and closed his compound eyes.

When he finally reopened them, there was a tiny blue flame or sparkle of electricity that was not there before in each lens. He nodded at his friends. "With this," he said slowly, "the two of you will buy yourselves enough time, or privilege, to make preparations to leave."

"To leave? To leave what?" Tzara-9 asked. "What is he talking about?"

"Tell her," Rxgr-14 said. "Tell her everything, and leave with her. You, Tzara-9, Szafair-2, and everyone else the princess is recruiting. It all makes sense. I felt it when I flew with her, her plan. She's going to sneak you all out through the secret tunnel to the surface. She was testing your loyalty, showing you the way. You'll need capable tunnelers, especially at first." His voice dropped an octave and took on an echo-like quality as if many voices were speaking: "Seek Emnf-4 in Avern-Z9. Her work is exceptional, and she'll be sympathetic. She's lonely, like we are." He looked right through them, and the flames in his eyes flickered wildly. "We don't belong here."

The royal guard burst into Avern-Y6. One of the royals spread his wings, then whipped them rapidly, which lifted him off the floor just enough to float above the survivors as he cast a scowl across the gore-splattered chamber. Then he started pointing in four directions, each with a different feeler. Columns of soldiers poured into Avern-Y6, breaking off in the different directions, opening more room for new winged leader-led columns to file in behind. Every soldier who'd participated in the mayhem hung their heads in shame. Tzara-9 and Lnzt-16 hunched together instinctively. No one dared drink a drop or even move. The big-winged, needle-shaped male in charge went up to the nearest soldier and began hissing, demanding an explanation. The interrogated soldier looked over at Lnzt-16, Tzara-9, and Rxgr-14. Rxgr-14's remaining antenna was slack down the side of his head. Lnzt-16 turned to Tzara-9. Her compound eyes flickered fearfully, but then she said, "He's right."

"I know," Lnzt-16 said. "But I can't."

"Don't be afraid," Rxgr-14 said.

Lnzt-16 looked at him angrily, then forlornly.

"I am what I am," he said.

"What's that?" Rxgr-14 said sharply. "You choose who you are with each moment." He looked at his friend. "Just like your mother."

Lnzt-16 looked at him for a long time, then nodded unsteadily.

"And promise me you'll leave," Rxgr-14 added.

Lnzt-16 nodded again. Rxgr-14 looked at Tzara-9. She nodded.

Rxgr-14 was briefly overcome with a sense of peace.

"Now, do it. Hurry."

The needle-shaped male's wings flapped louder, floating their way. Lnzt-16 turned his head so that his mandibles were perpendicular to Rxgr-14's neck, then he hesitated again, and said, his voice barely a whisper, "I'm sorry. I can't kill my *mon frère.*"

Then Lnzt-16 was weeping. Tzara-9 watched with incredulousness, then with tenderness. Lnzt-16 turned to her and said raspily, "I love him."

The words broke Rxgr-14's heart at the same time that they repaired it. Then Tzara-9 looked at Rxgr-14, and she said, "Me too." Her words did the same, and he found a meaning resounding in them that had neither floor nor ceiling. Tzara-9 then skittered around the edge of the divot, knelt on her forward feelers, and locked eyes with Rxgr-14 as her mandibles widened around his. When their chitin touched, saliva gushed out of Rxgr-14's throat on reflex and coated Tzara-9's much larger mandibles, just as saliva gushed out of her mouth and glazed his face. He was blinded, and a flowering numbness took the pain of his missing antennae away and then undid his broken feeler with a feeling of oneness that sank down his spine and spoke its strange, wordless language to every fiber of his body. He felt again like he was flying, only without moving, like flight without time, like movement without exertion, like he was still and it was the world that was flying through him.

When Tzara-9 whipped her body and separated his head, he didn't hear the suction and the snap. There was a second of surprise, then it cut to black.

GARBAGE

ON A DOG-ASS COLD SUNDAY MORNING IN FEBRUARY, after trudging twenty minutes through shin-deep snow-drifts, I arrived at my favorite café, flung open the door, and was rewarded by a warm wave of air redolent of freshly baked pastries and freshly ground, exotic coffees. I was certain I'd made the right decision in leaving the house. Uncoiling my scarf, looking around, however, I realized that everyone else in town had had the same idea, and there was only one remaining empty chair. It was at a table already crammed with four other people. I went for it on instinct, only to stop short when I got closer. What I hadn't been able to discern from the café's entrance was a mug and a copy of *The New York Times Book Review* spread out in front of the seat. The claimant must either have been in the bathroom, or was one of the several people standing in line to order, perhaps going back for a refill or a treat. There happened to be a woman studying a textbook to the left of the vacant seat, and I assumed she was the companion of the person who was missing. In fact, I remember thinking, she is precisely the kind of person I wished I could be, an intellectual who is the companion to another intellectual. Isn't it just typical, I thought, that not only do I get to not have a seat, I get to be taunted by almost having one, and even further toyed with by having my attention drawn right to the person in this café I would most want to be like or become friends with, only to have that opportunity taken away the moment it dawns on me as a possibility. Then, as if confirming my status as a waste of space the world has no place for, someone got up from one of the low, slanted, uncomfortable, drafty-ass seats along the back window. You'd think it would be impossible for even the winter wind to blow clear through glass, but, somehow, as soon as you sit in one of these seats by the window, you feel it. Your toes go cold, and then your socks feel like they're wet even though they're not, and then you can't enjoy your coffee. The perfect perch, I thought, for someone like me: lonely, irascible, unfriendly, combative, and deranged.

I navigated toward it, grinding my teeth. I dropped my scarf on the slanted seat and my hat on the window sill, then I rushed back to stand in line and wait to buy the coffee and maybe a treat that I knew I didn't need but which I'd probably buy anyway. I'd recently read an article that had suggested one way to lose weight was to remember that all your unhealthy cravings weren't the result of some evolutionary imperative to hoard sugar like most people thought, but were actually just the product of marketing and loneliness. What we secretly craved, the article said, when we buy things we know we don't need, is the social web it lets us take part in. The sense of purpose and version of justice we get to experience when we trade something we have that someone else wants for something we want that someone has, the article argued, was a need we would go to virtually any length to meet when it wasn't met in our personal lives. The article suggested that if we interacted more with friends and family, we'd be less prone to filling that void with the inferior substitutes of capitalistic exchanges with anonymous entrepreneurs and their low-wage employees. Then we'd all be wealthier and thinner, but I guess the economy would collapse, or perhaps have to change.

I'd never seen this barista before. He looked barely fifteen. Because he was new and young, the line the rest of us waited in was long and slow. I'd reached the middle when I realized I'd left my phone wrapped in my scarf at the window. I looked at my scarf and hat from across the dining area. I didn't want to lose my spot in line, and I also refused to suffer the indignity of having to walk all the way back through the maze of chairs and tables, asking people to scoot up, interrupting their conversations, in order to get it—just to have to do it all over again on my way to get back in line.

Without my phone, I was noticing things I'd normally not given a shit about. One was a lady with a stroller with a kid in it who I knew wouldn't become a genius. She was rocking the stroller with one hand while studying the rows of colorful juices in the display case like she was trying to figure out what juice *would* make her baby a genius. Spoiler alert: even the green ones supposedly packed with antioxidants contain something like two-and-a-half servings of 26 grams of sugar each. Sugar's all you're loving when you crack it open and drink it and think, "Ahhhh, I'm finally healthy! I'm finally doing something smart!"

Fuck all these people, I thought: the two cute dudes who get everything they want just by flexing their dimples—they should be taxed; the bearded scholar crouched over a book I knew was poetry from how spare it was on the page, sipping his mug through that mask of hair between him and the

world, broadcasting smug discernment before scribbling his
own inane fragments in a notebook with one of those medi-
um-fancy pens that's like $5.99 for a two-pack—a clown with-
out a circus; the teenage scarecrow bopping snowboots on
her barstool footrest, leaking huge puddles of snow on the
tile, intermittently glancing up from a novel whose thickness
bespoke its genre—fantasy—to gaze through the fogged-up
window, woefully unaware that her real life would never be
the magic epic she was programming herself with such books
to endlessly yearn for it to become more like—a mouse fash-
ioning her own mousetrap; two cops, one fat and one skinny,
the fat one cutting a bagel with a plastic knife, the skinny one
chuckling, probably at something casually sexist or racist the
fat one just said—with their big black guns on their uniformed
hips and their big black belts hung with human-hunting tools
practically screaming out for people to stare at and imagine
them being used, inspiring in me unwanted fantasies of running up and grabbing the skinny one's gun and firing two
shots into the pressed copper ceiling and further shattering
the complacency of the café by shouting something completely insane like, "Hitler's back, baby!"

Not that I'm a Nazi—far from it, I hope. It would just be
fun watch lucky people try to maintain their benign personas
at the sudden advent in their midsts of something so obviously
evil. Maybe somebody would be a hero and put me down.
Or reason with me and surprise me with their reasoning and
somehow save my soul. Besides, what if I *did* have to disarm a
cop? What if this was the eve of the people's coup and I was
a key operative upon whom national liberation depended?
What would I do, just jump on his back? Or charge like a bull?
Would I be able to get that little snap thingy on the holster

unsnapped before he threw me off, bowed me in the face, and then put me out of my misery? Would I even have the nerve to do it at all? Or would I just stand there petrified, perhaps even by the fear of success, while the only chance the revolution had slipped away forever into history. Like a match I let blow out when all I had to do was move it one inch closer to the bonfire whose light would let others, others I'd never even know of, know that courage is possible.

Then there was the conversation the two girls ahead of me in line were having. I had no idea who they were talking about, but whoever it was, they kept calling her 'garbage':

"She's garbage."

"I know," said the other. "Fucking garbage."

Then, the first one said it again, as if it were a new idea. "She's a garbage human being."

"Oh my God," said the other, "garbage."

"I mean, she's just garbage."

It was almost like they were in a contest to see who could speak the ugliest about this person, but they'd both agreed beforehand to only use one word, so they just kept saying it in slightly different ways, but then, after a few rounds, they'd return to old iterations as if they'd forgotten them or agreed to pretend to forget them. I desperately wanted one of them to say to the other, "You've already said it that way." But neither did.

"I mean, it's like, she's just…" the one on the right squinted, seeking a new way to put it. She had amazing blue ombré waterfall hair that was dark on top and got lighter and bluer at the ends. She looked like a futuristic comet.

"She's just garbage," concluded the comet.

"I know," said the other. She had helmet-like bangs and her otherwise long black hair shined and swished like a curtain.

"And I'm not even, like, angry, or even care really? Does that make sense?" the blue-headed one said. The one with bangs nodded. "It's just that she's *garbage*."

"She's fucking garbage," agreed the one with bangs.

"She's a garbage human being," the blue-haired one said again, pulling out her phone and doing something that seemed unrelated.

"Ugh, she *is* garbage."

"Garbage."

"Ugh," the one with bangs said, checking her phone, too. I waited for another garbage to drop, but the pair was perfectly silent, just doing stuff on their phones. Then the one with blue hair put her phone away. Then the other did. Then they looked around like I had just been doing. The one with bangs leaned out of the line and looked at the barista, whose skinny arms were struggling with the espresso machine. Then she said something to the one with blue hair I couldn't hear.

They both had hair I wanted. My hair is unevenly curly and looks like a mullety bridal veil, curly on top and straightening out to my shoulders. The only thing that prevents it from looking completely gross is if I don't wash it. It's almost cool-looking, then, in its oiliness—like I might be some kind of avant-garde theorist who spurns norms of hair-related fashion, or rather, one who establishes such norms before they become the mainstream. But rarely am I able to achieve this delicate balance of intentionally uncool coolness because I always wash my hair. If I don't wash it, my scalp itches like crazy and I can't stand that feeling. I think it goes back to when I was little, when my mom, who was so beautiful, always made a big deal about washing my hair. She gently scrubbed the shampoo into my scalp with firm fingernails while humming show tunes and telling me I was an angel. I think it programmed me to where I have anxiety if my hair isn't washed. I just wish I'd have inherited her sweet disposition instead of my father's, but shit in one hand and wish in another and see which one fills up first, as my dad used to say. What's truly heart-breaking is that I'm sure there's even some fancy conditioner out there that would resolve all my hair drama forever, but if I suddenly got good hair now, it'd just make me regret the preceding thirty-seven years of hair-related angst even more. Few things leave as bitter a feeling in your soul as learning so late that something you've hated about yourself all along was easily within your power to alter.

There I was, envying their hair, mesmerized by how uncreatively nasty they were being to this unnamed person, growing more curious about who their enemy was and what she must've done, when they started calling her garbage again completely out of the blue.

"I'm serious," said the one with blue-hair. "She's garbage."

The other looked surprised, as if she, like me, had been certain they were through with the topic. She inclined her head in solidarity, but then didn't actually say the word, perhaps indicating her desire to retire it.

"She *is*."

"Like—total garbage."

"And I hate that we even care. It's like, she's garbage. Why do we care?"

There was a pause, and the blue-haired one finally leveled her eyes at the one with bangs and said, "She's a bitch."

A different look spread across the face of the one with bangs, worry or perhaps even disagreement.

"I mean, isn't she?" added the blue-haired one. "I mean, she is."

"Well…"

"You know she is."

The other one thought about it, then said in a clarifying tone, "She's garbage."

The blue-haired one shrugged and the line inched forward.

Maybe she was garbage, I thought. Maybe she was the worst person ever. But it just made me love her, whoever she was. I pictured her as a waif in rags crouched in a cobblestone alley in eighteenth-century Paris. She had dirty cheeks and fierce, innocent eyes, like Cosette on the cover of *Les Misérables*, hopelessly besmirched by a bleating and distant clique, friendless, penniless, and unable to make her own way. But then I looked at the clique in front of me more closely, and they seemed to be in their own purgatorial version of friendlessness. I remembered being in high school, and, insanely, feeling sorry for the people who were popular because of all the things that had probably made them so. I was a pariah who no one thought twice about terrorizing, but even when I looked at those I envied, I saw their meanness or indifference or willingness to be self-destructive or to flaunt their wealth as the likely consequences of various horrible parents. All the jocks I imagined had violent, alcoholic dads, all the cheerleader-types were the spawn of sniveling, materialistic moms, and all the people with dyed hair who did drugs and got laid had charismas tempered in the forges of blistering divorces of fools who should've never been married.

I was suddenly put off by my own self-righteousness, and tried to rein it in. Whoever this girl was, I didn't know if she was garbage or not; and whoever this pair in front of me was— wasn't puffing myself up like some kind of heroic judge of their behavior a quintessentially repugnant quality? Whether they were right or wrong in their evaluation of someone I didn't know, who wasn't present, was none of my business, and while they easily could have shit-talked her less conspicuously, what right did I have to lord my superiority over them, even in my own mind?

Maybe garbage girl had punished them in countless ways over the years, separately, so that the abuse she unleashed was unique to both, and maybe this was their first meeting—and what I was witnessing was an awkward accord between two strangers who were victims of a common villain, and lacking the common ground I might have otherwise wished them to have, their alliance had cohered around the one epithet they could both agree on—garbage. Who was I to critique that? And were there not a hundred other possible explanations for their behavior that didn't merit the bilious condemnations of a misanthrope like me?

No sooner had I anointed the two girls saints and re-confirmed for what felt like the hundredth time that I was the most superfluous person in the café, than they both, without warning or indication as to why, exited the line. Watching them walk away, I wondered what I'd missed. They hadn't discussed leaving, so how did they know to leave the line at the same time? Not even a simple "Let's get out of here?" Maybe they knew each other well, actually, so well that they could communicate basic ideas without words. The theory that their endless repetition of 'garbage' was evidence of a brand new friendship suddenly seemed naïve, and my attempt to arrange the world into an order that enabled me to feel redeemed for rejecting my earlier, harsher judgments seemed suddenly just as vain. And yet this attempt to arrange the world blew on like wind in my head, dying down to nothing in one instant only to swell back up in the next.

I envied how easily they navigated the tiny tables on their way to a large checkerboard setup near the back that was half-obscured by a column covered in art. There they conferred with an older woman who could've been a relative, a boss, or a coworker, but surely, I thought, not garbage. She was too old. I don't think people refer to old people as garbage. It would be like calling an old person uncool. It's redundant because all old people are automatically uncool, at least in the estimations of the youth-drunk young. Plus no one would be that openly mean to someone they were actually here with. The slanderers seemed to be acting friendly toward the older woman, but they were too far to overhear. I shrugged the whole thing off and turned back around. At least they'd removed themselves from the line, I thought, looking back at those behind me. We seemed like pilgrims to me, and now we were all obviously better off. I started to like the pair again in their absence. Maybe they really were angels. We usually only imagine angels as agents or harbingers of epochal change, but is it any crazier to believe they would work tiny miracles, like, say, removing roadkill from freeways, causing you to find your keys when you'd lost them, or moving a line forward by leaving it? Why not, I thought. And suddenly even the bearded poet I'd observed earlier seemed like he could be heroic. The strollered mother's belabored juice selection seemed suddenly sweetly motivated, and the puddles underneath the fantasy-lovers' snowboots glimmered with promise, if not out-right magic. I love this café, I thought.

The barista took the money from the rumpled boy who'd been in front of the now beatific girls, then glanced at me through the gap. I stepped into it. I prepared to order. "Large coffee," had barely left my lips when I saw in my peripheral vision the girls—bangs sashaying, blue comet blazing—dashing through the café to reclaim their spot. Now, the three of us were standing at the counter more or less equally, and they were looking at me like I'd committed the ultimate crime by stepping into the gap they'd vacated. I was just about to step backward out of it on instinctive politeness when the one with blue hair tilted her head at me imperiously and said, "Rude, much?"

She stared at me like I was nothing, like I was sub-human, like I was garbage. Her voice—"*Rude much?*"—ringing in my head. I felt like everyone had heard her and was watching. It was more humiliating than the girl with blue hair could have known. Hate welled up within me like magma ascending the central shaft beneath a volcano, but I kept it under control. I simply stared back with my mouth hanging open. The effect, I knew, was like being looked at by an inbred or a ghoul. Then, when she blinked, I mimicked her inflection and said, "Maybe not ruder than what you did?" I indicated her friend with my head so that they would know I was using the 'you' plurally.

"We?" said her friend.

"Us?"

"What did *we* do, lady?"

"Held up the line," I said, "yakking with your step-mom over there. I don't know if you two have noticed, but you're not the only people in this café." I gestured theatrically. "In fact, if you look around, you'll see that it's actually quite busy. Bustling even. It's cold outside, and everyone's come here for refuge."

"She's not our step-mom," said the blue-haired one, ignoring the latter half of my commentary.

"She's our friend," confirmed the other.

"We were getting her order."

"But we're sorry if *you're* in such a hurry."

They were a formidable tag-team. Then the blue-haired one gave me the look. Most people avert their eyes when we interact closely, but when they truly look at me, it's almost always only a prelude to war. Her eyes seemed to tremble in her skull, almost as if my humanity—the fact that we were the same species—was too much for her. I saw she too was terrified, and as lonely as me, and in her own version of this story, she was the stalwart protagonist bravely facing down the belligerent other.

I felt like I had no choice, though, so before she could do anything to humiliate me, I faked a sneeze. The trick is to lift your cupped hands a split-second too late, so it spritzes your aggressor. It's surprisingly effective for making people flee, as the fear of contamination, I believe, is one of the few primal impulses stronger than the desire to dominate those of low status who dare challenge yours.

"Gugh!"

"I'm sorry," I said. "It's just allergies." I wiped my nose on the sleeve of my sweater. "And, no, I'm not in a hurry." I gestured at the pilgrims. "But maybe they are." I looked back at two moms in whose legs were intertwined toddlers, a trio of musicians holding guitars whose brain-dead expressions probably weren't being faked, and a gangly comic-book-nerd-looking guy who was kind of like of a male me—with rosacea splashed across his cheeks and chunks of dandruff in his sideburns. In an alternate universe where I was an Empress, he would've made an excellent sycophantic advisor. In any case, I was hoping for more solidarity than I got from the crowd.

The blue-haired girl tilted her head at me, like the silence of the line had made her point for her.

"Okay," I said, gesturing with my hand. "You can have your spot back. But can I tell you a secret? Do you know what I do when I see a long line like this? I get my order ready before I get in it." I bit my lip as if in deep thought. "Or like, I think of what I want, or what my party wants, *while* I'm in it. That way, when I arrive at the counter—if I've timed it correctly, of course—I can order what I need without causing any delays. Now, I know what you're thinking. You're thinking, lady, what if I'm at the front of the line already, and I still don't know what I want? Well, in such situations, I just step aside, out of courtesy, say, for the other human beings in the line, because they have humanity. Because they matter. Because they might be having a bad day. And then I'll just slide back into the line whenever I'm ready, and it's all done really organically, without making a big fuss or calling attention to myself, or without calling anybody rude like you did, because I don't know what kind of bad day—or bad life—the people waiting behind me might be having. And you know what's really weird? Everyone else in the line almost always understands. The barista understands, the other barista understands if there's two—everybody understands. It's almost magical how no one has to have this explained. It's almost enough to make you think there's some kind of hidden pattern that emerges when human beings decide to be decent to one another. I think it's called a social contract, but I'm not sure if that's the right word for it. Have you ever heard of a social contract? Or if you haven't, have you ever heard of the Golden Rule? It starts off 'Do unto others,' and then it goes on to say, 'as you would have them do unto you.' It's funny, I've never actually said it out loud before. I guess I've never had to. Isn't that funny? Isn't that just odd? That something that's never needed to be said before suddenly needs to be said out loud? Anyway, I'm sorry I got snot on you if I did, and now I'm sorry for what I'm sure feels like a waste of your time. Let me try to summarize what I'm saying because I know it's Sunday, and I know you probably have fun, important memories to craft and activities to delight in before the work week kicks in like I do. The summary, I feel, is necessary for the rest of the world's sake, because I want to make sure you don't go on not understanding how lines work on a basic level, but also, if you already do understand it from what I just said, I don't want to waste more of your time on a Sunday, so that's why it's just a summary rather than a laundry list of increasingly vivid examples of the particular principle I'm compelled by conscience to clearly articulate. Basically, when you're in a line, with a lot of other people behind you, instead of calling someone 'garbage' over and over who's not even here to defend themselves, think about what you might want to order."

I hadn't known I was going to end there, but when I did, I knew I was done. Immediately, my back broke into a full summer sweat. I heard the echo of my own voice in the sudden silence and realized it had gotten louder and louder. I usually fuck up when I try to be a smart ass, but the thickness of the silence sold me on the likelihood that I hadn't.

"Oh my God," said the one with bangs said. The other one just teared up. Before I could backslide into sympathy, I stepped to the counter, perfectly prepared to nudge either of them aside with my hip, but they both moved.

"Large coffee, please" I said to the barista, who had just watched the whole thing and done nothing. "And can I get some skim in it?"

It took him a moment. "M-milk's over there." He pointed to the side table. I didn't look because I knew where it was.

"There's only half and half and soy," I said.

I felt the girls' eyes on my back. The sweat was already cold under my shirt. My armpits were dripping. I pointed to a sliding-door fridge below the espresso machine. "There's skim in that fridge." The barista turned. He squatted and opened it. When he found the carton he looked at me and smiled, impressed, but then he started to pour way too much into a silver pitcher, and I stopped him and told him that all I needed was a little.

RETURNING TO THE DRAFTY WINDOW seat with my coffee, I noticed again the five-person table with the open seat, the seat I'd assumed someone was saving with the mug and the *New York Times Book Review*, and which was still vacant. That didn't make sense at all, since everyone in line when I'd walked in had gone through it by now, and it was an unusually long time for an intellectual who would've been reading the *New York Times Book Review* to stay in the bathroom. So, out of curiosity, I detoured and peered into the mug and saw that it was bone-dry. A rookie error not to have checked that more thoroughly earlier. Whoever had left this mug, I realized, hadn't been claiming anything. They were simply gone and had left their mug un-bussed and their illustrious reading material behind, possibly as a gift, but in a placement they didn't understand would be interpreted as a staked claim by someone far away who had just entered the busy café. They'd probably been here earlier this morning when it wasn't as busy, when a mug and a *New York Times Book Review* wouldn't have been interpreted the same way.

I felt almost victorious, as if this was my prize for making the garbage-haters cry. I claimed the seat with my own full, steaming coffee mug, bussed the empty one, retrieved my scarf, hat, and phone from the sub-optimal window seat, and then worked my way into the new one. The intellectual to my left, who I'd also noticed upon first walking in, looked at me and smiled, then she slid the book she was reading over an inch. Perhaps I was emotionally raw from my earlier confrontation, or simply weary from life, but her gesture of hospitality struck me as profound. It was like I'd arrived in a little pocket of heaven. There was no draft, the seat was comfortable, and the company was utterly kind. Had she slid her textbook over further, it would have indicated a fear of contamination. Had she not slid it at all, it would have indicated a stubborn territoriality. Sliding her book toward me would've been downright aggressive, intentionally crowding me out. That she'd slid it just a centimeter, though, toward herself, was unambiguously a gesture of welcome. She'd made more room for me, or maybe more importantly, she'd wanted me to know she would give me room if I needed it. I knew instantly that she was a good person, and my pride at triumphing over the people in the café I could not stand softened somewhat into gratitude

for those I admired. I wanted to tilt my head into her view
and say hello, and tell her thank you, and describe all I'd been
through, or at least compliment her kindness or something,
but as soon as I thought about doing this, I was pulling out my
phone and opening my favorite game, a kind of high-speed
Boggle. When the game screen loaded, though, I felt like I
was dying. I felt all the hours I'd poured into the game instead
of living life, and I swiped the game away. I stared at all my
other apps on the screen, then at my neighbor. She had wispy
hair pulled in a bun through which you could see her pale,
purplish scalp. This made her even more wonderful to me.
Slightly thinner hair than normal was a memorable physical
quality for a generous person to possess, I thought. She had a
tiny diamond stone in her nose, too, and her ear was riveted
top to bottom. She had had loving parents, I believed without
knowing why, maybe the way she seemed so calm. She was
going to be a doctor, it seemed, from the drawings of organ-
elles and cells I could see in her book, or she was a doctor
already, an admirably ambitious one, at the peak of her powers and still unsatisfied with what she knew of biology.

I started weeping and hid it with my hands like I was rub-
bing my forehead like I was tired. I thought it was going to be
only a moment of emotion, but when it didn't stop I pulled
the *New York Times Book Review* under my face and turned the
pages in rhythm to muffle my sniffles. I could have asked her
what she was reading, what she was studying and why. I'm
sure she would've answered me as kindly as she'd slid her textbook over. I didn't feel like I would have been bothering her
at all. We could've talked about her scientific expertise, and
maybe I could have learned something. But where was the
will to initiate that conversation? I felt like it was in me, like

pieces of my mother are in me, or how pieces of all people are all within everyone—just buried. I slurped my coffee quickly, and then, jacked on caffeine, noisily folded the *New York Times Book Review* in half and slid it to the center of the table so that future patrons who wanted to peruse it could do so without confusing it for a claim on the seat I was leaving.

On my way out of the café, I bussed my mug, and I passed the pair to whom I'd read the riot act, recovering with their older third party, and I think I said I was sorry, but it was a blur.

The sun was shining when I walked outside. It was still cold as hell but felt at least ten degrees warmer. The sun on the snow looked like melted butter on mashed potatoes, and I wiped my tears and realized I was hungry. Underneath the snow all around, I could hear the meltwater starting to trickle. "It's Spring!" I thought to myself as a joke, since it was still the middle of February.

I think I went to a diner next. I don't remember. In any case, as I was walking wherever I went, I kept wondering, every time I saw someone else outside, whether they were garbage, and each person I passed, I decided that they couldn't have been, no matter how rotten their pasts. I even passed some actual garbage—big black bags leaking egregious shit, tossed right out onto the snow—and decided that it wasn't either. Maybe I even passed you.

K-4

KINDERGARTEN

MRS. CARSON WAS TALL AND broad-shouldered and kind. She could've been a frontier schoolteacher.

All the girls in my class had a crush on Dusty Lang. He had lipstick stains on his face every morning from where his mother kissed him when she dropped him off in her T-top, and a bumper sticker on his Trapper Keeper said ASK ME ABOUT MY EX-WIFE, I swear. Candace Fisher had a crush on Dusty too, but she was my best friend.

Early in the semester, Candace and I bonded over our shared love of *Charlotte's Web*, the cartoon not the book. On the playground, Candace pretended to be Fern, the human girl, and I was Wilbur, the pig. We never found anyone to play Charlotte, not that we tried. I think we were too young to confront what it would have meant to want to play Charlotte. Hell, maybe we're all still too young.

In any case, I'd crawl on all fours across this row of spray-painted tires half-buried in the sand, oinking and grunting, and Candace would walk behind me, whipping me, petting me, calling my name, etc. I remember being embarrassed every time we played *Charlotte's Web*, but I also remember how much I loved it, and how happy it made me that Candace enjoyed it too. I remember every day walking out to the playground, feeling shy, overcoming it, asking her if she wanted to play *Charlotte's Web*, and she always did, and it always surprised me.

It felt like Candace and I were really in love that year. Whenever I thought about her, my stomach kinked up in that terrible, exciting way that it does when there's so much you want to say to someone, but can't, or don't know how to in a way that would do it justice, or are maybe afraid of ruining whatever it is by putting it into words and making it official.

But I remember that feeling completely unknotting, unkinking, whenever we were playing *Charlotte's Web*. During that fantasy, I felt profoundly alive and free, like I had everything anyone could ever want in life.

1ST GRADE

Mrs. Vincennes was mousy and wore thick glasses. She was all business, one of those teachers who showed affection so sparingly that, when it happened, you knew it really meant something.

She had more trouble with students because not everyone loved her. She would bust your balls, and she didn't think anything anybody did was cute. It wasn't about cuteness for her. It was about education. I respected the fuck out of Mrs. Vincennes.

In this class, I was in love with Jenny Meachum. Jenny was pretty, blonde, quiet, and smart. We were the two smartest in the class. The problem was, she was in love with Scotty Dillard, who was my best friend. Scotty was not as smart as me, but he was cuter and he had a gold chain.

When I told Scotty I liked Jenny, he shrugged and said, "Yeah, me too." He was tying his shoe and didn't even look up. I watched the cross on his chain swinging back and forth above his laces until he finished and stood.

Soon they were together, Jenny and Scotty, and I was miserable, because I loved Jenny because she was so smart and pretty. I would see her and Scotty laughing, passing notes, and my stomach would tighten, and my heart would hurt, and I'd feel like a hideous loser, a failure, a fraud in my own skin. Scotty and Jenny were neither cruel nor unobservant, though, so it wasn't that long before they proposed something.

Cassidy Lastinger was Jenny's best friend, and Cassidy Lastinger had decided she might like me. Maybe me and Cassidy Lastinger could go with each other?

SOON ENOUGH, ALL FOUR OF us were hanging out at P.E., and to be honest, I didn't think Cassidy Lastinger was all that great. She had curly hair and spaces between her teeth. Whereas Jenny's smile was understated and aristocratic, Cassidy's was unselfconsciously out of control, vaudevillian even. There was something unbridled about her laughter, too. I decided to give her a shot, though, despite my own suspicions that, deep down, I was only using her to get closer to Jenny.

Cassidy, Jenny, Scotty, and I would walk the playground playing games I don't remember the rules of anymore. Perhaps that was because these games always felt forced and dull, and perhaps they felt that way because we had to come up with activities that appealed to all four of us. I suppose I was learning the real value of intimacy, and that the sort I'd shared with Candace Fisher in kindergarten was going to be difficult, if not impossible, to recapture. I did feel my tolerance of Cassidy Lastinger, though, burgeoning into respect, if not affection. For instance, after every math and handwriting test, Jenny, Scotty, Cassidy, and I would compare the results to see who had the highest grade. Despite hers always being the lowest, she never shied away from the competition. After seeing she'd been beaten yet again, Cassidy would just shrug and say something wry and self-deprecating like, "Guess I should've studied, huh." She seemed to be above the academic rat race with which we were obsessed, and I wondered more than once what, if anything, Cassidy Lastinger knew that we didn't.

Of everything on the playground, Cassidy loved the monkey bars the most, and she was better at them than me. The more I got to know Cassidy, the more I wanted to have a crush on her instead of Jenny, but it was futile. Jenny's smile took me away to somewhere magical, while Cassidy's seemed to be merely real. I was insanely jealous of Scotty, and I sometimes wished he'd get sick and miss school, or that his parents would get a divorce so one of them would move to Florida and he'd have to go with them so I could have Jenny for myself. Scotty was clueless as to these dark wishes. And he never went anywhere. Mrs. Vincennes observed all of these proceedings with such a well-practiced detachment that it gave me the feeling that she was actually always listening and watching—and with greater attention than anyone had the capacity to realize—kind of like God.

Every day I found myself feeling more and more guilty about not being honest with Cassidy. Eventually I told her we had to break up. I really liked her, but I was in love with Jenny, and it was wrong to go with someone when you were in love with their best friend the whole time. Cassidy Lastinger took it badly. She told me the first-grade equivalent of "You're a fucking idiot. You wouldn't know love if it bit you on the ass. You're gonna live to regret this. You're gonna be alone for a long, long time."

2ND GRADE

I WAS SINGLE THE WHOLE year, and my teacher, Miss Dumas, was the first unmarried teacher I'd ever had. Miss Dumas was kind of ditsy, kind of a bombshell. She wore purple lipstick and reapplied it after lunch every day. It grossed me out, but at the same time I found the ritual mesmerizing and I couldn't peel my eyes away. She had an enormous bosom. This was also the first time one of my classrooms had a paraprofessional, the term our school district uses for a teacher-in-training in the classroom. So, Miss Dumas was always trailed by the extremely tall and stern Mrs. Blackshear. Whereas Miss Dumas wore billowing dresses of patterned pastels, or every once in a while, jeans that showcased her curves—Mrs. Blackshear only wore stonewashed jeans with a tucked-in silk blouse and a tight vest with a western frill. She was also the first person I'd ever seen with a tattoo—a small snake curled around a sword on her forearm. It was rare to see it, and so I was always looking for it. Mrs. Blackshear was Miss Dumas' enforcer. There was a really gross, wild girl in the class named Tiffany Simmons who could whistle by putting her tongue up to her nose and blowing upward really hard. It was a really loud, extremely annoying, bizarre-looking way to whistle, and I was secretly always trying to mimic it.

Tiffany got made fun of a lot for her body and clothes, like having boogers visible in her nose, or getting caught digging her underwear out of her crack, or having bugs in her hair. She was sort of like the second-grade equivalent of a hippie, but she was self-aware and fairly fearless. For instance, if someone made fun of her for picking her nose, she wouldn't just run away (which is what I would've done), she'd try to wipe it on them. One time this kid Rawls pushed her, and instead of pushing him back, Tiffany tried to lick him.

This didn't always work to protect her from humiliation. She was often crying, snot-streaked, and alone in a corner of the playground, wondering aloud why everyone hated her.

From a distance, I admired her as any spineless worm admires any iconoclast. I never stood up for her, and I never befriended her. Had it been Nazi Germany, Tiffany would've been one of the innocents ripped from their homes in the middle of the night and "relocated" without explanation, and I would've been one of the ones watching from some upstairs window, wringing their hands and feeling horrible, but not lifting a finger to stop it. I was a real piece of shit back then, and when I look back now and try to figure out why, I never reach a satisfactory resolution. One answer might have been that I was reeling from the Jenny and Cassidy debacle. To be sure,

I missed both terribly, and Cassidy Lastinger's parting words still echoed hauntingly in my mind. But I don't wholly accept this rationale, as it seems to me like I'm trying to let myself off the hook for being a coward. There's nothing more disgusting and cliché than a man who blames his defects of character on some past heartbreak, is there?

Truthfully, I suspect that even if I and Jenny had been together in first grade, I still wouldn't have reached out to Tiffany Simmons in second. But why not? How can I see that something is the right thing to do, but not do it? I remember thinking that repeatedly during that year.

I don't know why everyone picked on her so badly, either. She was actually kind of cute. Her clothes were dirty, sure, but, back in those days, whose weren't? After all, this was James T. Bumblefuck Elementary, not Harvard University. Were we so backward that Tiffany's smidgen of imagination made us too painfully aware of ourselves as the rubes we were? God only knows what happened to her. I never saw her after second grade.

One day out in the hall after lunch I was standing against the wall, waiting for the bathroom, and when no one was watching, I tried to touch the tip of my tongue to my nose and blow as hard as I could. I tried for a long time, and then, right as Mrs. Blackshear swept past in her swishy vest and stone-washed jeans, the whistle inexplicably worked.

It was like a loud and beautiful birdcall. It pierced the corridors of the school, yet sounded faintly sad, like a whale song. Mrs. Blackshear whipped to me without batting an eyelash and spat acidly, "Tongue in your mouth, young'un."

Thinking about this later, I found it perplexing that Mrs. Blackshear's reprimand had focused on my tongue being out of my mouth, and had not at all addressed the disruptive sound I'd made.

More importantly, whenever I've tried to make that sound since, it's never worked. That was the only time it ever happened. Tiffany Simmons, on the other hand, whistled like that every day. Now it's been so long since I've heard it, I'm not even sure I remember it right. Maybe I'll never hear it again.

3RD GRADE

MRS. RAY HAD BIG EYES and big hair and looked like a shell-shocked war veteran. Every morning when we filed into her classroom, she looked up at us like we were aliens, like she had no idea how she'd gotten here to be teaching these particular human beings. Third grade was also my introduction to the cool kids at my school, who'd thus far never been in any of my classes. I think this might've been the first year they tracked students by test scores and shoved high-scorers into certain rooms and low-scorers into others. Whereas before, randomized classroom rosters tended to promote social parity by forcing clean, rich kids to learn alongside dirty, poor ones, which kept all alliances more or less loose—now all the rich kids were clustered in a few rooms, and powerful cliques with non-porous borders began to form.

Some of the cool kids were: Richie Myers, the third-grade equivalent of Hercules (backwards hat), Nessa (short for Vanessa) Evans, the stylish dresser with dyed blonde hair, and Cody Jones, who was skinny, sly, smart, and wealthy, and who was the first person in our school to wear sunglasses at recess. Also, in this class were Scotty and Jenny, all the way back from first grade. Scotty wore the same gold chain he always had, but he'd plumped up, and now it looked tiny around his thick neck. He was no longer anywhere near alpha-dog, and Jenny had suffered a case of early-onset acne, and had gotten wispy, and, I'm ashamed to say, poorer-looking, especially compared to Richie, Nessa, and Cody. Most likely, Jenny had always been poor, but in first grade I'd just been too naive or infatuated to notice. Now when I looked at her, instead of seeing her face and feeling butterflies, I saw only her poverty and felt only pity. I wondered why before I hadn't seen it. What had even made me aware that such a category as "rich" or "poor" existed?

And if you think I was happy in the slightest to see Jenny knocked off the pedestal she once so effortlessly occupied in my mind, you've got me all wrong. I was sad for her and Scotty and bore no ill will toward them whatsoever. In a weird way, I felt guilty, like I'd surpassed them, and not because of anything I'd done. It was only dumb luck. I'd won a lottery none of us were even aware that any of us were playing, simply by not yet having suffered the indignities of poverty, acne, or any of the other ravages of age. I was still bright-eyed and bushy-tailed, as they say. Neither cool nor excluded from coolness, I lived resolutely in the middle.

Anyway, Mrs. Ray, poor woman, was cognitively absent the entire year. I remember one day she got really angry at us for something, but no one could figure out what we'd done. Then later at recess Cody called her, casually, "Crazy Ray," and everyone laughed. I laughed too, but then felt bad for laughing. Not because I didn't think it was funny—it was because it was true—but because I hadn't thought of it. I think that moment is when it began to dawn on me that my envy of Cody wasn't just casual. It was primal. I didn't understand why, but it bordered on actual hatred. And I would be lying if I said it didn't frighten me.

There were no girls in third grade that I was in love with that I remember. Nessa Evans, with her leopard-print backpack and high-tops with blinking lights, was practically incomprehensible to my simplistic perception of aesthetics. Plus, what would happen in fourth grade was so emotionally epic that I might've had hundreds of girlfriends in third grade and not remembered any of them, the way no one remembers who they talked to on the phone a week before Kennedy was assassinated, or what they had for dinner the night before 9/11, even though, for all they know, it might've been the most amazing phone call or meal of their lives.

4TH GRADE

IMAGINE A MORE SOFT-SPOKEN MARILYN Monroe. That was Miss Forrester, and I was in love with her. She was nice and smart and was always happy to talk to any of her students. Most importantly, by some insane stroke of luck, I was her teacher's pet—a distinction I'd never enjoyed before. It wasn't without its disadvantages, of course. People made fun of me for it, but similar to when I was playing *Charlotte's Web* with Candace, it felt so gratifying to fill the role of pet that I was emotionally immune to any embarrassment from it.

Then, halfway through the year, Miss Forrester's boyfriend, a sheriff's deputy named Officer Alton whose cruiser was sometimes parked beside the school, proposed. Miss Forrester's stapler was labeled with white masking tape and FORRESTER was written on the tape in Magic Marker, and as a joke, the teacher next door, the mean and shrill Mrs. Templeton, who we could hear shouting at her kids through the cinderblock walls, stormed into our room and tore the old masking tape off the stapler and balled it up and threw it at Miss Forrester, who just looked confused and offended. Before Miss Forrester could do anything, Mrs. Templeton peeled a strip of fresh masking tape from the roller and smoothed it onto the stapler and wrote TAYLOR on it with new Magic Marker, and then Miss Forrester understood, and the two of them laughed uncomfortably. I don't think they were friends. When Mrs. Templeton left, Miss Forrester explained to us the joke: Officer Alton's last name was Taylor, and that soon she herself would be Mrs. Taylor, not Miss Forrester.

There was nothing inherently frightening about the transformation of my favorite teacher's name; after all, she was still the same person who doted on me and called on me and listened to me and whose angelic face and melodic voice made learning about long division and earth science and world capitals almost narcotic. But how quickly a Forrester could become a Taylor—that planted within me a seed of unease.

I avoided discussing it with my girlfriend at the time, who was none other than the incredibly brilliant, vivacious, and irresistible Cassidy Lastinger. That's right, the one from first grade whose heart I'd broken and who, within the first few weeks of fourth grade, had taken me back. Her teeth had filled in, her smile was now kinetic, and her laughter was somehow even louder and freer. In a way, she reminded me of the tongue-whistler, Tiffany Simmons, only more in control of her social image, and comfortable moving among every clique. Of course, I never told Cassidy about Tiffany, but in my mind it was as if Tiffany Simmons had been a kind of prototype—a novel innovation too unique to function—and Cassidy Lastinger was somehow its second-generation fulfillment: cuteness, confidence, imagination, and popularity all rolled into one. That we had a history together gave me an in, and so I worked it.

Cassidy and I passed notes back and forth constantly. In them we covered topics as far ranging as the subjects we studied, the other people in our class, and how cute we thought each other were, which was very. My main male friend that year was a guy named Sam Washington, a really skinny dude who was equally athletic and charismatic. He was poor, but he was a cut-up, and he ruled the field when we threw the football at P.E. Mine and Sam's alliance formed naturally and yet offered key strategic advantages. His status as class clown took the edge off mine as teacher's pet, and mine as teacher's pet probably saved him a lot of grief from Miss Forrester/Mrs. Taylor.

Rawls was also in our class (the same kid who bullied Tiffany back in the day) who everyone hated. I always felt like I was in charge of the class, and had a responsibility to be nice to everyone. Just to give you an idea of how sad Rawls' situation was, he'd spray-paint his shoes white every few months instead of buying the new ones he needed. But I told him they looked cool and that I wished I had a pair. He seemed to appreciate it, even though I knew he didn't believe me.

If second and third grade were characterized by fear and cynicism, partially due to my dawning awareness of competition and tension between different socioeconomic classes, and partially due to the aftershocks of first grade's heartache, fourth grade was, comparatively, a utopia. Even Nessa Evans, who was also in our class, smiled with admiration whenever I said something even mediocrely clever, which was the maximum level of cleverness of which I was then capable. I knew I was too good, or perhaps too boring, to actually interest her, but that didn't make her attention feel any less satisfying. Under the paradigm of this low bar, I thrived, raking in attention from Nessa, Miss Forrester/Mrs. Taylor, and of course, Cassidy Lastinger. And I had Sam Washington as my best friend. And I even looked out for hard-luck kids like Rawls. Everything was perfect, and the fantasy that I had achieved a universally satisfactory resolution in the intertwined narratives of my private and social senses of self was so engrossing and bolstering to my self-esteem, that I had no reason to question whether it was real, or wonder whether I deserved it, or imagine that it could ever change.

A week or two after Miss Forrester completed her metamorphosis into Mrs. Taylor, Cody Jones transferred in from Mrs. Templeton's. He had apparently been in the wrong class the whole time, and now he was in ours. When he walked in the classroom, all the girls practically gasped. Then the boys saw his shoes, and they did too. He would've been an impressive enough specimen in any footwear, but he was wearing those new kinds of shoes that you could pump air into by pressing a button on the tongue. He was the first person in our school to have them. There was a poster on the wall behind Mrs. Taylor's desk that featured a big cartoon heart with a smile on its face, reaching forward with a white-gloved hand and giving a huge thumbs up with the caption "You can do it!" This poster had always made me happy. I truly believed it. But when Cody Jones walked in, I turned back to look at it, and it seemed insipid.

Cody and Nessa Evans became an item immediately, something I wouldn't have minded at all if I'd been blind. If I'd been blind, I wouldn't have seen how jealously Cassidy looked at Cody and Nessa. Especially when Nessa was laughing at all the actually clever and sometimes cruelly surprising things Cody said. There was significantly less gusto in my and Cassidy Lastinger's note-swapping thereafter, and, like a fool, I chose not to address it until it was too late. When Cody dumped Nessa after only one month, for no reason that anyone could discern, my life became a waking panic. There was a week where I tried to be his friend: we traded baseball cards at recess, and I gave him better deals than I would've given anyone else. And when I was playing football with Sam Washington, like a backstabbing bootlicker of the lowest order, I would deliberately throw the ball to Cody instead of Sam. But Cody was like Scotty had been in first grade. He didn't give a damn about me and my transparent attempts to secure his allegiance. He was happy to accept any favors I threw his way, and, for all I know now, my pathetic appeasements sped rather than slowed him on his beeline for Cassidy.

Meanwhile, I could feel her slipping away, and I knew that once she jumped ship, there would be no begging her back. She had a long memory.

On the day I'll remember for the rest of my life, Cody and I were sitting on top of the very monkey bars Cassidy Lastinger and I once climbed together so long ago in the innocence of first grade. Cody and I were flipping through each other's baseball cards, intermittently surveilling the playground rather than playing on it, looking from our classmates to the cards and brokering deals over the latter.

I ask the reader: in all of literature, has there ever been a finer, more hideous example of the death of innocence and triumph of toxic masculinity than two boys, so obsessed with status and its loss or acquisition that they perch above the field of life instead of living on it, wasting precious recesses comparing possessions, bartering, albeit indirectly and unconsciously, over the affections, real or imagined, of distant women they didn't deserve? We weren't even friends!

Toward the end of recess, Sam Washington raced up to the monkey bars and looked up at me and told me to climb down, he needed to tell me something. I felt bad, but I had to play it cool.

"Just tell me from down there," I said, bouncing my foot on a lower bar, which caused dirt to shake out of the bottom of my shoe. I watched Sam watch it fall to the ground where he stood. Then he looked sharply from Cody to me and said with his eyes, "Fuck you. We're through." Then he said with his words, "Rawls stole Cassidy's backpack, and he won't give it back." I squinted across the playground and saw a commotion way the hell down by the swing set. I looked at Cody, then back down at Sam who was already walking away. He stopped. He turned around and said the fourth-grade equivalent of "I guess I'm only telling you because we used to be friends, and I know you really like her." He spat into the dirt as if to clear the idea of any remaining friendship between us from his mind, then he dragged his foot through it and walked away.

I felt so bad I wanted to disappear. I turned to Cody, who hadn't even looked up from the Trapper Keeper in which I kept my baseball cards. He just kept flipping pages, looking at the faces on my cards, completely uninterested in my real-world turmoil. I must have looked pretty lost, though, because

I remember he suddenly shut it and sighed, "Well? You gonna go kick Rawls' ass, or what?"

"Right," I said, looking at his pump-up shoes.

I climbed down the monkey bars and walked quickly to the swings, or maybe I ran slowly. I felt like an executioner, uncowled by circumstance and cursed with just enough conscience to hate himself to the core for what he was about to do, but not one ounce more. The whole class was standing in a semicircle in the sand that spread out from the swing. Cassidy was sitting on the ground and crying. People were laughing at her. Rawls was holding her backpack over his head, laughing. On the backpack were four faces of some boy band the name of which I don't remember and whose music I've still never heard. She'd gotten it recently at a concert that her mom and dad had taken her to, and it was her prized possession. It was exactly the kind of thing Rawls, with his spray-painted shoes, would've stolen—an emblem of comfort, an emblem of familial happiness, an emblem of beloved men. I didn't want to fight Rawls because I felt sorry for him. I don't even think Cassidy wanted me to. It wasn't who I was. I was a peacemaker, I think. At least that's what I was when I was at my best. Maybe a more indicting term would be a person desperate for everyone to like him. But seeing Cassidy crying on the ground, just looking up at me, there was almost a dare in her mortified eyes. She, too, I think, knew that Rawls was the real victim here, in the grand scheme of things. It made me wonder, just for a second, if this whole damned damsel in distress thing had been engineered—if only subconsciously—to throw a wrench in the social order. My stomach knotted. I suddenly felt that I and every single one of us was doomed. I looked around, but Mrs. Taylor was nowhere to be found. This was the world we lived in now. A playground with no teacher. And love, to the extent it existed at all, was a bridge whose bricks fell out from under your feet as you walked and then sprinted across it.

I jumped into the circle and fought Rawls. It wasn't glorious. No punches were thrown. I yanked one strap of Cassidy's boy band backpack while Rawls yanked the other. We were evenly matched. I saw fear in his eyes, nothing more, but he never backed down. I didn't know what to do. I didn't want to hurt him, but I couldn't bear the loss of my status that losing to him would have set in stone. I realized that if he wouldn't let go of the backpack, I could sling him around and around until he got tired, so that's what I did. It eventually became like a merry-go-round that, when it got too much for him, he released. He went sprawling across the grass ass over head. He rolled all the way to the half-buried tires, and for a moment an old memory of Candace as an innocent farm girl and me as a happily whipped pig flitted through my imagination and made me loathe who I'd grown into even more.

Cassidy Lastinger got her backpack back. That made it that much more surprising—and yet somehow not, the more I think about it—when that afternoon during social studies, she wrote me a note with one line: "What would you do if we broke up?"

Without thinking, I replied below her handwriting: "I'd probably cry." I immediately regretted this response, but when she didn't pass a reply back, I thought that perhaps brutal honesty had inspired enough pity in her to stay my execution a while longer.

The next morning, Cassidy cut me loose in a note written on pink notebook paper. She even asked Mrs. Taylor if she could switch seats to be next to Cody. Cody became the new teacher's pet, and Mrs. Taylor showed him all the affection she'd once shown me. Sam Washington and I were never friends again, and by the end of the year Rawls had grown into a dangerous and unpredictable bully.

I think I cried myself to sleep every night the summer after fourth grade. No one was as strong and smart and fun and wise and loving and alive as Cassidy, but she was gone now, and part of the cool kids thereafter.

Reflecting back now as the depressed, disgusting, zit-faced shipwreck of a fifth grader I have become—adrift in a middle school social order I have not even the energy to attempt to scrutinize—I stare blankly at my teachers and classmates, see nothing familiar or extraordinary in their faces, find no totemic magic in their names, and know they see me the same way.

I regret the fight. Because of my status, because of Rawls' lack of it—because of a hundred things—it was unfair and unnecessary. Yet had I done nothing, I'd regret that just as much. And wouldn't I have lost Cassidy to Cody either way? Or to someone or something else? And by what right did I even call her mine? What force drove me to obsess over whether I was "going with" someone or not? And what is the point of these regrets? Why do I have them? And what's the point of a life if all it is is an endless piling up of regrets? Followed by interminable analysis?

Masturbation, which I discovered that summer, felt like finding a magic power, and I don't mean that in a positive way. I mean it like how winning the lottery feels good but ruins the winners' lives. I'd lie in bed awake at night gratified briefly only to writhe, sleepless for hours beneath the enormous weight of guilt that it brought down. I didn't do it that much, I don't think, and when I did, it wasn't particularly sexual. It was more mechanical, engaged in specifically to distract myself from an all-pervasive anguish. It left me hollow, penetrated by oblivion, and lonelier than I had been before I'd done it. I used it then, I realize now, the same way a grown-up might take a drink, or shoot heroin, or go to a movie, or open a book, or seek any other form of escape.

THE VOID

I T WAS THE MORNING. I WAS MAKING FACES AT ELWAY, MY eight-year old terrier, while waiting for the teakettle to boil. That's when a rift in reality opened near the far kitchen wall. Through it I could see into a kind of void. It was shaped like a winking eye, had ruffled edges, and at first was just hovering there, undulating, kind of like it was looking at me.

I glanced at Elway. He looked from me to the void, more confused than afraid, I think, and so I tried, for his sake, to remain calm too. That's when the void began speaking:

"I would like a face like yours," it said. Its voice echoed coldly, but was also awkward, as if it wasn't used to speaking in this language.

"And shoulders like yours," the void quavered. Its center seemed to comprise a cauldron of vaguely gaseous elements, but the more I looked into it, I felt fainter, almost hypnotized, and the less I understood what I saw.

"I'd also like a posture like yours," the void added. "And shoes like yours, too."

"Shoes?" was the first thing I said. "But I'm not wearing shoes." I lifted my foot so it could see. "I just woke up."

The void rippled once, like a pond a stone had been thrown into, and then was instantaneously placid.

"Exactly," it seemed to seethe. "I want shoes that are not shoes."

Then something like a chuckle rolled out from within it. I felt a wind, and the teakettle whistled, startling me.

I turned around and nixed the stove, hoping the void would be gone, somehow, when I turned back to face the kitchen wall.

It wasn't. It was still hovering there, watching, possibly waiting for confirmation that I was afraid. I don't know why I thought that, but I did think it, and as soon as I did, I didn't want it to know my fear. It felt like some kind of tense board-room negotiation, but I had no idea what the stakes were. I was only sure it wasn't money or property or status or power.

I scooped the tealeaves into a sleeve and set it in the cup, trying to pretend I routinely entertained interdimensional vor-tices. I poured the hot water over the tea and dipped the sleeve several times. Then I turned around to see the appearance of the void had still not changed.

"Shoes," I said. "Uh, okay." I nodded. "Anything else?"

"A nice apartment," it announced, "like this. And I'd like a nice day of the week, like this one, for the date to be on. And a nice planet like this one, too. To live on." Then the void dimpled and said as if it hadn't been talking to me previously: "You there. Answer me now. Is it cloudy out? Or sunny?"

I frowned at its tone, then looked out the window on instinct. It was shaping up to be a beautiful day, actually. After tea, I had planned on getting dressed, walking to the co-op, doing some shopping, and then meeting a friend for lunch at my favorite café.

THE VOID

"Sunny," I said. Then I blew on my tea.

"Thank you," the void answered, "for confirming what I already knew to be true about the weather!"

Mirthless laughter thudded from somewhere within it. I felt a prickling on my skin, and the room got hotter or colder, but I couldn't tell which. I glared into the center of the void, trying to find its mind or its face, but peering into it only made the void shrink until I could hardly see it at all. Maybe it's like a distant star, I thought. Looked at straight on, it goes away.

The relief at having discovered something vanished when I turned my head and saw the void anew. Through the corner of my eye, it seemed not to have shrunk but stretched out, expanding to fill, or replace, the entire apartment. I wasn't across the room from it, I was inside it, on its edge. This frightened me so much that I looked at it directly again, causing it to shrink until I could hardly see it. But still it was there.

"Well," I said quickly so as not to stutter. "Will you be staying long then?"

The void flickered and changed into several shapes which, in all my knowledge of geometry, I had no reference point for. Then I felt my back go cold, like the sun had gone out behind me. Like if I turned around, everything would be missing— the world replaced by the void, cold and cruel and airless.

In front of me, it pulsed lavender and violet and a strange shade of black that also looked like a new shade of orange. A ghostly sparkle moved across the tear in the air it occupied almost like a smile. I smelled ozone, or what I thought was ozone, or what people mean when they say something smells like ozone without knowing how ozone actually smells, which I didn't.

"I ask if you're, uh, staying long because I don't think I've brewed enough tea for two." I gestured nervously to the kettle. "And if you're hungry, I'm out of eggs, too. Uh, I'd actually planned on going shopping later this morn—"

"What is eggs?" the void shouted. "And tea?" It looked at me then scrutinizingly, like a corridor of dimness receding into eternity. "What is tea?"

I lifted the cup. "You mean this?"

"Yes, what is that?"

"Uh, a beverage."

"And a beverage? What is that?"

"Something you drink."

"What is drinking?"

"It's a… what?"

"What is it?"

"A process where you… there's a fluid, and you… you pour it into yourself."

"When?"

"What do you mean when?"

"When do you do that?"

"Whenever you want."

"When do *you* do that?"

"In the morning, uh, usually. For tea, anyway."

The void was silent.

When the silence got awkward, I added, "But some people drink tea all day. And tea's not even the main th—"

"Yes," the void hissed. "'People.' Say it again."

"What?"

"Say the word," growled a mouth of clouds within clouds inside the void. "'People.' Say it. I want to be people. Now say it."

I stared at the void for a second. "People," I said quietly.

"Yesssssss," it said. "Yesssssssssss." It paused and then the colors changed shape and the shapes changed colors and then they resumed their enormous empty dimness. "People," it whispered almost vulgarly.

"What about people?" I asked, unsure if I should have.

"People," it repeated to itself like a zombie. "People. People."

A new hum emanating from somewhere caused me to look around the room. It sounded a bit like the score in a horror movie when the main character is walking toward some gloomy door that should never be opened. But it sounded like it was coming not from the void but from all around.

"Uh," I said. "Yeah. People. I get it, I think." I laughed nervously.

"People," it replied creepily.

I looked around again, nodding. "Yeah. Uh-huh. Well, there's certainly lots of people on Earth, I guess."

The tendrils of its edges danced where they met reality. "Yes! There are, aren't there? Lots and lots of people here upon the Earth, home of the people, and the planet of the vibrant sky."

Its sinister cadence and oddly poetic diction set off some kind of alarm and woke in me a sense of responsibility I hadn't felt before. The hum was louder too. I suddenly felt afraid not just for myself, but for all the people on Earth.

"Actually," I said, "I'm not sure there are other people around here, frankly, in all honesty."

"What?"

I shrugged as casually as I could under the circumstances. "Yeah," I said. Then I turned to the window, and when I saw what I saw, I moved to block the void's view. Across the street, my neighbor, a widow about my age, was throwing a ball with her poodle. I squinted as if staring out at nothing as she bent down and picked up the ball and threw it into the side yard, and the poodle raced around her house after it. It was so innocent that I felt like an astronaut seeing Earth from space for the first time—while also pretending not to be seeing anything of any importance.

I shook my head, as if confirming the emptiness of the view, then faced the void again. "See? There really is no one here. In the world, I mean. I'm sorry if you came here expecting otherwise." I hesitated, trying to seem improvisational. "It happens all the time, actually. Expectations, I mean, uh, getting squelched under the, um, best laid plans and all that." I forced laughter. "I'm sure you'll agree it applies, you know, to whatever you are, too." When it didn't react, I lifted my teacup at it. "You do agree, right?"

It was silent.

"I myself didn't expect to find you here this morning, yet here you are. So that's all I'm saying. And you—you've come here in search of…" I cleared my throat, "people I think you said?" I glanced around again as a pretense. "Which, as you can see, aren't here. It's almost kind of funny isn't it? Me and you, I mean, not being that different. In that both of our expectations are apparently out of whack with the actuality of our given situation."

The void flickered rapidly, then stopped. Then it flickered rapidly again, then stopped.

"I'm sorry you've come all this way," I said forcefully, "only to have to return. But you better get going. I'm sure it was a long journey, and the sooner you leave, the sooner you'll get home."

"But you are here," it snarled.

"So?"

"And you are a person."

"Oh," I said. "Is that what you think?" I waved dismissively. "Because I'm not." I thought about how far I might be able take this, which was not very. "I'm not a person at all," I bluffed. "Now, it's time for you to leave."

"You're lying," it intoned evenly. "You are a person."

"Um, would you like some tea? Did I already ask that? I could easily brew more."

"I have the tea already!"

"I-I was saying… that… I must look like a person, and I… definitely sound like one… that's not up for debate. But there are no people here, so, I can't actually be one. Maybe you have the wrong planet or something. There's a lot of them out there. There's more planets than there are grains of sand. You know that, right?"

"No."

"No, you don't know it, or?"

"No, as in you're lying."

I pursed my lips in anger. "What've you come here for?"

"The question is what have you come here for."

"What?"

"What have you come here for?" it said mockingly.

"Are you an alien?"

"You are the alien," said the void. "Life is. Matter. Being is only seeming. You view yourself as so important because you breathe and walk and drink tea. But you are the visitor, not me. You are the interloper. This is my domain. It always has been.

You do not know because you are blind to all that does not emphasize your own significance. You know only what you want to know because that is how you propagate, the meme of your own meaning. But your propagation has come to an end. It is time for you to know the truth. You are a dream. I, the sleeper. Only nothing is real, and now it grows tired of its slumber." Its voice then took on a multi-dimensional inflection, almost like a chorus. "Nothingness is rising!"

Shattered static radiated from the void and touched everything in the room, and the formerly amorphous void grew sharper and realer. It was no longer a hole in reality, but a sphere around which I could feel the reality of my kitchen curving.

"You've come to what, then, invade?" I asked, frowning and feigning bravery.

"No, you have! You have invaded! You are the invader!"

A noxious strobe light expanded in the sphere, and the sphere expanded the room. The light inside appeared like faults to separate planes whose impossible tectonics turned my mind and stomach like they were perpendicular sprockets linked by a single axle. I heard my teacup clattering against the saucer in my other hand.

The void grew—or shrank me—until nothing was familiar. Reality bled away like a painting doused with mineral spirits. I found myself on a featureless scaffold in a shrieking field of pure abstraction. It was so startling that I fell, but down became up, and then I was standing again. I fell again. The same thing happened. I realized that nothing was changing at all. Falling, I was standing, and vice-versa.

The void itself I saw outside and inside, and beholding its violent conundrum almost broke my mind. Its color had no color, and the parts that had no color were purple, mauve, magenta, deep blue, shallow black, wide orange, skinny green, death white, furry brown, despair pearl, and futility gunmetal. It looked like a balloon exploding from having been filled with too much air, and then like a tub of water whose plug had been pulled. And where was I? Did I have a body? Had I ever had one, I wondered worriedly.

I had no sense of time, and, surprisingly, felt humiliated by that. It was like being naked in public in a dream, only there was no public, so I couldn't isolate the source of my shame. Then I felt sorrow. As if I knew the whole world was extinct already, and I was all that was left, and this left me with guilt, and the guilt morphed on into other negative feelings.

"Wait," I whispered, confirming only as I did that I still had a voice.

"Nothing to wait for!" thrummed the void. "Whatever it is, is done."

"No!"

I tried to think about Elway. Then I thought about the lady across the street, her poodle, and the kid who mowed the neighborhood's yards. I thought about everyone else I'd known in my sixty some-odd years, my siblings, my parents, my colleagues, old teachers, old sweethearts, their families. I remembered coworkers from my first job working at a fast food joint. I remembered historical figures. I remembered names from newspaper headlines, socialists and fascists, moderates and neo-whatevers. I pictured the forsaken, the drug-addicted, the lost whose faces I'd only glimpsed once on a sidewalk, in a parking lot. I pictured victims of wars, the incarcerated, the limbless, the sick. I thought of the "blood-dimmed tide" from that Yeats poem. I even thought of murderers and oppressors with a surprising nostalgia for their mere fact of having been at all, and I concluded that even if that nostalgia made me some kind of monster, that flaw made me authentically human, and it meant I had been, and so part of me must still be alive.

"If it's over," I said into it, "then why am I still here?"

The void was omnipotently silent.

"How is it that I can be speaking?" I insisted. "I know you hear me!" I shouted louder, "I hear myself!"

Something vaporous churned, and the void was bulging and flattening. Then it was popping and writhing. Then it was blowing and bowling. Then it was spewing and fraying. Then it was leaping, and then it was weeping. Now I was inside a kaleidoscope. Now inside a Big Bang. Now inside the Devil's speech bubble. Now in a blueprint for rain. Now in a bullfrog, now in a tadpole, now in a snowglobe of mud. I was a snowball fired from a tank. I was locked in a box in a vault in a bank. I was in a whale, in a well, in a star. I was in a shadow in the mouth of a worm.

"You speak because you are nothing," it said, the voice coming from within me. "You are nothing now."

"No!" I shouted. Then I told it my name. I yelled out my address. I named my occupation. Purely as a form of defiance. "And sure, I'm lonely!" I added. "And not by choice! Everyone I love is dead! But I'm not nothing! I try to enjoy life! That's hard enough! And I'm not a saint! But I never claimed to be! And that's more than you can say for some people! But even they're not nothing! No one is!"

Everything slowed, and, like a time-lapse photograph of a stormy sky, the trippy, many-tentacled void de-metastasized instantly, and where it shrank, the aspects of my kitchen reassembled. Elway. The fridge. The furniture. Elway was hiding behind the couch arm, panting in terror. The saucer was still in my hand, and I let the teacup slip off it and didn't fully return to my own body until the teacup cracked apart on the floor.

"Hahahaha," the small-once-more void laughed. "Simple fool. You have betrayed yourself."

My breath was shallow as I stared at the spilled tea and fragments of shattered ceramic, then looked back up at the void and said, "I'd rather be a fool than whatever you are."

It laughed again and said, "People. You said you never claimed to be a saint. That it was more than you could say for most *people*."

My sense of defiance faltered, as did my relief at being back in the apartment.

"So?" I tried to say calmly.

"So there are people," it said. "So this is a place with lots of people. As I knew. You lied before."

Elway whimpered. I glanced over. He was drenching the couch arm in slobber. Out the window, my neighbor and her poodle were gone.

"You misheard me," I said, inclining my head. "I misspoke."

"You spoke the truth!"

"Fine." I was disgusted. "What are you going to do, murder everyone or something?"

"Oh, more than murder. In fact, you've already glimpsed what I shall do. To all people. To their dreams. To the trees and the rocks. To the stars and the seas. First, everything will feel the fear of extinction, and then it will feel the distinct absence that is the feeling of feeling extinct. All matter. From the widest wave to the tiniest particle, being will be stripped down until all but a single wish—to be—remains, and then that wish will vanish, too. And I…" it hesitated, "I will finally… be…"

Its voice trailed off.

"Be what," I said.

"That's just it," the void replied austerely. "The thought is unfinishable. It is being itself I will end." Suddenly, indescribably energy exploded across its exterior and it shouted, "It could have no description!"

I leapt backward in fear, jabbing my back on the corner of the table. I cried out. The room shook like a bumper hit by a pinball. The void's laughter jackhammered through everything. I felt powerless and rageful on behalf of the world, and my back hurt too.

I threw the saucer at it. The saucer passed through it and exploded on the white kitchen wall. The void laughed harder.

"What is not, cannot be harmed."

"I don't care!"

I grabbed a mug of pens off the table and slung them. The lightning tracing the surface of the void discolored. There was a book of poetry under the mug, and I threw it too, and then book after book off the shelf between the table and couch. Each time a book hit it, the void laughed and shifted in shape. It took no damage, but I felt better after every object I hurled. Elway started barking. I had no idea if he could even see it. From his perspective, maybe I'd gone crazy. I pulled the silverware drawer out and flung it in whole, hoping for some mystical interaction between my grandmother's silver and the void—she'd been an amazing woman, after all, and far ahead of her time—but it didn't work. I threw open the fridge and pulled everything out: hot sauce, ketchup, mustard, a sparkling water, the butter dish, a jar of beets, blueberries, a bottle of champagne I'd saved for some reason, a half-carton of eggs, a quart of milk, the box of baking soda, and a block of white American cheese. Then I yanked out the crisper and threw it so hard at the void that the plastic shattered and the celery alone seemed to send a ripple through the ether. But nothing did anything to silence the laughter or slow the general advance of the void, so I jerked the fridge off the wall and knocked it into the void with my shoulder. The freezer door cracked a floorboard and disturbed the void's whorling colors like a cannonball landing on soft seafloor. Then I threw the dish rack through, too. I opened the cupboards and threw the bowls through, and the cups, and the canned beans and boxes of pasta and bottles of spices. From the sink I slung the cutting board, the butcher knife, the saucepan, the skillet, and even the teakettle into the void, shouting maniacally, "Have some tea!" I opened the cupboard above the sink where I kept the liquor and threw liquor bottle after liquor bottle through, too.

And yet none of my outburst changed anything but me. I stood before the void, sweating, heaving, and staring into it as fiercely as any barbarian ever stared across a battlefield at an impossibly large imperial legion clad in brilliant mail. Like a good warrior, too, I was ready to die for my cause. In fact, I wanted to. Discovering this felt like finding a door that had always been hidden in the cellar of my mind but which I'd lacked the appropriate desperation to open, and which, once opened, allowed a cool wind from another realm through. I let it blow all over me until I felt coated in something like mystical armor. I even looked at the void differently. Staring into it now, its ravenous desire to simply be struck me as pitiable. Its envy of the living seemed so petty, in fact, that I envied it. I envied the freedom of not existing. With a glance, I bid Elway a forlorn goodbye, took a step back, then ran barefoot across the floorboards toward the void. Lightning scissored across it. It rippled and strobed and imploded and grew, as if trying to frighten me, but I dove through the center.

"Hey!" I think I heard it cry in protest, but I was already traveling through the sound of its voice like a tunnel. The meaning of its words warped around me. I pulsed like electricity through a cord. Though through my beating heart chugged currents of dread, I moved at the speed of negative curiosity. I glanced away—to the side in a sense—and could discern familiar shapes beyond the wormhole's lurching walls. A shaky silhouette of Elway peered from the couch as if through an evil veil that fell on the other side of time. Beyond his head, the kitchen window let in a ghostly vision of the neighborhood. Behind me, the ransacked cabinets and sidelong refrigerator—taut black cord still plugged in—shimmered like mirages in a desert of shadows. Still hurtling forward through the void, I felt like a swimmer doing a kind of hyperspace backstroke in one of those one-person exercise pools in which you can swim forever without going anywhere.

"Where are you now?" I said, as the void.

"You know where," I answered us, letting my momentum propel me faster and faster through the nothing until I had reached the speed of pure prayer.

"Stop," the void urged.

"Stop what," I said. "Becoming you? You threatened everyone. What choice do I have?"

It seemed to take a deep breath, and then it shouted, "Leave me!"

"Isn't this what you wanted?"

"You are... I am... We are not one!"

With these words, the door that opened in the cellar of my mind when I decided I was unafraid to die blew off its hinges—and an ocean of cold wind filled the cellar, and lifted the house off its foundation. The foundation rained down dirt, and its roof rose into the sky. I felt alive and whole in death and emptiness, and tenderness in my antipathy toward the void. I did not even pity it anymore. I simply felt like it, and like it was me. And I could hardly believe my own thoughts when, in that moment, I decided that I would try to love it. Not just to join it as an act of defiance or self-destruction, but to genuinely love it for what it was, and what it was not.

And then it was easy. Or rather, for one small moment filled with a serendipity that has yet to return to me, it was easy.

"I'm sorry," I said. "I'm sorry for hating you, and I'm sorry for being you."

"Silence!"

"When all of that which first existed burst into being, you probably weren't even consulted, and ever since that you have been ignored, if not insulted relentlessly, by everything that is, or is made, or remade, or which remains. I'm sure that it must feel to you extremely unpleasant, if not utterly unbearable."

"I have no feelings!"

"Whatever their equivalents are, then. I'm sorry for causing them, on behalf of everything."

I could hear Elway panting in the galactic distance.

The drone of a weedwhacker; the brakes of a garbage truck.

The sound of people walking by. A jet overhead.

The open freezer straining to freeze the world.

The teakettle on its side, dripping on the floor.

My heartbeat in my ears. My own breathing.

Thoughts hopping from synapse to synapse in my head.

A shard of a word or thought, caught and released.
And I saw my own thoughts as they were: little cords
of naught wrapped around aught, data in a vacuum,
being in nothing, one in zero, and zero
in one. Picture and frame, a song and a silence
whose symbiosis had so irked my former enemy, the void.
"I'm sorry we are one," I told the void sternly, meaning it.

I told it I genuinely wished that it could be nothing and take away everything without losing its nothingness. "But you can't," I said. "Because if nothingness is all there is, then it's no longer…"

I trailed off, hoping it was a sentence the void could finish.

"Nothing," it finally said.

"Right," I added.

"You tricked me."

"I didn't mean to. It's just what happened."

"I'll be back," said the void bitterly.

All around me, the coil of absence through which I was vaulting began unraveling tendril by tendril like the bird's-eye-view of a terrible carousel slowing down at the end of a ticket's worth of time.

"I know you will," I said sadly, and I might've wept if I'd had a body yet.

"Wait," I said, and the void clung to me for a moment more. "When you do return, I swear I'll welcome you."

My body was returned to me, then, and tears flooded my eyes, and through them I whispered, "I love you."

Time rained down again, and the kitchen rushed into being. I wasn't a doctor, but even I could tell my nose was broken. My lip was busted, and I tasted blood. I felt like I'd been punched in the face.

I touched the bridge of my nose and winced. From my mouth to my forehead was tender. I blinked twice and thought I was looking up at the cloudy sky for a second. Then I realized I was eye-to-eye with the white kitchen wall. I could even see the direction of the grain beneath the coats of paint. Below, on the wood molding, was a bit of my own wet blood.

I rolled onto my back. Elway, who had jumped off the couch, barked twice and skedaddled over to me and began licking my face.

I pushed him away and scratched his head and looked around at the thoroughly destroyed kitchen. Where my hand lay, the floor was sticky with liquor, and I was lucky that I hadn't cut myself on the broken glass.

"Hello?" I asked, not altogether certain who or what I was addressing, but there was no answer.

In a small mirror above the sink, I inspected the gash across the bridge of my nose. I then glanced back at the blood on the molding. My tongue felt something strange on the front of my tooth, and I turned back to the mirror. Upon closer examination, I noticed a piece of enamel missing from my front right incisor.

I went to the window, still tonguing it, wondering if any neighbors had seen or heard the racket. Down the block, a man in a bucket hat was fiddling with the threads on the head of his weedwhacker. He appeared to suddenly solve whatever problem he had been trying to solve, swung the weedwhacker down, pulled a cord, and resumed gracefully slashing the grass around his house's bright red brick foundation. Through the open window I could smell the grass and the gasoline and for a moment felt expanded in my fear, and then, somehow, un-alone. A sparrow swooped into and out of view.

Then another. Then a squirrel leapt off the raincatcher of one of the houses and landed on a power line, then it changed its mind and leapt back onto the roof. I watched the power line bounce until it was settled. I watched the squirrel on the shingled eave struggle with what to do next. Elway cautiously nuzzled my leg, and I pet his head absently.

LOST IN TRANSLATION

I HAD ALMOST FINISHED TRANSLATING THE NOVEL OF SOMEone unknown in my country (I've decided against identifying him to protect his reputation) when, one night after grading papers at a bar, I walked home to find my front porch window shattered and the deadbolt unlocked from within.

I walked inside as if entering a dream. Up to that point, if my life had been a novel, it would have been the sort of slow-paced, middling, pseudo-literary meditation on bourgeois ego so over-represented in American fiction. As the shards of glass cracked under my tennis shoes, however, I wondered if tonight was the night my life finally changed genres.

I set my keys and graded papers on a table by the door and walked down the shadowy hallway. Maybe I was drunk, or delirious from having just read so many of my students' idiotic arguments, or both, but I remember feeling strongly a spine-tingling curiosity. At any moment, I naively hoped, some beautiful spy was going to jump out of the dark and press into my palms some secret artifact, or map to its location, and entrust me with the continuation of a mission upon which the fate of democracy or even humanity hinged.

"Why me?" I would stammer. "I'm just a part-time college teacher!"

"I know it's not ideal, but it has to be you!"

"Are you… hurt?" I would ask, looking down at the blood leaking through their shirt.

"I've been shot in the stomach."

"Oh God. You need a doctor. Let me take you to the——"

"There's no time! I won't make it. Look, I know we don't know each other, but you have to promise me you won't let my death have been in vain. You have to deliver this to…"

And on like that. Soon I'd be sending out an email cancelling all my classes, tossing a pistol into an open suitcase, and racing to Egypt on a cargo plane to prevent a determined cabal of neo-Nazis from acquiring a shard of the Cross, or a lock of Mary Magdalene's hair, or a map to the Garden of Eden.

Fully deluded in this manner, I tiptoed to the end of the hall, gingerly entered my own bedroom-office, and saw that my mattress had been unceremoniously flipped over.

Something about the blatancy of this fact was sobering. It hadn't crossed my mind that whoever had broken in was just a normal burglar, probably someone from my community who had less money than I, a drug addiction, or some other desperate circumstance reflecting the social and economic iniquity that characterized our capitalist system.

Imagining whoever they had been more realistically now, I took a step back, suddenly worried they might still be in the apartment. A quick check of the rest of the rooms revealed no one, so I went back to the bedroom-office.

My dresser drawers had been emptied onto the floor. There were the clothes I worked out in; the clothes I taught in; the good underwear, the underwear with holes; a crushed box of condoms; some expired fish oil supplements; some ankle socks that had always been too small; a puka shell necklace a girl I'd dated in college had given me when she told me she just wanted to be friends; an old postcard of a meadow full of wildflowers that I'd never sent to anyone; etc.

The sight of my actual belongings all dumped out like that smashed any lingering fantasies. I suddenly felt sorry for the burglar. How desperate and out-of-touch would you have to be to break into a random apartment and expect to find loot under a mattress? Who even has cash anymore? Whatever the burglar's other struggles were, I decided, they were also hopelessly lost in a past that was gone forever.

My pity evaporated, however, when I saw that my desk was empty and realized my laptop was missing.

A broader inventory of the apartment revealed the only other missing item was my old microwave, which truly puzzled me. Aren't microwaves like $20 brand new? Why would anyone risk breaking and entering for something worth so little? I never used it, and I probably couldn't even have given it away. In fact, in this way, I even momentarily reconsidered the burglary as a potential blessing—but then I remembered the laptop, and the laptop's loss was profound. Don't ask me why, but I hadn't backed anything up. Gone were hundreds of pages of notes and all of the translated drafts of the novel.

The police suggested I check the local pawn shops over the next few weeks to see if the laptop turned up, but every pawn shop dealer I spoke to explained emphatically that they would never buy anything if they suspected it was stolen. Not that I believed them, but I begged them to break that rule in the case of my laptop. I showed them a picture of the model and told them that if someone brought in anything that looked like that to please buy it, no questions asked, no matter how stolen it looked, I'd pay double. But they said they wouldn't do that. It would only encourage criminals.

There were no laptops in any of the pawn shops I checked, though in one I did find a VHS set of *Twin Peaks*, so I also bought a VCR, and I watched the entire series over the next few days instead of doing any work.

The author had sent the original-language hard copy of his novel by mail, and that particular copy I still had, but I found it difficult to look at now. It sat there on my desk, butterfly clip-bound, coffee-stained, waiting to be re-entered, waiting to be re-translated—but I had lost all motivation.

While I genuinely believed that I'd be doing the world a favor by ushering this writer's work into English, I was honestly more interested in the thanks the world would heap upon me in return. I'd dreamt every day of the better jobs and social connections and greater academic and literary credibility that completing the first major translation of this author in English would bring me. Thus, the prospect of starting all over from scratch was demoralizing. I was thirty-seven, and I'd have liked to have had children before forty, but who was going to marry some penniless part-timer professor with eighty grand in debt and only two chapbooks of his own unacclaimed drivel to show for it?

Even if it had been ignored critically, with a complete and beautifully rendered translation, I'd have been able to claim some sort of artistic martyrdom. Such a version of me might still have enough appeal to draw an acceptable mate with whom to have children on my preferred timeline. Without the translation, though, my only prospects were the day-drinkers from the dive bar down the street and the other, even sadder teachers slaving away at the same sad, underfunded community and state colleges I'd taught at for years. I'd of course fooled around casually with several, but that all-important personal connection that didn't wither in the clear light of day had thus far proven elusive.

Dating fellow teachers was its own extra level of hell anyway. Everything became a competition: who had the worst students, the most grading, the most degrading pay, the least job security, the most meetings, the most total commuting, the single-longest commute, the most mercenary administrators, and, of course, the most debt. That all of this relentless whining was justified did not make it any less toxic to the happiness of anyone I knew. While at first the loss of the laptop meant the loss of my golden ticket out of a doomed milieu, in the subsequent clarity of my depression over its loss, I realized that no one new was going to have loved me more for translating the work of some other person no matter how wonderful the final product turned out.

My whole plan, the plan upon which I'd staked my early-to-middle adulthood, I learned, was not only naïve, but was bitterly, ironically naïve, given that I was a teacher, and it was my job to be the opposite of stupid. Re-translating everything from scratch then—dumping even more years of life staring into the laptop screen with even less chance of success than before—was simply not going to happen. Instead of throwing it away, and hoping perhaps that the laptop might somehow turn up and permit me to finish the job, I pushed the untranslated hard copy to the back of my desk and forgot it—or tried to. Even there, it seemed to mock me, however, so I stacked a bunch of textbooks I was supposed to be reviewing on top of it too. Later, because I could still see the edges of the manuscript pages poking out from beneath the textbooks, I put my printer in front of the stack and then draped a track jacket over the output tray of the printer, completely covering not only the manuscript but everything touching it, too.

The pile, of course, was an even more obtrusive reminder of all the lost time the manuscript represented. Plus, on a purely practical level, it utterly cluttered my already small desk. But because it still seemed sacrilegious just to throw his manuscript in the garbage, I used it as an excuse to do some spring cleaning. I put the butterfly clip-bound pages in a cardboard box with some other stuff I no longer needed, including a book on the history of ballet that had been in my bathroom for ten years, some old scarves and hats, the ill-fitting ankle socks, the expired fish oil supplements, etc.—and set it all out by the street.

I checked the box whenever I left or returned to the apartment, and each day, something new would be gone. The manuscript was the last to go. When I realized that probably no one would take it, I resigned myself to letting it be ruined by the rain, which seemed poetic, and therefore slightly better than throwing it in the garbage. But then one day, before any rain had come, the box was empty. I wondered what kind of person would take three hundred plus pages of text in another language off the street. Probably someone had seen free scrap paper and gotten it for their kid to draw on. Or perhaps some punks who had wanted to start a fire had seen it as free kindling. As I crushed the cardboard box into the recycling bin, I decided that I was happy not knowing, relinquishing the author's book to the universe for whatever purpose the universe saw fit to give it.

I walked back into the apartment free of foreboding for the first time in what felt like forever, wondering what new vaguely literary paths to self-actualization might now be open to me. Maybe I would become one of those people who sold tote bags online with Henry James or Virginia Woolf quotes on them. Maybe I would write book reviews, or reviews of reviews, and submit them to some arts-centered online dumping ground. These ideas failed to capture my imagination, however, when I realized anyone with a computer and free time could do them. They lacked the romance, the exoticism, the whiff of self-sacrifice, the glimmer of public service, and the writerly nuance I believed I was capable of, that translation demanded. And yet translation was too depressing to return to. And so, because I had no desire to be admired for any of the things I feel like I could have done, and because I wanted to be admired for the one thing I no longer had any interest in doing, I did nothing.

For weeks I woke up grumpy, drained, and exhausted. I couldn't go to bed unless I'd had a few drinks, and no books or movies or TV shows entertained me. I switched therapists, but where the last therapist had been too supportive, the new one was too smug and prone to lecture, for some reason, about the failure of psychoanalytic theory, so I switched again only to end up with someone who couldn't even remember our appointment times, and switched again after that only to end up with someone who had potential, but who was too new at their practice to be very helpful to a buffoon as prone to self-pity as me. I even bought a new phone. The new phone was beautiful, but so big that I dropped it all the time and could hardly get my hand around it and it fit in none of my pockets. Before long the screen was cracked and I tried to go back to a smaller one, but they wouldn't let me without paying $250. I got a new laptop. I quit coffee. I quit sugar. I took up smoking, and then I quit that. I got into yoga. I started meditating. I got an app that tracked the length and frequency of my meditations. Nothing changed.

I think when life is good, we see its diversity and are gratified by its abundance. Even its conflicts seem an important part of the hidden continuity between outwardly dissimilar things, almost like the glue that holds everything together. But when life sucks, we see only fragmentation, and fragmentation is lonesome. Every fragment becomes a reflection, and then an amplifier, of a formless sadness within.

What happened next was initiated, ironically, by some of my worst students. It was one of those hot, sweaty, evil teaching days when your hangover just won't cool, and the void won't let go of your soul, and you can feel a thrumming drumbeat between your ears, a distant echo of war and chaos and plunder that inflects everything you think and do, and then at school all your students do is whine and cheat and lie and throw tantrums and stare at you in stony silence and break your heart and ignore your assignments and even when they actually try, disappoint you. There you are in front of the classroom, grinding your teeth, hands shaking, hair thinning, temperature rising, eyeballs aching—and you come within inches of throwing your hands at the ceiling and shouting, "You know what, Amelia? Class cancelled! You know why, Jerome? Here's why, Ansley. Because we're lost! We're doomed! All of us! Even me!" And you swing your finger around like a preacher. "But especially you! And the only evidence I need to make this thesis statement sing is right here. That I'm the one appointed to be your shepherd. A total loser, someone for whom no dream has ever come true, nor should it have, since all his dreams are hopelessly narcissistic. And that fact that you're still listening to him is proof that you're just like him." But of course you don't do that. You bite your tongue. You internalize. You go into that fugue state you go into, which you don't wake up from until you've left campus, both regretting even thinking what you thought and yet ashamed of not having had the guts to say it. You feel guilty and stifled in a hundred ways you haven't even the energy to unpack, and the only remedy is to do something recklessly stupid.

Even though it was after 5pm, I pulled my Honda into a corporate coffee shop, got a giant cookie and the biggest coffee they had, dumped a shitload of cream in it, sat down by the window, opened my new laptop, and started working on some original poetry. I never drink caffeine after 5pm—ever. I stay up all night. I work myself into dizzying spells of meaningless anxiety. My dreams, when I do sleep, become ghoulish. It makes me absolutely insane. But I had to do something to reassert for myself some semblance of purpose, and the combination of poetry and caffeine had called my name.

The coffee capably worked its sorcery, and for all of an hour the writing was practically glorious. Then I realized my bladder was about to explode—my ruminations had been so beautiful I hadn't noticed—so I asked a lady next to me to watch my laptop and went to the bathroom.

When I came back, I casually perused the document I'd just spent the last hour typing furiously into. Instantly, I saw that it was wordy, vague, and overflowing with expository bellyaching, its uncensored bitterness filtered only through the thinnest veil of pseudo-intellectual "lyricism." The only thing it seemed to be "about" was my own privilege—unintentionally so. When I'd left the table to go to the bathroom, I'd been convinced it might be the next great American poem—that once-in-a generation poetic artifact of ignominious origin that would go on to be read in classrooms until the fall of the empire, and maybe beyond, but when I returned, I saw that it was disgusting, and I slammed my laptop shut in disgust.

I drove home dehydrated and sweating, still jacked on caffeine, having squandered the initial concentration it had given me and dreading the anxiety that would be its price on the back end.

I cleaned the whole apartment when I got home. It was hot and I was trying not to run the AC, so I stripped to my boxers and blasted Chopin and swept and mopped and dusted the blinds and all the books on my shelves. Behind the table I keep my keys on, I even found some broken glass from the break-in I'd never swept up. After the living room, I cleaned the kitchen. After the kitchen came the bathroom. The bedroom-office came last.

My desk sits over a cast iron radiator. On cold winter mornings I can do work and be heated and soothed by its humming and wheezing. Cleaning behind it, however, yielded a surprise. Amid some cobwebby essays by students whose faces I'd long since forgotten but whose names still felt faintly familiar, was a second butterfly clip-bound hard copy of the novelist's untranslated manuscript. It was actually the first—I suddenly recalled that when he'd sent it to me originally, I'd promptly lost it, so I'd requested a second copy, which he'd agreeably sent through post, and the second one was the one I'd been working from, and which I'd left in the box on the street.

I stopped cleaning to ponder whether this find was an indication that I should foray backward and translate the whole thing again from the beginning. I might be forty-five or fifty by the time it got published, but that's young enough, right? To have finally established my brand? To have gotten my mini fifteen minutes? And cash it in for a job? Or adulation? If nothing else, I had nothing better to do. It was Friday night, and I was a hyper-caffeinated loner dusting and sweeping to Chopin.

On the other hand, I'd already rejected this path once. When I'd set the manuscript out in the box with the scarves and fish oil, that had been that. I'd not looked back. Wouldn't restarting again, now, be retroactively wasting all the months that had elapsed between the first time I quit and today? If I stayed quitting, all that time would remain progress. Toward what I didn't know, but it didn't matter.

Around 2am, I was still too caffeinated to sleep, so I made popcorn and opened a bottle of wine. I sat on the couch with the popcorn in a bowl on the cushion to my right and the glass of wine balanced on the cushion to my left with the untranslated manuscript in my lap. Between sips of wine and handfuls of popcorn, I turned the crinkly, untranslated pages hesitantly—not intending to translate anything—just to read a few of my favorite passages. And, okay, maybe translate a little, but only if I was really feeling it. I suppose that removing the pressure to create great art helped me relax a little.

Upon skimming the first few pages, however, I grew alarmed. I tried to allay my fears by reading on, but the fear intensified. The same text I'd once considered a wry and unpretentious confrontation of the aesthetic crises of our time now seemed woefully insufficient. The tone of the story was sour, its narrator unironically moralistic and snide, oozing unchecked ego, as if the world itself would have been lost without his pronouncements. The other characters felt either like pale reflections of people who'd wronged the writer in life, or utter stereotypes whose purposes in any scene were only to incite and then listen to the narrator/protagonist's relentless grandstanding.

Worst of all, the narrator continually digressed into long unfunny commentary on the nature of literature as he saw it. I knew I'd been in love with this kind of shit at some point in my youth, but I couldn't now for the life of me remember how or why. And of all the things upon which I could have pinned my hopes of shedding my unsatisfactory circumstances, I'd chosen the shepherding of *this* into English? I couldn't believe how bad his novel suddenly seemed, and how retroactively stupid that had made the first seven years of my thirties.

I tabled the pages and sentenced myself to bed, tossing and turning, bitter, nauseous, sticky, drunk, and yet not drunk enough to simply pass out.

I'd reevaluate the manuscript later, when circumstances had conspired to make me feel okay enough about things in general to assess more reliably how bad or good the manuscript actually was. Only then would I know exactly how much to regret my life—completely, or just a lot.

WHEN SEVERAL SOBER RE-READINGS THE next week failed to restore my faith in the work, I actually felt a bit relieved. I dropped the manuscript in the trash and thought at least I'm back to zero with this nonsense. At least I can finally move on, whatever that means. Thirty-seven wasn't that old. Some people never even make it to thirty-seven. From that perspective, everything I have is gravy. I could move to Vegas, right now, just start doing drugs and see what happens. I could go on a Caribbean cruise and never come back. Even if I knew I was unlikely to act on them, such fantasies seemed to liberate my future from my past, and for them I was grateful. Then, a few days later, I received an email from the novelist.

Early on, he'd tried to make our author-translator relationship more collaborative, but I hadn't been interested in that. I'd found my precious caterpillar and wanted to take it into *my* cocoon and turn it into *my* butterfly. I wanted to wow him—and the world—and privileging the privacy of my process seemed like the best way to achieve that. Looking back, he was a saint to have trusted me at all. When his email arrived saying he hadn't heard from me in a very long time and asking me how the translating was going, I felt doubly bad because I'd just disencumbered myself of his work for the second time, and he'd had no idea that it had happened even once.

I don't know if I detected a hint of mockery in his otherwise polite email, or if I was still irritated at him for writing what was, in my updated opinion, dreck in any language, but I was unproductively forthcoming in my response. I told him I was sorry, I'd not only lost all the work I'd done, I'd lost interest in his work as well, and I wouldn't be able to continue in good conscience in my capacity as his translator. Then I lied and said this decision was recent, and the only reason I hadn't emailed him yet was all my teaching duties. It was a real gem of an email, I thought, perfectly balancing pettiness with self-pity, and I regretted it as soon as I hit send.

He replied almost immediately. He was disappointed, he said, but he understood if I wished to discontinue the project. And he signed it 'Best,' and that was it.

What a classy guy, I thought. I was completely surprised, and I castigated myself for having been a jerk. This was a real human being, and if not a great writer, maybe an okay one, if only on the grounds that he was kind. That's the key, I thought. Kindness. That's what's missing. Being humane. Maybe if you're a kind, humane person, you can write something bad, but that's still a net win for the world. Maybe this guy was exactly the kind of hero I needed to learn from. And for a moment I thought about what it would mean to change into someone more like him.

An email a moment later, however, reversed my opinion. He said he was sorry to send a second email, but he had to get something off his chest. He said there was no reason for me to be rude about his writing, and I could've easily kept my newfound disillusionment to myself. Then there was a beefy little paragraph calling me out for stringing him along for so many years and then not informing him of my decision immediately, even if it was recent, teaching schedule or not. He then went into several aspects of his own teaching and administrative duties that were substantially greater than my own, but which, he argued, had not prevented him from respectfully and promptly emailing everyone he needed to email for going on twenty years. Then he said he'd felt betrayed because he'd completely entrusted his work to me and had been so respectful of my privacy and process.

I sent back an even more ill-conceived, one-sentence email that to this day still mystifies me:

> *Well, I hope that someday someone else writes something I can in good conscience usher into English… that redeems the act of translation for the both of us.*

It's not that it's even that mean, it's just childish and confusing. Sometimes I re-read that whole email chain to try to figure out what was I feeling that made me say that. Why would his faith in translation have been shaken? How would me translating anything new by anyone else redeem it for him? Was I trolling him? If so, why? What was there to gain? Sure, he'd disappointed me, but only after I'd outgrown his work, and how was that his fault? He never begged me to translate him, I sought him out. He never even knew I existed until I pitched him on it. And I didn't feel bitterness toward other things I'd outgrown. I didn't hate bands I liked as a kid even though I never listened to them anymore. And if I'd been a more collaborative translator, maybe we'd have copies of all my drafts in our inboxes. Even if his novel was bad, at least I could have finished the project.

When he didn't reply to the last email at all, in my opinion, he won. I thought of a metaphor for how I'd ended that chain. I was like a batter who'd swung and whiffed at two easy pitches, realized he was going to strike out on the next pitch no matter what, and so, at the climax of the third swing, had released the bat like a weapon, launching it from his hands, on purpose, toward the pitcher, only to have the pitcher, being a superior athlete, effortlessly duck, and then the whole stadium watch the bat sail silently over second and into shallow center. There, no one picked it up, but the TV cameras zoomed in on it, and its pathetic solitude against the manicured green grass evoked for all watching the miserable character of the batter.

I spent the next few days trying to write a poem that used that metaphor in some other, more universally relevant context. I was so enamored of the bat analogy that just thinking it to myself felt somehow like wasting it. As the draft of the

poem got longer and longer, I knew the piece was losing all
emotional and thematic clarity—but I pressed on, ignoring
my eyestrain, ignoring other duties, pouring even more hours
into it like I was still in my twenties, like poetry was the only
thing that mattered, and like as long as I was making it, my
time on Earth wasn't finite. I was stretching it out. I was cre-
ating new hours and new years inside the elastic simulacra
of language, not using up a fixed allotment. When I finally
realized the poem would never work, however, because, in its
inception, it had only been a paean to my own self-pity, and
therefore would have been agony for anyone to read no matter
how apt its metaphors, I surrendered and deleted it and knew
nothing about anything once again.

YEARS LATER, I ATTENDED A literary conference in Ann
Arbor. Except for the bare minimum necessary for personal
and professional communication, I hadn't written or translated a word or line of anything in years. Everything about
my life had been dominated by the pursuit of this career, and
all it'd done was drive me deeper into mazes of self-absorp-
tion. I remained a teacher for income, and I'd met someone
at a bar that I'd sort of fallen for. We'd even bought a house
together. We didn't have children and weren't married, but at
some point that stopped mattering too. I suppose I found that
by relinquishing all ambition—writing, translating, offspring,
or climbing any semblance of a ladder of dreams—I'd redis-
covered the ability to spend time with others and have it mean
something more than how much it hindered or advanced my
own long-term plans. I was old, but for the first time in my life,

I was content with who I was. I was sad, don't get me wrong, but I was also happy.

I was only at the conference at all because my department head, having rejected me for a full-time position for the umpteenth time, had paid for the trip out of guilt and had given me a ridiculously high *per diem* of $100. So, as long as I spent less than $100 a day, I was literally making money by eating free food. And walking through the room with all the booths and the young people so passionate about writing and invested in their blossoming careers gave me the feeling of a former major leaguer, who'd washed out after one half-season, eating a hotdog in the stands, enjoying the smell of the grass and cigar smoke and the roar of the crowd, but also, not caring who won or lost the game, and even being glad that he wasn't playing. I saw in the young people's faces the same ardent idealisms and vanities that had once driven me, and yet I didn't want to grab them by the shirt and shout that they were doomed. I felt happy for them, and then I felt proud of myself for feeling that zen—until I saw the novelist.

He was flanked by two large, vertical banners whose dark red color reminded me of those flags beneath the standards of a Roman legion. Each banner featured a picture of his huge bearded face in black and white and the translated title of his then just-released novel. Obviously, it was not my translation. I looked around that crowd, wondering who the new me was, but everyone in the crowd looked exactly the same. Then I thought his translator probably wasn't even there. Whoever they were, they were probably hunched over a laptop in New York or Los Angeles or Beijing or Berlin, putting the finishing touches on their next blockbuster translation. No good writer would even be here, I thought, glancing around resentfully, unless they had something to hawk.

I bought a copy of the book and then got in the long, twisty line of folks waiting to have him sign their copy. Despite his imperial posters, the novelist looked surprisingly down-to-earth. He just smiled at each fan through his Merlinesque beard, exchanged two lines of smalltalk, opened the cover, crossed out his name, and signed. I stepped forward when the line moved. Soon I was in the middle. Then I was near the front. Then I was three people back. Then two. Then one.

When you're young, maybe you read your own writing and think it's bad, but maybe somebody else says it's good, so you think it might be. Or you think you're great until someone you think is good tells you you're bad, or mediocre, or have a long way to go, and you believe them. And maybe you give up. You move on. Or maybe you don't. Maybe you try to get better. Maybe you ignore everyone and crank out epic after epic overflowing with your own unappreciated genius. The point is, you don't know. No one knows how good they are, and no one knows how good anything is, especially in the beginning, and there's something equalizing and honest in the universality of that uncertainty. But for me, that uncertainty was unbearable. I wanted to win, not be uncertain, so I wanted an insurance policy, and that's what made me a hack, and that's what made translation—an act I barely understood—a kind of sanctuary. I could be someone else, someone whose work the world was already sure was good. But serving myself first and the work only second, if at all, had made that sanctuary a trap.

This was just the personal reckoning I went through standing in that line. I know my experience isn't everyone's, and probably not even many's. I'd also like to emphasize that these

fears of inferiority were only the earliest seeds of my interest in translation, and that my sustained interest years later
can only be explained by a sincere belief in the power of the
art: the desire to share important work that would otherwise
go unread; to reinvigorate the status quo with new, untram-
meled modes; the desire to bridge different literary communi-
ties; the childlike joy of fiddling with syntax and diction like a
trapeze artist across the poetic gap between concepts drawn
from vastly different experiences; engineering empathy on
the sub-atomic level of context and syllable—all these virtues
eventually inflected my practice, too. That's the good that I
believe translation, or any kind of writing, can do. To excel
necessitates sincerity, and even if it takes a lifetime of failure
to learn it, an insincere person who learns sincerity has gained
the world.

When I got to the front of the line, I purchased the book
and asked him to sign it. He asked who to make it out to.
Since we had never met in person, he had no idea who I was—
until I said my name. His enormous eyes flashed recognition.
He inclined his head a centimeter and squinted at me for an
instant. Then I watched it dawn on him—the wasted years,
the rejection of his collaborative spirit, the juvenile emails—
until his eyes relaxed again and he looked at my clothes and
body and face and saw who I was, almost like a mafia don
inspecting a supplicant. When he finally smiled at me, his face
held a wry, almost mystical aspect. Then he hunched over the
book and with a big ballpoint pen between thumb and finger,
scrawled a meaty note.

His novel had been so arch, so knowing, so prancingly
in-your-face about the narrator's social perception and his
supposedly surprising diagnoses and dismissals of all manner

of hypocrites and dilettantes, I knew that if he bore any ill will toward me at all, he wouldn't be able to resist skewering me in the inscription. I watched him relish each stroke of the pen for a good twenty or thirty seconds, then he put the pen down and closed the book and slid it portentously forward. I took it and was about to walk away when I halted. I didn't feel right. I turned back and awkwardly apologized, suddenly and sputteringly—for being a pest, for being a prick, for informing him I didn't like his work—then I told him I was actually looking forward to reading his book, again, in this new context, and I lied and said I'd flown all the way to Ann Arbor just to meet him. I smiled and awaited his forgiveness. Instead, though, he looked over my shoulder at the next person in line and beckoned them forward. He snubbed me.

Still standing there, out of place in front of his throne-like setup, I looked at his novel in my hands, the back of my neck prickling, the tops of my ears suddenly hot. He was already in smalltalk with the next fan. I pretended to check my phone like I'd gotten a text. Then I pretended to look around the room like my friend had texted me to tell me where they were. I scanned the room and stopped, pretending to see the friend in the back corner where the exit was. I put my phone away and walked to the exit then, looking up and smiling as if both my friend and I were amused by the distance between us. The book felt heavier with each step I took, like I was the bearer of some kind of cursed or sacred relic. I imagined everyone in the room's face suddenly melting into steam and blood if I opened it, like my own personal Ark of the Covenant; his seething inscription glowing gold, heating the book from within, tempting me to crack it open, to free it, to read who I had become in another's eyes and reawaken the old me who had squandered so much in search of so little.

The book now rests on a shelf by my bedstand—unopened, and never to be opened—though sometimes I do still look up at it and wonder what is inside.